Melusina

The End of Dreams

Peter de Lissovoy

Also by Peter de Lissovoy

The Angels of Zimbabwe

feelgood: a trip in time and out

The Great Pool Jump (co-author, editor, nonfiction)

Invisible Car Dealer

Wisconsin

Cover photo: Geoff de Lissovoy, "Icelandic Horse"

ISBN: 978-0-9844139-9-7

Library of Congress Control Number: 2018912366

YouArePerfectPress

". . .through a glass darkly . . ."

Cigarette holder wigs me
Over her shoulder, she digs me,
Out cattin, that satin doll . . .

Baby, shall we go out skippin?
Careful amigo, you flippin,
Speaks Latin that satin doll . . .

—Satin Doll

The last person I could have expected to see in the club that night was M, who had never been there before to my knowledge, but suddenly swept in wearing a floor-length silverfox coat. And it was summer. This ornament made a strange impression on me, not only because it adorned her so gracefully, whom I was more used to seeing in tight blue jeans and a T-shirt. She was wearing her usual tight jeans, under the open silverfox garment. She placed herself directly before me, fists on her hips, flashing the fur outward, showing a bit of red satin lining. Raising my eyes reluctantly, I was struck dumb by the unexpected look of authority in her gaze.

Right behind her in her wake, a mere boy was following her, probably twenty years her junior. To avoid her eyes and hide my shock and jealousy that she had a youthful admirer, turbulent feelings as confusing as the ones stirred by her sudden bold entrance itself, since my brief unhappy affair with M had been over for years, I returned my glance to the lower blazes of her magnificent foxfire, the opulence of which reminded me that I had heard she had mended her ways and entered upon a successful career in real estate.

I had to look up. There was no way of escaping her stare and what was in it frightened me. She had come in and confronted me so directly, I had the impression I was going to be killed. The dim darting forest animals with their quicksilver pelts and molten-lead tails, through black trees in the moonlight, the satiny interior which showed at the level of her calves and

1

between her legs, the craft and money. I had always had reason to believe she held a grudge. I know I held one. Surprisingly enough, she seemed to have acquired power.

Stark fear (because you never knew what M might do next, particularly in public) and surprise gave way to justifiable irritation at this invasion of my privacy. After all, one thing you had a right to expect in a lowlife nightclub like this one was not to see M walk in, wasn't it? Why go into a crummy dive like this if you were going to run into prosperous people from your past like M, who always were trouble even when they were poor? If a guy couldn't hide out in a Clark Street tavern like this one, where could he hide? I liked it in here. Everybody was so threadbare and poor I could relax. Without effort I could feel rather well-dressed, even flush, and successful. I rested here comfortably at the bottom of the ocean of human striving, where things couldn't get worse, bereft of all illusion. She had ranked my pleasant blues, and disturbed my peace of mind by coming in here from way out of my past. I tried to tell myself rationally it must have been a coincidence, just bad luck, but the way she stood there looking at me accusingly, I found myself doubting it.

M was a woman who had made the chills run up the spines of a number of men in her life, I knew for a fact, and not only from the number of her divorces, which had never gained her a red cent, however, since she was too damned mean and careless to make out for herself properly, so bent on getting revenge never getting even. All this had changed apparently someone had told me, and by the evidence of that expensive foxfear coat it was so. And there was this handsome kid trailing after her. One moment she struck you dead with her primordial sexual appeal, thick strawberry hair, devilish loud laugh, leering slanted green eyes, high flashing cheekbones, and salacious flat hips. The next minute her allure had dissipated completely before your eyes no less than if she had changed into an alligator, which on occasion she actually did, just to show you it was no joke. She laughed too loud, gossiped too tactlessly, smoked too much, told people in the row ahead of you to shut up or eat their popcorn more

2

quietly, objected to the menu, criticized waiters and complete strangers at the next table, walked right out on you if you protested or asked her to be silent, or even if you didn't, told you you were a fool and a pushover not to complain at some minor offense only she discerned. In the end her moods were so mercurial and her behavior so incoherent, she left you without a moment's peace unless you could escape to some dim hole like this club to lick your wounds and congratulate yourself on your escape. And then, you know, the rubythroated salamander would show up to fetch you, changed back beguilingly into Melusina, in spite of your knowing better, and at home on your pillow, suddenly blotting out all memory of her outrages, transformed back into the most mouth-watering, smoking satin doll. And here she was again before me.

M had been a late blooming hippy and a beach-bum as a young woman, at the end of the seventies, she'd confessed to me, that improbable decade that the culture spent extending or repairing the ravages of the sixties or pretending they had never happened. M was oblivious of the culture, she was a natural force that had no need of it, operated outside it, and for that matter her beach that she was a bum on was not coastal but the shores of Lake Michigan. The midwest can hardly be said to have a culture in the sense that the two coasts have, so she stood out all the more, a revel without a cause. M was a picture with no need of a frame. She could have popped up and bloomed anywhere. As if she'd been some succulent tropical orchid, the very air fed her, with a little help from her friends, and many another cliché. M had no need of conversation, you imbibed a heady wisdom from her lips no matter what nonsense she was talking. Now when the rest of us were finally questioning the plunder and materialism of the Clinton-Bush years, she had lately discovered a way to make money, moreover in a way I had heard she enjoyed and was good at, dabbling in real estate. It was always her eccentric and confoundedly accurate timing that blindsided you. Now, in her late forties, she was getting rich,

3

quite a comeuppance had they known it, for various men who would have rather she suffered for eternity.

Her lifestyle had left its mark on her beauty, unfortunately. Through the years she drank too much, yes, had indulged the odiferous weed, in the long nights of youth, mornings as well. Rising late, stretching out her blonde body on the northshore beach someplace, she had caught the full brunt of the noonday sun, which like other males in her life, after a honeymoon of infatuation, seemed determined to punish her. Her facial skin had been affected, but she pretended not to care. "So, I'll have wrinkles," she grinned at me a little madly, lying on the beach, out of a silence and the blue. "I don't care. I love the sun too much." She had noticed perfectly well what the rays were doing to her fair and delicate skin, but she never stopped worshiping old Sol. I was not about to admonish her to seek the shade and risk a rain of invective as she equated me with her problems already. M always shot the messenger. I had learned to keep my mouth shut and not get involved in her thought processes. There she lay on the hot beach, her breasts concealed like white stones in a glade (green her color, even her bikini), while across those fateful cheeks and eyelids crisscrossed fine nets inquisitively as if laid there by the Fisher of Souls.

Strangely, her body remained quite youthful while her face began to age ahead of schedule. It made her a striking creature, though not for the entirely fastidious gaze. Never exactly admitting it to myself, never consciously avoiding that handsome but ever so slightly withering face of hers, I must have concentrated on the lips so tender, when tendered, and the fine breasts and bottom which lay like hidden oases behind the green palms. From those sheltered springs flowed milk and honey when the camels were not braying. Though she had joked hardbittenly about her incipient crow's feet, and promised she would not stop hanging out on the beach no matter what, it had never occurred to me that those were appeals for the delivery of a caress and hints as to the target. But I had a lot to learn, and I was going to learn it, and much more, late though it was.

4

Melusina

Leaning over me in the dingy, sordid fly-in-amber club (in which I was so at home), red high heels scraping the gritty littered floor, hunched slightly in silhouette with the dim light behind her, hovering in her silverfurcoat as in the mouth of a cave, boyfriend ineffectually striking a match to light a cigarette behind her as if he were trying to start a campfire on a moist night, her eyes gleaming cages, holding shards of moon, in the dirty lowlife ambience I loved and had deliberately chosen as perfect for my night out and she had violated, her delicately shattered skin aglow in a questionable luster, like a chamois, until she moved, frightening crags showing in shadows about her aquiline nose now tilted upward, she thrust out her open hand at me making it clear as crystal brought out to be broken that I could never be alone, nor escape from her, while she implored me with a violent shriek, "You must *touch my face!*"

Loud enough to be heard on the street! This wild cry of embarrassing longing and as if cryptic prophecy—and indecipherable at that—the inconsolable lament of a night creature, as I heard it, a howl (to my ears) not a statement, that silverforestfur of hers might not have been a coat at all but her own mane. In the desecration of the night the devastating power of her eccentric command was beyond all her raucous behavior and reptilian metamorphoses, in my memory, in its strangeness, and all of my present reality was completely altered. Although heads had turned, there was nothing at all and no one in the club but she and me. The boyfriend had gone off to gather driftwood for their campfire. Whoever I had recently imagined myself to be, lounging and concealed in a favorite hangout, I was no longer, and I confronted some abysmal absence—but of what?

Touch her face! Why not? Hadn't I often enough done that before? Or had I? I was afraid she'd finally gone insane. The moment was too intense to cause me humiliation, for her or for me—my usual reaction to her performances—for there was no room in my soul for other than unnamable overwhelming stirrings from dark depths, with which I responded to her from a full heart. Staring up at M, I even thought I knew what she

5

meant, though I had no rational idea. Uncanny chance to make amends—for what?—last chance to save my soul! That's the crazy feeling that inspired me. I had the terrifying intuition that to stroke those prematurely wizened cheeks of hers was opportunity of a lifetime and it was too late. Opportunity, for what? Could she still love me? My heart leapt. Touch her face! What black magic, had I done so, I wondered, sitting there in astonishment. Glancing at me with a look more of doom than regret she cried down ruefully, "But you *won't!*"

At this welled up in me an answering intimation of loss strong enough to make me do something about it, just as suddenly M swirled her furs about her and cut out of the place. All this had taken about sixty seconds. Her boyfriend threw his cigarette contemptuously to the floor. Searching for something I might hang onto I found my drink and knocked it over. I jumped up, ran to the door and out to the street. But they were gone.

Standing lonely in the streaking headlamps and glittering litter of the busy, yellow and shadowy Clark Street, I felt the sting of shameful self-recrimination. I had always blamed her weird and wicked personality for our problems. Could it have been partly me? Something cold, mysterious, and honest seemed to back off and stand aloof from me at the curbstone, to glance askance at me, an accusing unknown in the gutter. This *meaning* set off a lost, rich remembered music, which at once retreated, just beyond imagination. I felt the years that had sped by seemingly filled with experiences, leaving me prey to such a charge of superficiality, for so I understood M's taunt. Well, I hung out in a tavern like this one to avoid such doubtful disturbances. My feet sought their way back to the dirty solace of the nightclub, ground underfoot cigarette butts, candy wrappers, the small debris of everybody's thinly nourishing consolations.

I hurried back in for another drink, and as that didn't help much, found my way farther back into the recesses of the joint, back to the poolroom in the rear of the place where there were several scattered and scarred pool tables under uneven lighting, long fluorescent lamps depending on oily cords from the filthy ceiling. This room was another theater of heightened anonymity and affectless self-assurance that I enjoyed, for I wasn't that bad of a pool player. I found my way back to it like a wounded animal seeking its den.

A black guy got up from a crude bench and offered me a game of nineball at the one table that was unoccupied. I was glad I didn't know him. Distracted, and hoping for more distraction, I grabbed a cue, grateful for a chance to lose myself in a game. Though I couldn't hope to rid myself of upsetting memories of M, let alone what had just happened with her, at least I could force a separation and erect a barrier against my wild emotions, memories, and speculation by this sporting activity. I immersed myself in the spare ritual of preparation, rolling the stick on the table to ascertain its straightness and trueness, not that I cared, shaking out talc on my left palm and all over the place and rubbing it in between my fingers luxuriantly and forgetfully, chalking the cue tip overabundantly with blue chalk, lagging the cue ball too hard for the break, etc., taking my time about it, as if all this meant something, as it did in the aching wish to blot out the image of M in that foxy coat, with her preposterous wail of a command (or perhaps it had only been an *observation* on her part, as she happened to pass by).

My normal self-confidence and degree of self-regard always inspired in me by being in the abysmal nightclub with its adjoining rear pool parlor had almost returned when I noticed my opponent studying me indulging in this overlong chalk and powder business with amusement as if he thought I was quite a greenhorn. Well, naturally that would be the impression he wanted to leave me with to rattle me, as we had agreed to play for five bucks a game. I didn't think I'd ever seen him before and I was almost a habitue here. Maybe he was a hustler from the southside trying to intimidate me. He had won break or rather I'd lost it. I didn't let it bother me, and I didn't care, but as our play began I realized I had chosen my cue badly, for it was crooked and too thin for my taste. I wasn't so far gone but I picked out a new one from the rack, but it turned out to be about as smooth as

7

a raw branch you would tear off a tree, but there was little to be done about it unless I wanted more sneers for holding up the game. I couldn't keep changing cues. But it was too late even for that and my first five bucks was lost as my opponent dropped two balls on the break shot and was shooting with lightning speed and had cleared the table as I was still trying to pick out a cue.

Disconsolately I stood there watching him demonstrate his considerable skill and feeling I was being hustled. I should have bowed out then and there. My initial suspicion that he was going to try to sucker me disappeared as he seemed to be holding nothing back. If he'd been a real hustler, he would have let me win one. Well, maybe he would let me win the second one, and then I would quit, I thought wisely. He ran the table again and did so once more and we were on the fourth game and I was down fifteen bucks already before he missed one and I got my first shot, which I missed because there was a strange bump at one end of the green baize. I had certainly played pool before in this club and the tables were bad, but it must have been at another table, because this defect was outrageous, like the wood under the felt had buckled on account of the midwestern humidity. It was like a hill in a pasture, or the curved space the physicists tell us about. It occurred to me that my opponent's play had mostly been down at the other end which must be why neither of us had noticed this terrific hump in this table before. When the ball passed over it or even near it, it took a wild swirl and jumped off to the side or even into the air.

After sinking several more balls machinegun style, the guy's play now moved to that end and his shots began to be disturbed by the protuberance too, thankfully, which seemed to mystify him as if he hadn't seen it and couldn't see it, and his shots were careening outward all over the place for no reason at all. His mouth hung open briefly and his eyes blazed as a man bewitched. To me the hillock was as obvious as the smoky mountains and as a result I won two games in a row. It was a wonder why he couldn't see it, while by this time I was able to

8

aim my way around it. Well, all this made for an insignificant and tawdry adventure, but it somewhat occupied my thoughts at least, although it added another dimension to the weirdness that had befallen me in what I thought was a familiar and mundane watering hole. I felt out of sorts and tonight I was only playing pool because I couldn't think of anything else to do, after Melusina had come in and successfully broken my chops leaving me lonely for her again.

A handsome ravenblack-haired woman suddenly walked through the poolroom doorway, catching my attention and everybody else's too. Women didn't come in here, and she had a kid with her. Everybody stared at her. No woman had ever come back here that I could recall, even though times have changed and women play billiards all the time and there are many talented female players, some of them champions on TV playing at major competitions at Native American casinos and famous and better at it than almost all men. But this blasted place was not a room any of those glamorous lady champions would have sought out. All eyes went to this woman, including mine, and my heart to my throat, I don't know why, it was as if we had touched. In addition, in an uncanny way she looked familiar. I was sure I knew her but couldn't say how. I was sure she would come over too, I don't know why, and she soon did. Her expression was bland, superior, and dangerous. Women never came in here because why would they, particularly trailing children by the hand. She stood about six feet from the table and began kibitzing my game. "Oh you'll never make that one!" she grinned showing big handsome white teeth. She began giving me gratuitous advice on my shots, which I took silently just to show her how wrong she was and how cool and agreeable I could be. The more absurd her remarks and suggestions became the more mellowly did I respond to them, just to see where all this led. The black guy was pocketing my money again and eyeing me sardonically and indulgently like he didn't mind her interference if I didn't. Stuffing my money into his pocket he put on an air of helpfulness and gave me tips as unhelpful as her advice. I forgot about him and smiled at her goodnaturedly since by now we seemed to be flirting with each other, until my eyes happened on the kid she had by the hand, who was too short to see over the table and on whose face was an expression so disagreeable it resembled a snarl.

Who in the world would bring a kid to a sporting venue of ill fame like this one, let alone such a handsome woman with slicked-back blueblack hair, who clearly did not belong here either, in spite of her pretense at giving me advice on how to play my shots? It was not only improper but suggested abetting juvenile delinquency, something negligent or desperate, bringing a little kid into this joint. What could she be up to wandering in here irresponsibly with a child? She might be a drug addict or a prostitute, if so a good-looking one. The kid was just barely tall enough to stare at me over the edge of the table with a nasty frown. That hostile look on the tiny face had a force to it almost impossible to reconcile with a childish origin and I studied his diminutive form suspecting he might be a dwarf perhaps, not a child at all. Things had taken another strange turn, but at least I had been able to forget about M for a few minutes, I consoled myself, although now I felt annoyed at being affected by this beautiful but odd woman. It even made me absurdly feel disloyal to M who had just split on me again. I couldn't keep my eyes off the raven-haired woman, even if it was the corner of my eyes because I didn't want her to notice. She was very attractive. Why had she come in here and started talking to *me?* There was mystery here and while I walked about the table pretending to keep track of the game, I waited for it to reveal itself. An hour ago I had been oblivious and trouble free.

"Look here, take care of this kid for me for a while, will you?" She walked around the table after me leading him by his little paw. "I have things to do—*responsibilities*—unlike some people I know!"

What had she said! What "people" would that be? She had responsibilities! I should take the kid? My mouth must have fallen open and I almost dropped my cue stick. What was she asking of me! She must have imagined she had ingratiated herself with me somehow. I felt like a worse sucker than ever. She must have registered my interest in her and absurdly thought she could ask a favor. She had me confused with somebody else, I concluded, not even considering the impossible request she had just made. I stood there, pool stick in hand, wishing I did know her, but informed by the outlandish intimate favor she had just asked of me that I definitely did not. I let a little incredulity steal into my expression and raised my eyebrows in a friendly fashion not wishing to totally destroy our rapport. I wished she would explain herself, actually. My opponent was grinning so hard he was almost laughing out loud as he ran the table. I gulped and was about to demur and ask her if she'd like a drink when she cut me off loudly.

"I am now going to tell you something about me which you don't know," she said, stepping forward and putting her foot down assertively, almost on my own, dragging the kid behind her. I no longer had even the slightest notion what was going on and my mind began to wander. That much closer to it I could see it was indeed a child, not a midget, in spite of its worldly scowl, a mighty unhappy child. Her midnight hair slicked back into a wild feminine look of authority trembled like a grease fire.

"You still think I'm just some shady lady you met on the beach, but now that we're no longer together I'll tell you something. I am Mayor Daley's illegitimate daughter and that makes this kid of mine his grandson. I mean the *original* Mayor Daley. So take good care of him, buddy!"

For a moment I waited for her to realize her mistake, notice that I was not who she thought I was, whoever that might be, and cringe with embarrassment. She was feeding all this mystifying baloney, plus giving a little kid, to a total stranger. But she disappeared out the door in a cloud of dust, so to speak—so fast it reminded me of M's recent departure from the tavern at the other end of this dungeon. Then the game was up as I had recognized her under her disguise and understood that it *was* M—and it was I who was covered in confusion, for it was

Melusina all right, come back to trouble me some more, in a black wig, leaving me in charge of this strange kid frowning at me. I knew I'd recognized her—I took a step after her—it was that jet-black set of locks that had blinded me, plus the child, who was now standing alone by the pool table with its finger in its mouth, Mayor Daley's illegitimate grandson. That boyfriend of hers seemed to have shrunk up and changed into it, was all I could guess fancifully (but the whole night had become fanciful) because otherwise why would a little child stare so petulantly at me, who had done it no harm? Of course he didn't want to be left with me anymore than I wanted to be left with him.

She was gone so fast again, leaving me doubly forlorn. I ran into the barroom but she was not there, gone again. I had never heard about M having any kid. Could it really be she—who had now entered and left the place twice, abandoning a minor with me? Maybe it wasn't M at all, but some unbelievable mistaken identity. I stood there paralyzed in dim wonder and appalled that on my night out I was a babysitter. Less than an hour ago I had been half-drunk, numb to it all, and if not exactly happy at least not wounded, hopeless, and freaked out by lost love.

I started to take after her out into the street, for what? To howl at the moon, and bitterly protest that she couldn't leave me with her kid, anyway, if only under my breath, but the floor was strewn with charcoal—wet charcoal from a recent fire here, apparently, because it was still steaming. Somebody had gotten rid of something, burned up a lot of trash here in the barroom. You never knew what you'd run into in this evil joint. I stumbled in the pile. I would have had to pick my way through the mess. So I just gave up and stood there in the ashes. Anyway it was too late to catch her by now the way she moved when she wanted to. When M decided to vamoose, she could disappear like a puff of smoke. That was how I was pretty sure it was M, all right. Maybe these were the ashes of her cloud of smoke.

A poolroom bum came through the doorway with a bucket of more water and dumped it on the hot charcoal which was now awash. Satisfied the fire was out he began scooping up the sodden mass into the bucket with a shovel. A very macabre feeling stole over me as I watched the watery ashes being lifted stroke by stroke into the bucket and carried away. I stared into the black mass. The wild idea came to me that these were M's ashes, that she had burnt up and disappeared by spontaneous combustion. I understood that things like that had been known to happen. She had just burned and now was really gone, leaving me the child. Good luck! I realized I had let the kid out of my sight and hurried back into the poolroom to find him. I had almost forgotten about him.

I couldn't just turn this kid over to the cops, it would spoil my chances with her. I hadn't been thinking of her at all, when here she came again, and all I could wish for now was her. Loneliness struck me, the same old loneliness as when during our long ago love affair she would walk out and leave. What a welter of old emotions M had stirred up in me tonight! Maybe she did know the Mayor somehow. My opponent was waiting with his hand out for me to pay up another five bucks. He had run the table again while I was staring at the ashes.

It was not a welcome development having an ornery child on my hands. I paid up my wager and replaced my cue on the wall, because I had to keep my eye on him and I wasn't going to lose any more money either. I had walked back in the pool parlor without noticing where I was going, and looking about wildly for the pale snarling little kid, I suddenly couldn't find him. Panic had struck as I thought I had already lost M's kid not five minutes after she had entrusted him with me. No such luck. I saw him in a shadowy corner on one of the rickety chairs that adorned the place, his little face wrinkled up like a prune in the nastiest expression. Obviously he was not overjoyed to have been left in my care either, Mayor Daley's illegitimate grandson! Well, whatever he was, he was certainly the child of untoward events. I wondered if I should call the police and report an abandoned child after all. M would kill me if I did that, if she ever came back. What if she never came back? I didn't know how to take care of an unhappy kid. I didn't want to either. I stood there with my back to the table, my hands behind me caressing the green felt, as I stared at the kid.

How long was she going to leave him with me to take care of? My mind got down to practicalities and couldn't find any. The guy I'd been playing pool with gave me a grossly knowing wink and a smile of commiseration with my situation as he sauntered off looking for another game. It wasn't enough he had taken quite a lot of my money but he burdened me with his pity, irritating me all the more. Wreathed in shadow on his perch in the corner, his little legs dangling down, his feet about halfway to the floor, the kid radiated sullenness and defiance. I could barely make him out in the dark corner. He began to swing his legs in a childish yet very threatening way, harder and harder, as if he were winding up to fly around the room. That was about all I could see of him now, his thrashing legs, for the upper half of him had retreated into shadow. Mayor Daley (the son) was out there in one of the golden towers of the Loop somewhere, powerful, admired, dear to the hearts of his people, and I was left in charge of this bastard—what, his half-nephew? The family relationship M had sketched out evaded my comprehension annoyingly.

Above the kid's head a beer advertisement glowed in a stray patch of radiance cast from the battered overhead lamps. It was an ancient Hamm's Beer poster from better days with its promise of the drums of summer and sky blue waters blackened by the smoke of countless pool players' cigarettes. The old Hamm's Beer jingle went off in my head: "From the land of sky-blue *wa-a-terrrrrs* . . . Comes the beer refreshing . . . beer refreshing!" Nobody drank that brand of beer anymore, did they? Did it even exist anymore? But the advertisement lingered, selling those wa-a-terrrrs eternally. For a moment it brought a charming whiff of carefree vacations and being on a fishing trip in Wisconsin. I experienced a moment of false peace—false because it was over in the instant, real though Chicagoans' vacations and fishing trips had always been, but I was still here in the hellish poolroom with some sort of deformed and demented minor stationed under the beer poster like an insult to my intelligence. Next to the Hamm's Beer poster was the standard poolroom admonition: NO MASSE SHOTS.

Then along the wall a little farther I noticed another sign I had never seen before, which did not seem to belong here at all. Its fiery red letters vaguely disturbed me just the way they had been hand-painted on a rough strip of cardboard in the style of hellfire-and-brimstone evangelical highway billboards, each accusing letter seeming to jump up in red flames of woe and damnation.

> *If Through Cunning or*
> *Your Own Speculation*
> *There Is Not Enough Light!*

said the sign enigmatically enough. I objected to such a sign being placed in my familiar and comfortable haunts, but I knew it was meant for me.

It was natural enough that M would have remembered our first meeting as having taken place on the beach given all the time she habitually spent there on the funky brown sands of Chicago's great greyblue inland sea. She spent at least part of every day on the shores of Lake Michigan during the summer, and after they closed the beaches in September, she went on sunbathing anyway, though she didn't swim. She didn't flout the law by swimming, she was never a lawbreaker as such. Even in October I found her on the sand soaking up the last poignant rays of Indian Summer. I spent plenty of days at the beach with M during what remained of that season after we met. But we didn't meet there. It was not on the beach, as she remembered it.

She didn't work. She was living on some "savings," she told me. I guessed from hints she dropped that she had received a pittance from her last husband before he had left the States for his home in "the islands," what islands she didn't say. She couldn't have had much because she was living in the same cheap old boardinghouse for some of the more marginal Northwestern students that I was domiciled at. (We were past student age ourselves, or I was anyway.) That was where we met, in the shared kitchen of that dilapidated, patchily painted northshore Victorian that had once been some tycoon's mansion.

M loved recounting sordid tales from her lurid youth (she'd first married at seventeen), bragging how she'd gotten her revenge by making a scene in front of family and guests, walked out on her husband at a party given in his honor because he treated her like furniture, two-timed and three-timed the poor devil because he had taken her for granted so, all the while eyeing me like the next meal and not bothering to hide it. I thought my love for her was plain as day. I fell in love with her the morning I met her, although my first impression of her was irritating in the extreme. What that says about me I'm not sure. I surely did not think I would be up to treating her badly. But she suspected differently. In her gossip and her stories M wove a crazy anecdotal web of victimhood around herself, marked here and there by fantastic gossamer lumps where the bodies were buried, suggesting slyly it was the other way around after all in spite of her outrage. I thought she couldn't shut up because she didn't want to face herself and learn from her mistakes. How vulnerable the glee in her voice at her misdeeds. How she'd paid them all back! She'd been divorced twice by the time she was twenty-two. I never guessed in those days that her endless chatter recounting her pathetic victories was a clever ploy to hide (even from herself) her overwhelming power.

It was my opinion her heyday was over, and M in despair she never quite hid might even have to admit it to herself no matter how grudgingly and clean up her act, starting by treating me decently. But she might never learn. In the spiderwork of wrinkles that had already just begun to faintly bunch around her sliver-of-new-moon eyes when she laughed at her exploits, I thought I saw her future written and that she'd be her own next and maybe last meal if she didn't look out, unless she were caught by the Fisher of Souls in his nets by a lucky break for her. How little I knew was now attested—years later—by the ease with which she had left me with an orphan to babysit for, a kid of hers she had the effrontery to pass off as related to the Mayor of Chicago as if to scare me into submission, just like it was the old days of cheap wine and wilted roses on the Lake Michigan beach.

The real reason, I suspected, why she didn't care to remember where and when we had actually met was that she would have had to recall the rather awful old house near the campus where we had both been living at the time, and how in fact we had met in its dreadful kitchen full of students' odds and ends, spare bicycle wheels, and coagulated jars of healthy honey. That would have been humiliating for a woman whose tales of tawdry triumphs had always taken place in the finest northshore or Loop restaurants—and who could certainly afford it again now, so I'd heard on the grapevine, having struck it rich in real estate. She wouldn't want to remember that student co-op of ours and how down on her luck she must have been then when we had met, not even to show herself and me how far she had come. No tales of rebirth for Melusina, who considered herself a force to be reckoned with for all time. Our meeting must have been on the warm sands, M sprung from the waves naked and bejeweled.

I had come down to the kitchen about 10 o'clock one morning, my normal time for rising, and usually even later, after burning the midnight oil writing my novel. I preferred not to venture into that horrible kitchen till most of the other (juvenile) tenants would have gone off to classes on campus. Little did I know then that ten bells was M's customary wakeup call too. When I walked in, she was standing by the kitchen table smiling out the dirty shimmering window on some apparently sunny prospect in her mind's eye as she absently inserted a piece of pink meat between her lips.

I had seen this woman, a rangy strawberry blonde, several times at a distance in the hallways of the house, but our respective habits had so far just barely managed to keep us out of each other's way, out of harm's way, I put it to myself with a lurch of the heart. I don't know when she moved in, maybe she had been there before me. I noticed her only subliminally at first, a slightly disturbing, but passing, presence on the staircase. She was closer to my age than to the students'. That was a sign of trouble right there. She was clearly no student, unless a student of life, I observed knowingly. Each time I had seen her on the stairs or banging on the bathroom door I had ducked back in my room out of an instinct of self-preservation. M, though she stayed out late and got up late, was punctual, and 10 o'clock no later was her breakfast time, I soon learned, for she liked to head out to the beach just before noon. Unlike me she had a schedule.

To hide my discomfiture running straight into her like this, at last, at such an intimate breakfast time and place, beside the kitchen table covered with moldering crumbs from students' blueberry muffins, I found myself stammering, "Oh, what time is it!" inanely and pointlessly. (There was no clock in the kitchen.)

"What time is it?" she repeated my question and sneered at me. "You tell me. The body is a clock," she added abstractedly. "I am a clock. You are a clock. We are all waiting for the alarm to go off."

It was early and I was barely ticking, and I found this either sophomoric or above my head, either way, too clever by half. Out of self-defense, I was speechless. In fact I couldn't think of a witty reply to her characteristically hippy dip patter mixed with innuendo and sly wisdom, and I am rather a shy person. From the first moment, I knew M would always be ahead of me, but it was too late already. There was more on the kitchen table than the students' unappetizing condiments I noticed. M leaned down over a fine pink ham unwrapped from a nest of silver foil, fragments of it littered about the table. Knife in one hand, another piece of smoky pink meat in the fingers of the other floating upward to her open lips, she slowly straightened up and stared absently into the sunshine of the new day coming through the flyspecked window, glinting from her knife, sparkling off her greasy chin. It was one of those delightful mornings when the moisture from Lake Michigan seemed to ride beckoningly in on the very rays of light. It was a beach day if it was anything! Her lips were dripping from the meat, filling me with disgust, apprehension, and desire. Languidly she chewed the bite she had just taken with obvious and honest pleasure.

The next moment I was wholly taken aback to hear her say, "Oh look, I'm sorry, I'll pay you back!" Over her shoulder she glanced with some sort of appeal at me as if she knew me.

"What?"

"I didn't think you were home. I mean I've seen you around. I would have made it up to you. I don't eat other tenants' food."

"No—"

"I was hungry and it looked so good I just couldn't help myself—I mean, well, I did help myself. Ha ha ha." She giggled mellifluously but to me enigmatically.

She had turned toward me with such a show of mysterious guilt about what I couldn't imagine and an open plea for confidence and understanding regarding nothing I wanted to know about that I thought she was completely out of her mind, dangerous, and alluring. What the heck could she be going on about?

"You're confusing me with someone."

"No, this is yours. It was wrong of me to take some but I'll make it up to you. Here have some yourself!"

"That's okay!" I assured her. Not knowing what was okay—she was up to some inconceivable game with this meat—I might as well play along but I wasn't quite ready to participate. She was mistaken if she thought it was mine. Anyway, I suspected it was a trick. For what purpose? She looked like she had plenty of tricks.

She really did seem apologetic as well as confused, as if caught out. I had no plans that morning and she suddenly seemed attractive. I felt I had some incomprehensible advantage over her having to do with her odd notion that it was my ham, apparently. An unfair advantage like that could shift calamitously and the tables would be turned. All I felt, beyond a vague desire, was squeamish and embarrassed for her, as well as mystified by her mistake (if it was honest). I didn't want something to happen which would make life even more uncomfortable in this miserable house. I like my privacy, as a result of which I am far from quick on my feet. She looked like the type of woman that would require a strong character not to say a firm hand, qualities that even my abysmally small self-knowledge told me I was in extremely short supply of. Finally it struck me that she didn't care who I was, it was not her ham, and if I wasn't the owner I could be her accomplice.

"Here, have some of this," she insisted breathlessly. Still if I were the rightful owner of the ham I must be appeased. She blandished before my lips a piece of the succulent pink meat between her fingertips which were painted a shimmering orangish-silver color. I put out my palm either to refuse or to take the meat, I hadn't decided which, but she waved me off and forced the meat on her fingertips straightaway onto my tongue. I felt the touch of her finger on my lower lip. On the next bite it would linger for a full second on my tongue. What a way to meet somebody, especially M. After a shiver at the encounter I noticed it was rather dry stringy meat in spite of appearances, or perhaps it was my mouth was that dry.

"Well, I'm broke, I can't pay you back. But I have a couple Cubs tickets to a game tomorrow that I'll give you," she said.

"No, no, really. What?" This was getting deep. "Okay, but let's go together. What's your name?"

She had gone to the refrigerator for some orange juice to wash down the hunks of ham she continued to shovel into her mouth. By now she had done some serious damage to the ham so I could understand she felt she owed somebody something for it but why she thought that was me I didn't know because it wasn't mine. When she offered me another morsel I refused it.

"I'll just help myself then. What's *your* name? You must have just moved in recently. I've seen you around. I don't tell people my name as soon as I meet them. I'm a girl who has had to make her own way so you better watch out. When did you move in, I might ask."

"You don't scare me," I lied. That made her jump slightly, and she seemed to look straight at me for the first time, as if I had finally managed to say something that made sense. If I wasn't careful she would soon carve me up like the ham, and I could hardly wait. I felt her moving in for the kill, and I adjusted my feet firmly on the floor and took hold of the edge of the table with one hand.

"I don't live here," she said disdainfully, changing course. "My place is being decorated and I'm just staying here for a week or two."

"Oh? There's nothing wrong with this place. It's poor but decent—students and so on."

"I'd rather just live on the beach. If this was California where I used to live, but it's not—it's Chicago. They roust you out if you start sleeping overnight on the beach around here, not like California, where I actually live."

"You actually live in California."

"That's right. . . . I mean I'd rather be back there . . . but I don't think I will."

"Why not?"

"You know, the West Coast . . . there are two types of people, those who will always live in California, even if they

21

haven't gotten there yet—and those who are meant to stay there only seven years."

"So you're the second type?"

"I haven't completely decided."

Later I would discover just how much of a liar she was and that (amazingly) she had never been to California, let alone seven years, but at the time it seemed to explain a lot.

"Well, right, we're all relatively normal around here and only bums sleep on the beach and they aren't allowed in Evanston."

"Don't get me wrong, I love Chicago, and Evanston. Lots of good restaurants."

"You like to eat, I notice." I got off another zinger, which she didn't deign to notice.

"City of the Big Shoulders. The people know what a good meal is around here, I'll say that for them. In California all they eat is menus."

The wry comment, with a literary allusion thrown in, caused me to make a small readjustment.

"You know what Saul Bellow said," I said, "by the time an idea gets to Chicago from the West Coast it has worn so thin you can see right through it."

"How cute. These kids, or students or whatever they are, told me you were a writer."

"Is that right."

"Every guy you meet on the West Coast is a writer, usually a screenwriter . . . so they say! They just want to get you in the sack—"

"Yeah, well, I'm not like that."

"Look, do you mind? This is really good," she said helping herself to some more ham and washing it down with a slug of the orange juice of some student.

"Help yourself! Help yourself, I don't know what you are asking my permission for," I said.

She stared out the window and for a moment went off in her thoughts. Now and then her hand ran over the silver foil and pecked up more bits which she raised to her lips.

Suddenly she noticed me again. "I don't know . . . this isn't yours? You didn't order this? Is it your birthday or something? Anyway, it's yours all right, because your name was on the package."

On the package? She thought she knew my name already, and not only was she eating the ham of a student but had actually unpackaged it.

"Where is it? Let me see it."

"It's around here someplace."

One of the students was going to be hopping mad about this transgression of the cardinal rule of the communal kitchen: Thou shalt not eat other people's groceries. To say nothing of unpackaging them to do so. She'd even disposed of the box as all I could see were a few strips of silver foil surrounding the luscious red mound. Three-quarters mound by now, after all she had chomped up.

"You sure you won't?"

She gestured at the ham and halfway handed me the knife, turning to me a flushed look not so much of shame at her own thievish gusto but honest if slightly guilty bewilderment that I would not join her, almost—I swear—compassion or concern for me, for the delicacy of my manners or whatever. I thought the next thing she was going to admonish me, You really should eat! or some such absurdly motherly or sisterly advice from someone who was swiping from a struggling student. She went on smacking her lips loudly while she nibbled. Her show of sensual pleasure in the smoky meat mesmerized, attracted, and revolted me. Her gustatory performance was such that I could not possibly have joined in. I was sidelined by her, swooning, yielding, fixated, positively falling headlong into, my eyes glazed by, losing myself in her eating her breakfast, string of ham stuck to her glistening pink underlip.

"You eat that like there was no fucking tomorrow."

23

"Fuck you. This is good. And it's yours, you jerk. I said it was yours! You don't believe me? Find the box. That is pathetic. Don't even know what is yours. Can't even enjoy some of your own ham! I have to show you how it's done! It was sitting on the porch with your name on it. It takes me to discover it. I asked a student and they said it was you—I told you I have some Cubs tickets I'm going to give you!"

She threw the knife down on the ham like the murder weapon upon the body of the victim and snatched away her hand from the crime. But the way she did it I was to blame! I had succeeded in insulting her, at least. I was going to laugh at such melodrama but I saw her feelings were really hurt by my comment on her appetite and she was about to get really upset. She must be deeply ashamed of herself for eating up my ham.

"Hey, sorry, sorry! I didn't mean it that way. Eat, eat! Enjoy!" I was on the verge of laughing my head off at her, whether it was a show or not. I didn't want to hurt her feelings. She had just been wallowing in her breakfast. It was funny. "As far as I'm concerned, it's yours. If it's mine as you say, then I give it to you, okay? I don't believe it's mine. It's all yours. Maybe my mother sent it to me, I don't know, I don't think so. It's not my birthday. I just hope it's not one of these students' because they will raise a fuss. They will skin you. If it's mine, have it, eat the whole thing!"

"The whole thing! Thanks a lot."

"No, no, I mean, as much as you want!"

"I'm finished. Thank you."

We stood there for a moment, taking each other's measure. Finally I couldn't help saying, "I—I just admire you, you're so beautiful, when you eat, I mean, ha ha, you are a force of nature like . . . going through that ham, ha ha ha ha!" I just could not help laughing.

"Well, I'll be damned! Ain't we cool!"

"I just can't imagine enjoying myself quite so rapturously on a piece of meat like you are, standing up in the middle of the place, ha ha ha!"

"Well damn. You! Well damn! . . . You don't even know how to check out some simple goodness like eating a ham, do you! Your own damn ham, too. On a sunny morning!"

I didn't know what it was. She was over the top, and we were about to lose it, even though we had nothing to lose then. But I didn't want to lose it whatever it was. I didn't mean it that way. It was just that she was a handsome woman and the way she ate, sucking on the meat and chewing with her mouth open.

"I mean you get into it so much. I admire you, you're beautiful. It's just that I could not let myself go like you do."

"You think I'm a slob, is that it?"

"No, no!" She read my mind. "I mean you get into it, you get *after* it, ha ha ha ha."

"Boy oh boy."

"And the pleasure is soon over."

"What? What is soon over? What *isn't* soon over?"

"As if it is going to do you some good . . ."

"Of course it is good! Boy, you have some way of thinking! Not good? Do me some good? You mean I have offensive manners, I eat with my fingers?"

My mood suddenly fell. I recognized something fastidious in myself, or so I thought—something lukewarm, almost in the Biblical sense, I judged.

"Oh, give me some of that," I scooped up a mound of her shavings in the cup of my hand and ate it with my fingers.

"Can't you just enjoy?" she said softly.

"Oh yes."

"Might as well get into it instead of let it pass untasted."

"Yes, yes."

"Don't be a hypocrite."

"Don't be deceived."

"You're crazy, you know? You remind me of somebody I used to know in California."

"You have grease on your chin."

She grabbed a paper towel and rubbed her mouth. "I didn't know there were people like you in Chicago who don't know

25

how to eat a good meal! This zen guy in California used to talk like you do."

"I doubt that. I don't know anything. I like to eat too!"

"You should try to get some pleasure out of life."

"I get pleasure."

"Here, let me show you."

She wanted to feed me again, but I stepped back. "I don't let it take me over like the fucking ham was eating *me*, you know?"

"Man, you are some customer," she said contemplating me with overt pity like I needed help. Any shadow of doubt had long passed from her face and she was convinced that she was wholly in the right and I had a problem. She might help me. I was inclined to agree with her. I mean there was something to be said for both our points of view, but hers was far more appealing. I measured my pleasures, it was true. Poverty and being a starving writer had instructed me in this virtue. I thought I had sound philosophy on my side, at least up to a point. But in her presence I wondered if moderation too could be a vice. I bent over the meat and had some more. She had halfway convinced me. She had cut several slices generously for me that were lying there.

"Don't you ever like to *lose yourself* in something?" she asked insinuatingly, sidling up to the table and edging her flat hips against mine.

"In my writing," I mumbled. I was startled, but I liked it.

"That's a start. Better than nothing. Look at me. Do you think I'm a glutton?" She ran her hand down her lovely side and for sure there was certainly no indication her eating habits did her figure any harm. "But you write all night sometimes don't you, you let your mind just run wild. It shows. You get up late like I do. That's indulgent, even worse, in a way, letting your mind go, than a nice ham."

"How do you know what I do? What are you talking about. Looking for the truth in things."

"Oh, really?" she said drily but didn't press her point. "Here, try this part. This part's really good, that's the truth."

She cut me a new slice from a different side and it was now wonderfully moist and succulent. I decided to fix myself a cup of coffee. She rummaged around in the refrigerator and came out with a melon.

"That stuff in there is the students'," I said, but she ignored me.

Melon in hand she approached the counter by the sink and suddenly raised the round fruit above her head and slammed it on the edge of the sink, and it split right in two along a jagged seam clean as could be. Some juice splattered around. She handed me half the melon. My mouth was hanging open at her audacious feat. "Where did you learn that?"

"In the islands."

I scooped out the seeds and ate my half of the melon, amazed I could be so enjoying food that was not mine. I was hardly even guilty about it, I was swept up by her. She had made no pretense that the melon belonged to me too, like the ham, anyway. I resented being complicit in her crimes, but had some more ham too.

"Look here, we just ate a student's melon," I said.

"No, we didn't. It's my melon. I bought it in the grocery store yesterday, okay? It's my melon, okay? Want to see the receipt?"

"If you say so," I said doubtfully. I didn't believe her.

"My ex-husband is a season ticket holder. He still gives me tickets when he doesn't want them. I have lots of Cubs tickets to give people if they get excited about a lousy melon or something. I just give them a pair of tickets. That shuts them up. I don't go much myself. I don't really care for baseball. I would rather be at the beach."

"Baseball is a very spiritual game."

"You don't say. I thought you would say that."

"People have played a game like baseball for millennia."

"Hm. I'm glad to hear you enjoy something. Okay, I have your tickets."

27

"The batsman makes a circle, joins the circle, and returns to home, finds his home . . . believe me it is more than it seems at Wrigley."

"Whoa! In other words you wouldn't mind a pair of tickets! Say, this ham will last us for days. We won't have to go out for breakfast. It will go good with some eggs."

"If you go with me to a game. What are you going to do when it's gone?"

"What's gone?"

"When the pleasure is over."

"Are you starting up again? Get something else to enjoy."

"So it's not that much to get excited about."

"Who's excited?" A look of sunny irony was playing in her wicked eyes now. *"You're* excited. You know, I think we could be good for each other. I could teach you to love life more, and you could teach me to like it less! Ha ha ha, ha ha ha!" She threw back her head and tittered joyously, as if one's own laughter could be a meal in itself.

I studied her wide-open mouth, lips so full and red—and greasy. Was it better to be involved in life full throttle or be more detached and serene? Better to indulge to the hilt or seek eternal images? I had no idea. I was terribly attracted to her despite philosophy and personal misgivings it was in the nature of her message to me that I would overcome. I wanted her more than anything and had no appetite for anything else by now and I'd only met her. The ham was forgotten. I never did find out where that ham came from or whose it was, and she could care less. I made some attempt to wrap the silver foil around it and jammed it into the refrigerator. She didn't help. As for Melusina and me, I didn't quite realize it at the time of course, but looking back on the morning, that crazy conversation about a ham was our unlikely delicious courtship. I had been avoiding her in the hallway and now she had gotten under my skin.

"What time is it?" she asked abruptly, glancing about and wiping her fingers on her jeans. "I want to go to the beach."

"The body is found in time," quoth I, reflecting some meditations on reality I had been doing recently in the way of research for my novel, just stalling for time and trying to evade my fate, but no longer able to resist it.

"Just in time!" she shot back cheerfully right on target and ran upstairs to change. "My body is found at the beach!"

"That's good to know," I mumbled tentatively.

I finally tore my eyes from the burning red sign on the poolroom wall that I knew had been placed there just for me. One thing I really had no light on was how I was going to pass the time with Mayor Daley's illegitimate grandson. I couldn't even speculate on that subject. He had slumped way down in his chair, his toes nearly touching the floor. He had a real talent for slouching way down as most little kids do, when they want to, but this was dramatic, he looked positively bored to death and even ill. My nineball opponent was staring at me with a highly amused look over his shoulder.

Little kids like Mayor Daley's grandson, what goes on with them? One thing I could guess about his little mind, and something we probably did have in common, was how much he missed Melusina and wished she would come back to the poolroom right now and get him. I wished the same, so I could see her again, and get rid of him. But I knew her well enough to know she wouldn't be back right away, and it might be a while.

When I went over to the child, he looked so sad I felt very sorry for him, passed along as an encumbrance between adults. Well he was such a puny little thing and not a happy camper. I could remember quite well from my own childhood how unbearably tiresome adults could be and the life they gave one. Always being made to wait on things or to endure some sort of passage in grownups' time, or taken from place to place, in a car, or under the supervision of someone providing you with nothing purposeful to do. A dark sympathy for the poor kid rose in me— I wished so much I could think up some entertainment for him.

Then I had it—I remembered a church fair that was going on in the neighborhood. I'd seen an ad for some acrobats who were going to perform at this fair and heard talk of it. This prospect excited me. I wanted to see them myself and I was sure the little kid would love such a spectacle. All kids like acrobats and things like that. A small wave of joy washed over me at thought of such a distraction for us both and I felt like a kid myself. I was pleased with myself for remembering the fair that I'd seen advertised on a placard somewhere and no longer felt so annoyed at having been left in charge of this strange child. Instead I was glad I might be able to give him some happiness. This possibility even created in me some affection for him.

As we walked up the street together, I tried to picture for him what the acrobats would be like and he listened raptly and seemed less sad. I knew the perfect vantage point from which Melusina's kid and I could watch the church fair. A friend of mine lived in a third-floor apartment right across the street from the old cathedral. The windows looked out on the tall steeple so you felt you could have leapt out upon it and climbed its peak to touch the stars, or so it seemed in my mind's eye right now. The kid traipsed along beside me, or behind me trying to keep up, as in my anticipation I found it hard not to walk fast. He seemed no longer a wound-up little ball of fear and desperation, instead his eyes held that glazed expression little kids have when they are shifted around one too many times by their elders and have no choice but to follow helplessly but they still hope for the best. I so much wanted to cheer him up now because I couldn't help but be aware that I was in a better mood myself on account of taking him to the fair. Well, as always life had taken on a rounder look, a bit of a glow, as it usually did when M showed up even for a moment, even if she looked like trouble.

The next moment, because the fun he was going to have at the fair had not seemed to make any impression on him and he still remained perfectly glum, I was vexed once more at being in charge of him. I glanced down at him and I hadn't noticed till this moment that on one hand he wore a little baseball mitt, as if hopelessly asserting his little kid's wish that somebody would just throw him a baseball and play catch with him. This forlorn detail pressed on my heart. I wished I'd had a ball. I would have played catch with him though it was black night.

Then I was glad I did not. The mere idea of playing ball with Mayor Daley's illegitimate grandson while his so-called mother was partying someplace in that black wig and rapturous foxfire fur coat suddenly annoyed me again with intolerable futility. I didn't believe a word of her story, but I had no other explanation for this child who was undeniably shuffling along at my elbow. M's disappearing act was exasperatingly familiar, as much as her reappearance had been momentarily tantalizing, but this mysterious child she'd left me with presented a practical problem it was going to take more than a few pitches of a baseball to solve. This orphan was something new in the way of M's impositions on me. I had a sneaking suspicion it might take a heroic effort on my part to entertain him. I could only hope for the best from the acrobats and the games of toss and whatnot up the block at the fair. I put my hand on his tiny shoulder to urge him forward toward the church, picturing for myself how his little eyes would light up at sight of the jugglers and clowns. Once he got a chance to throw a ball at a target and win a prize, that would take his mind off his loneliness and little troubles.

We turned a corner and ahead of us was the church, all lit up for the fair, which was going full tilt, crowds milling around the arcades that had been set up on the sidewalk up and down the street. It was more impressive even than I had expected, and looking down at him I thought I saw the boy's eyes widen and gleam for sure. A thrilling sensation as one ascribes to childhood, after all, coursed through me, reminding me that the world could be full of wonder yet, even if alas it mostly isn't. It struck me that the kid was really going to have some fun tonight and so was I. Anyway, I was going to, I couldn't help about him. I hoped he would, I had begun to feel warmly toward him. It would have never occurred to me to come to the fair if I had not had this kid to contend with, and if M hadn't shown up and stirred things up as usual.

A few minutes ago I had been in the blackest mood and at my wit's end to have been stuck with the kid in the poolhall, and now the joyful sounds and colorful sights of the carnival beckoned wholesomely, and my own childlike excitement was like a fresh breeze off the lake out there in the dark. The crowds and lights and games and the prospect of the acrobats made a commonplace heaven we all may share if we have a mind to. As we passed the door of the apartment building where my friend lived, I decided it would be a good idea to go in and just say hello and arrange to come up later when the acrobats began their performance, so as then to gaze down on them from his windows. But I thought better of having the kid with me when I rang his bell. No, I did not want to take the kid with me because it might cast my friendly request in the light of an imposition, as if he could hardly refuse when he saw I had the kid with me. I would have been as bad as M. I liked to keep things simple. "Go in the back and play a minute," I told the child.

I hadn't seen my friend in quite a while actually. It would have been like blackmail, even rude, as if I were placing some responsibility for entertaining the kid on him (as M had done to me), and some of the genuine joy he might have felt to be generous, and I was feeling, might have gone out. Particularly if his wife was there who might have felt moved to take the child under her wing so to speak, I feared a shadow on our high spirits, and mine I viewed as precarious. So I sent my protégé into the backyard to play while I went up. The neighborhood was the type populated by young families and I vaguely remembered a teeter-totter out there as well as other kids' toys, alluring junk to a little boy maybe, and beyond the yard's perfunctorily mowed confines, a vacant lot with little boy–sized holes in the weeds that would captivate him for the time I thought it would take me.

Of course, I hoped he would not get lost or escape through the urban jungle, but at the same time I half wished he would. I flew up the stairs. My friend was not at home, but on his door he had taped a note: "Anyone who wants to watch the circus just come on in." That was just like my generous friend. I took a few steps inside. The rooms were darkened. Through the windows the floodlit church with fluttering flags and colorful banners seemed the center of a medieval festival. I pressed to the window and looked down enraptured on the throngs milling on the sidewalks. Booths and games, clowns, jugglers—chained to a lamppost was a bear wearing a party hat . . . I could hardly believe my eyes and could not take it all in. The church seemed displaced back in time to another, merrier age. Minutes had passed when I came to myself, and rushed downstairs to look for the kid.

Pale yellow light from the apartments' windows striped the backyard and the vacant lot behind it, a thicker jungle than I remembered. I couldn't see him anywhere and panicked. What if he had been bored and gone ahead of me out to the fair by himself? He might be lost in the crowds and I'd never find him. M would kill me. The backyard was a half-heartedly tended affair with a rusty swing set. The swings hung listless and forlorn. Beyond, the vacant lot was far ranker than I could have imagined, dense with tall grey weeds and household rubble, suggesting secret pathways down which a little boy could lose himself. For all the commotion and festivity on the streets, back here it was desolate and haunted. It was getting on ten o'clock on a moonless night. I should never have let him out of my sight.

Then to my relief I saw him hunched in the far corner of the yard, beyond the swings, and he had managed to make a couple of little friends with whom he was playing some game, huddled low in the dirt. Swells of organ grinder music and waves of tinkling laughter from the fair started up again as I relaxed having found him. The kid's friends on closer inspection were a couple of dirty nasty little brats. They wore peculiar brown peaked caps of a kind I had never seen before maybe denoting gang membership. From the peaks of their brown caps hung small gold bells. Probably they played some role at the fair, had been given costumes, and sold peanuts or something, and had been hired to be part of the atmosphere as the clowns were paid to stroll around. Instead they were shirking their duties and had wandered back here for a smoke and run into my charge, Mayor Daley's grandson.

The ragtag ends of the crowd pushed in through the alleys and shadowy backyards to gambol dubiously at the edges of the legitimate church festivities, these two juvenile delinquents having stolen in here through the tall weeds in search of trouble. But I didn't care, I was so grateful not to have lost M's little boy I could have hugged the filthy imps who had corralled him. I ambled over to where they were playing in a yellow-lit patch of dust. It was nice to see M's kid having fun and taking a keen interest in whatever game they were conducting. His bored look was gone. The crowd's chatter and waves of pleasure from the church fair once again cast their spell over me as I approached my little charge and his pals. Thinking passingly of what M would do to me if I had lost her kid overwhelmed me with gratitude to see the three of them.

Glancing over Mayor Daley's illegitimate grandson's thin shoulder I saw with repulsion that he and the boys were playing with two fat green snakes which were roiling and writhing over one another and in fact fighting under the prodding of the boys

34

who shouted at them and struck them with sticks. I was spellbound at the sight of the slithering reptiles.

At first I thought it was a fair fight between the two urchins' snakes, but as bad as that was it became apparent that the game was even more desperate. According to their shouts it was a titanic struggle between a "good" snake and a "bad" one. This cast a pall over me as the scene had shifted to nightmare. The little hoodlums were wildly calling encouragement to the "good" snake to take a bite out of the "bad" one, but the "bad" one looked in danger of overcoming the other. Mayor Daley's grandson was staring fixedly at the action, which was taking place in a makeshift arena that the boys had carved out in the dust with the point of a stick and some rocks strewn in a rough circle. Mesmerized, I watched this amusement, amazed that you could make snakes fight like dogs or cocks. Each time their favorite, the "good" snake, seemed about to succumb, the boys touched it with their sticks and goaded it into renewed activity, and whacked the bad snake within an inch of its life. In the center of the circle the snakes struck at each other's mouths.

"Wanna make a bet on em?"

"Your snake is going to lose."

"Well, bet on the bad one then."

"I'm not going to bet on either one of them!"

I grabbed M's kid by his reedy neck to steer him away, but he brushed my hand off with disturbing violence. I didn't think he had it in him. He was stronger than he looked. I looked at my hand which stung. Something powerful was going on here, as little kids' games can be so compelling you can't draw them away from them except with main force or the parental sort of authority I certainly didn't have.

The sordidness of having been asked by the scamp to wager on this death struggle increased the horror and I couldn't believe what I had found in my good friend's backyard. All at once one of the boys seemed to think that the good snake was in real trouble and he produced a line and fishhook with which he deftly snagged the bad snake's jaw, but not to allow the "good" one to escape for the "good" one instantly fixed a deathgrip on the other's neck and I believed I was going to witness the animal murder its rival. The sight of the "bad" snake being pulled over on its side by the boy's hook so the other snake could kill it seemed unbearably cruel and unfair and the next moment the idea hit me that the boys might be wrong or lying and the good snake might be the bad one and vice versa—or why should snakes be good and bad anyway? It probably just had to do with their property investment.

As much as I had no intention of getting involved, I was overcome with the feeling I had to end the abhorrence of this snake murder. Before I could think, I found myself yelling, "Cut the string! Cut the string!" Astonished at the vehemence of my own emotion, before I knew it I had hold of the boy's arm with one hand and snatched the string with the other but I didn't know what to do with it or what to do next because the snakes were unpredictably leaping about and the line was too strong to break. At this M's kid like a snake himself made a bold move. Of all the weird things I had seen concerning him tonight, this topped them all, as he thrust forward his head and darted forth his mouth this way and that and finally caught and bit the string in two with his teeth neatly, releasing the "bad" snake which instantly streaked off into the underbrush of the vacant lot. I stood rooted to the spot, staggered by the swift efficiency of his sudden move, relieved the snake had escaped.

"Okay you gotta pay us for that snake," said one of the boys with their strange caps. I didn't bother replying. The rascals pounced on their "good" snake at once and put it in a cardboard box. "Five dollars."

"Get lost." I was looking into the jungle where the snake had slithered. Without another word the boys headed for the street. About fifty feet away, one called back "You owe us." I felt victorious to have helped the snake get away from them.

M's kid squatted there staring from the arena into the weeds into which the "bad" snake had escaped with a look of forlorn affection in his little eyes. That won me over as much as his deft bite to free the snake had. I felt the same way. A murder had been avoided and we had even bonded a little in the act. All this confirmed my idea that the snakes were mislabeled for some reason best known to the avaricious miscreants who had just departed. I traced again the green glide of the "bad" snake into the fringes, an emerald gleam just out of sight as it hovered in there nursing its wound. The fishhook was still stuck in its mouth of course, but from a few experiences I had had fishing in Canada I understood that eventually the secretions of its jaw would rust the hook out which would fall away. Anyway I hoped so. I hoped it wouldn't die. By now I had more than a suspicion it was actually a "good" snake. I could sense its stunned outrage as it healed itself in the darkness, the grasses having closed over it in its bower.

Perhaps it had made a bond between us, for after a while when I took his hand he no longer pulled away but let himself be led toward the light and life of the church carnival round the corner. However, I could not forget the uncanny intelligence and deftness of the Mayor's grandson's swift nip of the string between his sharp teeth that had effected the snake's release to the undergrowth. What sharp teeth the Mayor's grandson had! I hoped he didn't bite me for any reason.

Lights, laughter, and music were the proper medium for us, and as we made our way into the happy distracted crowd around the church, it was a relief to be rubbing elbows with good folks in a well-lit place, and I hoped it would cheer the kid up, and make him forget all about the snakes, or at least not mention it to M later, who would not be pleased I had let him out of my sight in a back alley. He headed straight for a booth where an accurate or lucky toss of a ping-pong ball into the mouth of one of a hundred glass globes holding tiny fish in water won the patron the globe and the fish. The kid was very taken, and so was I, with the spectacle of rank upon rank of glittering clear globes rising one behind the other against the light emanating from the church, each with its tiny brightly colored fish nuclei like the flame of a candle, giving the impression of a staircase of watery votaries spread up before us. The light mirrored off the scales and fins of the little golden fishes and the water in every third or fourth bowl was colored pink or blue, an utterly lovely and wholesome sight, rather holy, and it made me smile to see the kid's eyes widen with childish lust for a prize, a pretty little goldfish in its round glass home. Then his eyes narrowed and he went to work.

With three tosses that my quarter bought him, he promptly won two fishbowls. I was astounded at his skill, and so was the black-haired woman who sullenly placed his prizes on the counter, who looked at him suspiciously and with an ill temper that she didn't even try to professionally conceal. I think we both hoped he wouldn't try again, or at least I did, because she was looking at him like he was a ringer. The firmness of his tosses and steadiness of his hand struck me too as outright ominous for one so frail whose nose didn't reach the countertop. His motions reminded me again of the way he had bitten that fishing line in two with his teeth. For a tiny tot he was weirdly adept and forceful. As I had no desire to add to the suspicion of the glaring woman who had lost two globes at once, nor to linger on the strange impression it gave me either, I took one prize and handed him the other and led him away to some other pastime.

With fishbowls in hand, sloshing water carelessly, I couldn't get away fast enough from memory of his ping-pong ball going off his fingertips straight into the mouth of a globe as if on a taut string. The combination of his piteous orphanhood and astonishing hand-and-eye coordination was uncanny. I couldn't bring myself to compliment him cheerfully on his aim, although a few moments before the thought of his winning anything would have warmed my heart. The one redeeming thing about having been left with this kid by M had been my idea that I could delight or amuse him. I should have won him a fish in a bowl but all he needed me for was to carry it. He didn't look satisfied either, but with his narrowed little eyes determined to win more prizes at the fair. I wondered what he would accomplish next. I could have thrown ping-pong balls for half an hour without hitting anything. He had his fishbowl in one hand and his baseball mitt on the other.

We found ourselves on the curbstone waiting for a parade to start, or that was my impression. A couple of guys ran past us right under our noses almost knocking the fish in their bowls out of our hands. My shirtfront was soaked already from my carelessness in transporting the fishbowl. More runners went by in colorful gear. A street race was in progress, not a parade, the runners passing us in a counterclockwise direction around the block. Now that seemed a proper spectacle. I loved a good footrace! A string of runners dashed by in the street before us, one after another, wearing shimmering tracksuits and numbers on their backs. I was enjoying myself at last and looked down at M's kid, but it was hard to tell about him.

When the last of the pack had gone by, to my alarm I saw I had spilled out all of the water and the little fish was flopping at the bottom of the glass bowl in my hands. I took a step back toward the concession to request more water from the woman but we must have walked farther than I had realized because I could no longer spot the booth. Instead I was standing next to a hot dog stand and I asked the black kid running it for water for the bowl. He extended a thick rubber hose from the sink and blew a hard stream into the glass. At the curb again, I was disappointed to see only an inch or two of water in the bottom of the fishbowl probably because the force of the blast from the hose had blown most of the water over the sides. Plus the fish was swimming sidewise looking shell-shocked from the force of it. Or maybe the elbows of the crowd had made me tip out the water inadvertently as I returned to the curbside. In the meantime M's kid had all his water in his bowl. My fish looked dazed as it floundered in an inch of water. It worked its gill flaps trying to breathe. I looked around vaguely wondering where I could get more water from a gentler source.

The runners flashed by on their next circuit, elbowing each other for position. It was an exciting race. M's kid seemed content watching the racers in their colorful shorts and fancy shoes kicking up their heels as they went by us, and I was grateful he was preoccupied. Strange, but at once it seemed the commonplace race that does indeed go to the swift, and nothing more, and the next moment an indication of a need for higher progress, of the kind I was sure I was not making. My fish was now completely out of water again. Its little body slithered about in a few drops at the bottom. I gasped for air too in sympathy. A chaos entered my heart. A fearful dryness invaded certain moist organs of my own. Some inner vial of my being seemed to cry out for a refill.

I pushed back into the mob around the hot dog stand but was unable to catch the black youth's attention who probably suspected I was not going to buy anything and only wanted free water again. I spied around for any water source and finally saw a Pepsi dispenser along with several unmarked spigots that I could reach on my own and I did so. Choosing what I guessed would be clear water, I pressed the button and shot a carbonated stream down on my fish. Not good! Frantic, I pressed the tips of my fingers down into the bowl upon the fish and squirted it up into my palm as I dumped out the fizz water on the ground. But at that instant I dropped the fishbowl which shattered at my feet. With the fish wriggling in my hand I avoided the crowd and ran out into the street.

The runners were taking another lap and I had to race back against the force of the colorful athletes dodging among them as fast as I could make it until I saw the game booth where we had originally won our little prizes and in desperation, beside myself to be holding a squirming fish in my hand, I began yelling at the black-haired woman when I was still a long ways off yet, demanding she give me a new bowl and some water, and when I got there she did this promptly, with no argument. However, it was not a round bowl at all, but a tall thin vase, and the water was quite strange, rather "heavy" I thought, a clear jelly. But as I examined my fish I saw it didn't mind and had begun to thrive though it had less space. Well, it was a water I had not come in contact with before. It might as well be better as worse. It was a "water that was not water," the words that came to mind. Its unusual viscosity had the benefit that I was able to make my way back to the corner without any of it sloshing over the sides, and the tallness and thinness of the vase helped also. There was something awfully familiar about that black-haired woman. Actually she looked a damn sight like M with her black hair as I had last seen her. I glanced back over my shoulder. She was extremely attractive and winsome it hit me with a jolt for a carnie barker. It was just that I was hoping we would run into M at the fair and she would take the kid back.

As soon as I saw M's kid standing there gaping at the runners going by I couldn't believe I had left him alone again and was overjoyed he was still there. I stood looking at him gratefully and he took a gander at my new glass in my hands. He reached out and pointed at it and I noticed that the woman had given me another fish, along with the water, perhaps to make it clear that this time I had better not come back. So now I had two fish. One of the little fish was green with flecks of cobalt and the other with red scales tipped with magenta. Magical and pretty little fish they were with long trailing fins like tiny peacocks. You know the kind I mean, magical at that. But you might not recognize the new water I had been given. I had the feeling if I tipped the vase upside down, it would not flow out.

The fish were so beautiful my hands began to shake for their beauty. I doubted my ability to care for them or keep their water in the vase. Heavy as it was, drops of it indeed began to leap out of the top of the glass into the air and to fall upon the pavement in fat tears. I was not able to care for these fish, I knew, any more than I knew what to do with M's child, Mayor Daley's so-called grandson, who—I had to face it—no matter what I thought of her story, was a mysterious child. The fish were almost out of water again, heavy as it was, it was just spurting skyward, I was in over my head with this kid, and the brightly clad racers were going by faster and faster sprinting for the finish.

41

Then it began to rain. You can imagine my pleasure and relief as I watched the vase fill up with rainwater, the pure and merciful rain. From the heels of the runners whole cups of water flew. The fishes revived and preened their feathery fins. The little red fish hovered slightly over the little green fish in a mating dance. Their bodies bloomed with health. The heads of the crowd around us began to turn. People stared upward and so did the kid and I, clutching our fishbowls. The acrobats were about to start their performance! A handsome young man with long flowing golden hair had stuck his head out a small window in the church spire. Now he waved his hand in a wide gesture betokening confidence, and gave it a flourish of bravado and good cheer. With a calm smile he leapt up onto the narrow windowsill, hanging onto the frame with one hand as he waved again and again to the crowd with the other, which, electrified, buzzed loudly, then fell silent. All eyes were on the young acrobat. The kid and I held our fishbowls for dear life like offerings we might need to make later to unknown gods. The sudden rain shower had ended and everything glistened with new life, and now the show began.

The acrobat with a graceful smile held himself erect for a long moment. Then he let go of the window frame and fell straight forward toward the pavement. The crowd gasped as one. Out went the acrobat's arms as his body reached the horizontal, from his flowing shirtsleeves wide tricolored banners emerging which unfurled and took the air. His toes gripped fast to the windowsill, while his "wings" held the breeze, and his lithe figure buoyed on the air, as gently he rode the invisible currents above our heads.

If the acrobatics had now begun, I thought, watching the long-haired artist above my head flying straight out from the windowsill on his tricolored banners like kites, or *wings,* it was time for the kid and me to go upstairs and take advantage of the fine view from my friend's picture window. I figured he'd be thrilled to be so close to the action. Now the kid and I were gazing straight across at the daring young man on the flying—well, no, he looked as though he were on a trapeze, he was doing a perfect imitation of it, his hair flowing in the breeze, and his body now rising, now falling, at more or less a ninety degree angle from the church steeple—yet it was a feat even more spectacular in its way than a trapeze act because it seemed to defy the law of gravity, his toes hooked onto the windowsill, his muscular arms outstretched and in his hands the multicolored flags powerfully holding the air. Looking right across at the acrobat, the window-to-window outlook we had on him and the church steeple gave the illusion we were all floating and flying through the air, I, the kid, the daring young man, everybody, the whole carnival. It seemed to me I could sense the earth slowly spinning, or had clear evidence of it. With the ground and the crowd in the street obscured from view we seemed to turn and hurtle steadily together through space on the bright banners. In my delight at this, and sure that my ambition of entertaining Melusina's kid had been royally fulfilled, I squeezed his shoulder, and looked down affectionately and proudly into his sickly little face, and shouted out my pleasure, pointing.

43

"Wings! Wings!"

But he was not delighted by it, for he only scowled more ferociously, and concentrated his attention on squeezing his baseball mitt between his little hands. There was certainly something wrong with him. Or maybe not—the fact was he just wished somebody would play catch with him. Maybe he was feeling ill. I jumped up to throw open the window all the way to catch some fresh air, realized I'd already done that, and leaned on my elbows on the windowsill so happy to be that much closer to the marvelous acrobat and to watch the crowd below who were noisy and gape-mouthed, loving it, unlike M's kid. I wished he could be excited as I was, but I wanted to forget about M's kid, who was sick, sulking about something, or was just plain too ill-tempered to be charmed by the amazing spectacle.

It was more than that. Something about him disturbed me, I suspected he wasn't a little kid at all. But it was hard to acknowledge my suspicious feelings, because then I would have had to ask myself, if he wasn't actually a little kid as he more or less appeared to be, and was supposed to be, having been characterized as such by M, then what was he? I preferred to evade this question and not think about it, observing again that he would rather play catch with somebody, and then it hit me how likely this was. But selfishly I would not play catch with him, I wanted to watch the amazing show. I wasn't aware of any baseball or any kind of ball in the vicinity either.

The flags or kites in the acrobat's hands were shimmering red, gold, and royal purple. Not only were we flying through space, but we had leapt across centuries in time, and the sights and sounds and atmosphere seemed to me more and more those of an old medieval church festival, and the church itself was an old stone Catholic cathedral from the middle ages. Monks in their cowls could be glimpsed in the doorways. At one corner of the church, in the torchlight, the bear danced on its chain. The acrobat flying on the breeze right across from me less than fifty feet away worked one hand loose from the flag that had been bound to it by a kind of brace, and threw his "wing" down to the crowd, and now he managed to stay aloft on just one banner, or wing. A happy boy below caught the one he had cast off and waved it back and forth above his head. For a few moments the acrobat flew one-handed. Then, just as he seemed about to fall and crash, a comrade in the church window extended a new wing out to him, this one green and white striped.

Out of the window now cascaded flag after flag, dozens of flags, thrown out the window by carnival workers, souvenirs fluttering down to the upthrust of hands of the crowd below. On the street, coming out from the church, gaily dressed performers handed out more and more multicolored flags to everybody. What a feast for the eye! Banners waved everywhere in a frenetic, climactic display. It was suddenly a winged crowd. I yelled down from the window, and three of them were sailed up my way. I managed to catch one of them and bestowed it at once on the kid, who disdained to take it. He had the ludicrous haughty expression on his face of refusing to be taken in by a trick.

My disappointment seemed to have no bottom. In my trembling hand I held the miraculous gold-red-purple spurned flag, which he wouldn't even look at. I couldn't believe such an obdurate child. There was no question that this was a child with his own ideas, a look stealing into his now wide-open eyes of intense perturbation, of having suffered about as much as he intended to on my account. This completely passed my understanding but I was arrested by the force of stubbornness in his small hunched up frame. I felt his *will* confronting and contradicting mine. My sense of disappointment regarding being able to entertain this kid until M came back for him became so strong it verged on fear.

If all of this did not divert him, nothing would. I tried to remember or imagine what it would be like to be a little kid forced to do what the grownups wanted. But what child did not like a circus? In his gaze which cut right through me I read rejection of all my joy and infatuation with the astonishing flying feat of the winged acrobat not as a sullen child would have rejected it, but almost as a jaded or perceptive man of the world would have deigned to be impressed by a mere feat of strength or even a cheap magic trick. That really was annoying because this was a first-class entertainment that had me spellbound and completely on air myself.

If it was a trick, it was a damn wonderful trick. The flags were so pretty, any child should have adored them. But there was something ancient in his little eyes. In some children one senses a wisdom beyond their years, but that didn't mean they refused to have fun; the wisest child is amusable. He was just plain ornery and a bad job as a kid all around, I decided, and when I heard some of the television cameramen begging members of the crowd to part with their flags at least for long enough for them to get some close-up shots of them—videocameramen from a TV station who had been wandering about and now had stationed themselves right below the apartment window—I threw down our unwanted flag onto their heads.

"The kid doesn't want it!" I called out the window incredulously, unable to contain my annoyance.

One of the cameramen called to the others, "Hey, somebody doesn't want their wing!"

I stared down at the crowd and the colorful flags soaring and fluttering restored my joy. It was the sort of thing that makes grownups think of being kids again, and I did. That's why they wanted to put it on the news and why the camera crew was here. I turned around to stare at the kid as if to say I guessed I'd showed him, if he was going to be so ungrateful and undelighted, by throwing his wing into the street—but he was nowhere to be seen. He'd slunk backward into the shadows somewhere. Maybe he was going to take a nap. He'd been looking unwell. Then as my eyes got used to the shadows, I saw him fading backward out of sight, not walking on his little legs though but disappearing straight backward as if he'd been on wheels. Just like that he was gone. He reminded me of the snake darting into the weeds.

This happened so fast I doubted my own eyes. He'd glided backward like he'd been on skates. I gazed into the dark jungle of the apartment. I had not turned on any lights, the better to view the spectacle across the street. A thin radiance stole in from the candles, torches, and beacons of the fair. I sensed the kid back there somewhere against the wall. Then I felt him move, caught a glimmer of him. He was in the corner of the room, and then I saw him. He had changed into a powerful looking dwarf. I had had this feeling about him before, that he was not so much a kid as a dwarf, and I was right. Far from frail and sickly, a pair of hulking shoulders clad in a white-knit polo shirt loomed momentarily in the crepuscular corner. What shoulders, like barrels! He wasn't any taller, the shoulders remained not three feet above the floor. They rolled at me.

The hunched power of those shoulders uncoiled in a lightning spasm. The kid's arm reared back, and wham! he hurled a silver bat at me that barely whizzed past my ear, about the shape of a golfclub, or a hockey stick, and disappeared straight out the window like the flag had but with inhuman violence. It went by my head like a bolt of whistling silver light, fast as a bullet with overpowering force. It would have killed me, driven straight through my brain and maybe taken my head off, never stopped going, had it struck me. The huge shoulders under the white polo shirt rotated back into shadow. For a long minute I crouched waiting in fear for him to throw something else. Was his aim bad or had he just meant to scare me?

The moment passed like the strike of a wasp or a hissing snake that had somehow missed its mark. Some elemental force had missed me or warned me. It seemed impossible that it should have missed and I was still in once piece. Monstrous and deadly instinctual power sank below the surface, retreated back into the depths, restoring an ordinary night that would not be the same. I gazed out the window to the ground, where the moonbright silver bat thrown by Mayor Daley's dwarf grandson now lay in a rough circle with three flags abandoned by the videocameramen in a patch of yellow sand or dust flickeringly illuminated by the festive lights. The silver bat was "flag"-shaped too, that is, roughly shaped like a banner or flag on a staff, though the flag or

47

head was very small, like a golf club. What's more the club head was really a small scrolled flame that mystifyingly burned, a torch never diminishing. The staffs or handles of the three purple-and-gold flags and the burning silver bat joined inward at the center of the circle, with the multicolored squares of cloth and the flaming tip of the bat describing the circumference, making a sun-wheel, which now began to spin, faster and faster.

The crowd pressed in to see this new spectacle, spinning and sparkling in the yellow circle of sand like a roman candle shooting sparks and brilliant flames. They murmured and pointed at the fireworks but didn't press in too close because it all looked like it could go off and explode more violently. The videocameramen were photographing it again and again from every angle for the late news. Maybe the bat was only a candlestick my friend the owner of this apartment had brought back from his world travels. I marveled that the spinning and burning sun-wheel in the street below had somehow been rendered into motion by the monstrous strength of M's little kid from the poolhall. I slumped to the floor in a near-swoon of deadly fear and the sickening realization I had very nearly had my head smashed in by the inhuman velocity of his silver missile. And I had thought his problem was just that he was being taken around my boring grownups who wouldn't produce a ball to play catch with him, when he had a silver bat on him that would have not just knocked the ball out of the park but into the next state or rather just pulverized any ball and burnt it to a crisp. Awe and dumb fear eclipsed my irritation at Melusina for having left me with such a "child."

He might throw something else at me. If I stayed on the floor I was a sitting duck and he could just crack a chair over my head. My idea of being at a cathedral fair in a setting out of the Middle Ages came over me again but this time with no charming sense of romance and make-believe but queasy realism out of nightmare that no longer had anything quaint about it. I seemed to have been removed back to an age of rude transformations and cruel tortures. That silver bat or candlestick spinning in the yellow sand below me had a look and shape to it that were remote, atavistic, and magical. It had put a scare in me and almost beaned me. It was made of silver or lead yet the tip of it was visibly burning and giving out sparks. I had brought the kid to see a circus fair and he had turned into a vile dwarf who'd propelled a burning brand at me. Unlike the kid, I was certainly not bored, anyway.

The bat had come out of the darkness at me from primeval mists hurled by an orangutan from the underworld. Yet at such close range, it could have been no accident it had missed, could it? Had I been mercifully spared for the time being? From what, and for what? What was I being warned about? The guilty speculations that this thought now triggered were more horribly confusing than the whizzing bat itself. On the kid's swollen face there had been a look of petulant outrage and snarling furious annoyance, but not quite outright murder yet. The whole strength went out of me and I stared into the far shadows of the apartment waiting for a new attack to come. I don't know how many minutes went by with the little guy skulking back there and me paralyzed with fear and wonder. What was this about? The strange thing was I seemed to have an idea, but I couldn't put my finger on it exactly.

Melusina burst into the apartment scolding us both at the top of her lungs for disappearing into the city and hiding from her, for making her search the list of our mutual friends before she'd guessed where we'd gone, etc., and now where were we hiding, the place was too dark, and she couldn't see a thing— accusations, lamentations, and the lamest threats concerning Mayor Daley, as if we could be fined or given a speeding ticket. She went so far as to imply there could be a charge of kidnapping against me, unless she personally intervened! That really did it. It was more like an attempted murder charge, in my mind. I loved M, wondered what she could be talking about, no longer believed a word she was saying, but was relieved, forgiving, and overjoyed to hear her voice and didn't care what she yelled, her voice was like music from a happy time when life on earth was sane, lush, abundant, carefree, and earthy, in a normal, ferociously feminine way, without club throwing dwarfs. I didn't even think to blame her for him. I felt rescued from the kid, and especially from myself, like on the morning I'd met her.

She now rounded up the kid and bundled him off to another room, saying he needed a nap, and came sinuously, wordlessly, silently back to slide on top of me, caress me head to toe, make love to me, and push an enormous load off my heart. And it came to me that it was true, she did know Mayor Daley, she was something else, a miracle, I had known that since I'd first met her, and she had one surprise for me after another, but it had been so long since I had seen her that I had forgotten. I lavished my love on every inch of her, measuring every curve of her body with my fingertips like the points of a compass on a map of the world. We made up for every last absence and created raw new grievances needing an eternity of forgiveness. In her octopussal power, we swam and writhed in serpentine coils of sex. In greasy rings of gray taut flesh like rodents swallowed by pythons of our desire, over and over we turned for an hour, striking death blows. She changed into a medium-size Florida alligator (I was used to this as I've said) and we glided together at last through the swamp and came to rest in the silky mud, our tongues lashed together like moorings after a hurricane. When all the damage had been done, M got up to turn on a light. We had been doing all this on the floor and I ached, had carpet burns on my knees, and felt black and blue. But sane again and grateful, for a few moments anyway. That flame thrower dwarf was sleeping it off somewhere, hopefully locked up in the bathroom, I'd almost forgotten him, and I was thankful to M for that.

Then I wondered in a stupor, through all the love-crazed interlude, might I have still not touched her face? The lights came on. My hands were outstretched in front of me to catch her from leaving, feeling for her lips. It wasn't M, who had vanished, but in the room with me was the wife of my friend, the owner of this apartment, who apparently had just come in, by her preoccupied demeanor. She jumped about a foot in the air when she saw me. My hands were almost on her mouth. The stealth with which she had entered, what if she'd come in fifteen minutes earlier?

Another crazy thing was how much she looked like M. Could it have been? I sincerely hoped not. The resemblance caused me to stare fixedly at her, and finally she asked me what in the world was wrong. Apparently my expression was even more disturbing than the outrageous fact that I had been naked on the floor in her apartment when she came home and had my hands outstretched as if to grab her by the throat. She told me to follow her and went into the kitchen.

"Your husband left a note on the door saying we could come in and watch the street fair," I sounded lame to myself, though it was true.

"You don't look very well," she commented offhandedly.

"I don't think I could begin to tell you how strange a night this has been."

"You look a little done in."

"Well, what do you expect after the past hour or two?" I asked sharply, suddenly thinking it was M after all, kidding around as usual. I peered at her suspiciously.

"What? *O-o-okay,*" was all she said in a distant way, as if she was in the know and whatever it was, it was really *o-o-okay.* Never has such *okayness* been put into that simple word in my hearing. It was said in such an offhand, certain manner. The essence of *okayness* tolled like a bell and I felt *okay* again. She radiated from her clear kindness and a thousand reassurances. Whoever she was, I felt that even if she was M, at the same time she thankfully was my friend's kind wife, although she might be someone else altogether.

M must be in the bathroom was all I could think. I took a step in that direction, but not more, because of the murderous kid sleeping back there. I didn't wish to stir him up and went on tiptoes. Through the crack under the bathroom door a little light seeped onto the floor of the darkened hallway, so that's where M was I could see, and the latest little mystery was solved. My friend's wife said to me with such mercy in her voice and the most wonderful kindly smile that I never doubted it, "Well, come and have a cup of tea."

Her modest, generous, and confident tone made me the more curious and I rushed to her side. I don't care much for tea and felt this was a fault to be overcome. Her kitchen was very cheerful and brightly lit and clean, and she seemed good and sweetly strong. It would be a blessed drink of something. She seemed full of light. Her face was glowing.

"You're so radiant tonight, you look like a goddess," I said, laughing. Without ever thinking or weighing my words, far from giving her a compliment, I was just reacting and stating my honest opinion or expressing my true feeling.

"Well, I am a goddess," she said with a small smile, seeming to reply from some good-natured off-hand level, so peaceful and in control, and sweetly reasonable, that I believed her outright past any cavil. Clearly this wasn't my friend's wife in any ordinary sense of the word, not tonight. The kitchen was an extremely pleasant and even sunny place, in spite of its being near midnight. Don't ask me how it could have been sunny at midnight, I'm just recording events as they occurred. When a goddess appears, it's hardly surprising if it gets sunny, whether it's night or not. Not only sunny, but shady, through a window the shade of an old elm or oak crept in refreshing as a drink of cool water. The season had changed to springtime, with its pleasant breezes blowing in the doorway and passing clouds alternating sun and shadow, delightful. Even the weather, the time of year, had skipped a beat.

Through the doorway were some woods, green and shadowy. It was far from that vacant lot with gangbangers and snakes. Out the back door I could see a dark man emerge from the pleasant trees and approach us innocently and leisurely. There was a measured, unhurried purposelessness in his gait that fixed my stare.

Some rattling of tins or pans returned my attention to the kitchen. On the stove was a big round silver tea kettle with an old-fashioned curved spout. That the kettle and the kid's silver bat were made of the same material was obvious, but the effect couldn't have been more different. I wouldn't say it was silver, it had a leaden look at the same time it seemed about to burst into flames. I'm just calling it silver because otherwise it would be indescribable. Big old tea kettle as it was, it seemed to grow bigger as I looked at it. It was almost as if the silver bat of the kid's had been changed by the goddess into that teapot, as swords will be beaten into plowshares. The goddess said nothing more. She was no longer in the room. She like the teapot were growing bigger and bigger. Now she contained the room. Now she was a presence all around the room and the kitchen was more or less in the place that would have been her womb and us inside her, or I was, as M was still in the bathroom down the hall. The kitchen itself was glowing and becoming curved like a reflection of itself in the round tea kettle. There was a roundness to everything.

I looked at the kettle (which by now was huge) more closely and saw at the end of its curved spout its whistle in the form of a little red crown. I thought it looked like a bishop's red hat. This red knob or hat had four slits in it to let the steam out and make it whistle, and this reminded me of the chess piece that is called the bishop. It all gave me a feeling of harmony, a feeling in short supply this evening, so I was deeply grateful to the goddess who had risen out of sight. The tea kettle had grown so big I was squeezed into the corner of the kitchen cozily by it.

The dark man had reached the kitchen door, his face as round as the tea kettle, with frizzles of gray hair and beard radiating from it on all sides in a perfect circle from chin to crown, like on an old print the anthropomorphized face of the sun showing the points of the compass, or the way the winds of the world puffed forth from his round cheeks on an ancient seafarers' map of the seven seas. As he came in, he brought with him the fresh breezes of spring, sun and shade, and the smell of the salt sea and distant climes. Crossing the room his presence suggested a filmy, flickering insubstantiality as though he were no more than a moment's fancy (but this whole night had begun to seem a moment's fancy to me), or the advent of a different reality too new to tell.

"Haven't we met before?" he said to me with an easy smile as he came in bringing with him a burst of sunshine. "Been a long time," he added. He was that sort of charismatic, graceful and enigmatic individual whom it is all too easy to think we have met, if long ago.

"Where have you been?" I asked without thinking, not knowing why.

"The islands," he replied promptly. He seemed to emerge from the waves. He had that breezy air. He sat down in the corner by the stove. The tea kettle began to whistle. By now the tea kettle had grown larger than the room so that we must have been inside it, and its whistle was like that of a steam engine.

"This is Black Sun Man," the goddess introduced us from an impossible height above the kitchen. He was at moments translucent so that you could see the chair he sat in right through him. She poured us cups of tea. Black Sun Man looked the part of his name. He had that aura that he was at the center of things and the planets moved around him. Invisible forces spun from his hand as he raised his teacup. You had the feeling that things would unfold the way they were supposed to if you only stuck by him. After a few minutes he had become steadily solider and I could no longer see objects on the other side of him right through him. It made me so happy just to be in the same room with him that I forgot all about Melusina and her dreadful child. It looked like he intended to stay.

"Hello, Black Sun Man," she said sweetly and with a slow-forming big smile as she came up behind me and walked up to him seated in the corner and took his hands in hers. His head was large and perfectly round like the globe. He smiled back at her in a familiar way bright as the kitchen light gleaming off the kettle, and sipped his tea. I wondered how M knew Black Sun Man.

"I'm hungry," she admitted, to us both.

On the stove sat that teapot as big as a pumpkin and just as round. The goddess said (from above and all around us), "If you're ever unhappy, just put on this tea kettle," and I thought that I would. But as many times as I tried later, in the long days ahead, I never could.

Not just to keep the conversation going, as the Black Sun Man, M, and the goddess were happy enough to sip their tea in silence, but I wasn't, because my thoughts had begun to return to the dwarf locked in the bathroom, fearing he could very well break free again, and to cover my panic I felt like needling M about it, I said, "How's Mayor Daley's kid coming along?"

"The Mayor came and got him."

"Oh yeah? . . . I thought you were in the bathroom."

"I was. I mean before . . . He was asleep in back. The Mayor came for him. Go look around."

I was sorry I had asked. Black Sun Man smiled at me easily, the tea was warming and refreshing, and if that kid was really gone, I was glad to hear it and didn't care who had come for him. I was happy to take M's word for it, even if most of the time I didn't believe half the things she said. Okay, Daley had rounded him up, if she said so. I was more than ready to have that vicious dwarf go back into the mists or wherever and didn't wish to think of him further let alone check up on him. I was ready for life to get back to normal or even better to continue in the peaceful way of this kitchen. Black Sun Man smiled and stirred his tea peacefully. His promising and guileless round face fringed with humorous frizzles seemed to gaze out on a happier, more permanent, nonnegotiable realm, if I may say so, a Mayor Daley–less one.

Now Melusina was hungry, famished, she said, and I began to be hungry too, for it had been a long night. In time the body must be fed. Because of the circumstances of our first meeting, over that mysterious ham unwrapped in silver foil, which she had slurped up with such gusto that fateful morning, I would always associate M with a good appetite. But right now she looked so queasy that I wondered if she should just lie down. The way she had dyed her hair black lately made her seem the more pale and gaunt, so I wasn't sure. I was sorry to leave our companions, but I needed to take care of M, who wanted a real meal, a hamburger at least, she said. She looked like it.

We said goodbye to Black Sun Man and the goddess. Little did I know how long it would be before I saw them again. I regretted our leaving them even as we did. As soon as we hit the dark street I was sorry we had left those friends. There must have been something good to eat around that kitchen if we had asked. It was a mistake to leave so fast but the kind of mistake you can't have avoided making. M was insistent on going out. She was an expert on finding good things to eat almost out of thin air, so I followed along. But I felt in my bones it was a serious error to have left Black Sun Man and the goddess. I was soon proved right. M was out of sorts, impatient, and bent on traveling, so we did. Something was eating on her.

It was past midnight and most of the crowd was gone from the street. The church bazaar was over and all the church booths were closed down or in the process of being broken down. But the post-fair was in progress, that is, little knots of people were performing desultory games and rituals of their own here and there, a few couples were strolling about like Melusina and me (if we could be called a couple), and various bits of harmless mayhem were breaking out or trailing off, it was hard to say which, the kinds of things that go on after such an event.

"So you like your friend's wife," said M suddenly out of the corner of her mouth sarcastically.

"*What?* . . . She's a friend." I didn't allude to her being a goddess, and was a little surprised if M hadn't noticed.

"Right," she said icily. I didn't know what she was talking about but felt guilty just the same and decided not to reply again. I mean of course I certainly rejected that interpretation of things.

On a corner a black dude and his obvious accomplice in a knot of eight or ten kids were conducting a shell game. At least the accomplice was instantly obvious to me, and we didn't pause to see if anyone was being taken in. The appealing and exciting tawdry element always drawn to a carnival atmosphere was mostly what was left in charge of the street by now. Such an element adds motion and color to the carnival, but at midnight when this element briefly takes control, and is all that is left, the mood feels as though it may turn ugly or dangerous any moment, and one is reminded how all human events go too far in one way or another if one hangs around long enough.

So M and I didn't linger, but pushed past the circles of kids passing around bottles and reefers. It was as if mother church, who had drawn the throngs to her with open arms, had now folded those arms resignedly and even knowingly with good grace. No one was shooing people away or anything, no cops were present, and I was reminded how the church like the sun and stars is always there for one and all, even if it has to close its doors overnight sometimes. It would open them again in the morning, for all.

A greasy frying odor in the air momentarily suggested something burning in hell. Then as we walked on, the smells clarified themselves into their individual components like bratwursts, french fries, and hamburgers, coming up from a bulkhead attached to the back of the church building. M turned to me, and we laughed together, happy to find somebody still serving food, as there were no late night restaurants in this neighborhood. All sense of evil dissipated upward.

The old-fashioned cellar doors were flung open, people stepping up out of them with steaming plates in hand. But we were late. The fair was over, and this kitchen was shutting down, too. At the head of the stairs a guard was encouraging people to come out and doing his best to prevent others from going down into the cellar. Last customers with their hot dogs and sauerkraut were being hustled up the stairs.

The people running the kitchen were trying to close up, but late-night hungry people like us kept pushing down the stairs obstreperously. Looking at the solid cellar doors flung open like broad wings, one couldn't have helped expecting concrete steps leading below, or at least something very substantial. On the contrary, down the bulkhead past the arm of the guard who was discouraging us, rude wooden planking, not very sturdy, led to the cavern below.

The makeshift wooden steps pivoted on big hinges at the top, and a little guy with a red beard down below was trying his best to fold them up by flinging these stairs upward where perhaps they would hook to the frame of the cellar doors and shut things off. Somebody with a plate of hot dogs overtook this functionary and stamped on the bottom rung pushing the stairs back down and stepping up them. Before the guy could try again to raise them, I ducked under the guard's arm, grabbed M, and started down the steps, forcing them down, keeping their base pressed against the floor below while M followed after me or so I thought. Biding his time, staring frustratedly up at me, the red-bearded church official waited for us to come down. He bent over, grasping the last step, ready to fling the collapsing staircase upward again the moment Melusina and I got down. It was just a matter of finding the moment when nobody was actually on the stairs and he was going to close up shop. He didn't seem to mind that we had made it inside, but clearly hoped we were the last.

How would we get back out again? It didn't matter, M and I were starving.

Despite his being a church worker, there was something Mephistophelian about his little red pointed beard, he wore a flame colored shirt, and I glimpsed an official badge. Something about him was oddly familiar. I didn't like the way he was ready to grab the steps and fling them upward the moment I leapt off them. How were we going to get out with our food? It made me nervous that he had leaned over and had hold of the stairs that supported me and M. They were flimsy stairs and bowed beneath our feet. It wasn't until I had come down close to him and was about to open my mouth to say something to him, that—glancing behind me to take M's hand at the same time—I realized she was not right behind me.

Unaccountably, she had lingered behind, her delicacy of feeling come out at this moment, never one to force her way in— except when it came to the men she was involved with of course, who by their attraction to her leapt into another class of being, one without rights to live, as the deer leaps into the sights of the huntress, who otherwise is a good mother, sister, etc., and far from murderous. But now she was shy, even though we had to eat. She was still lingering at the top of the moveable staircase. And that would have been fine if she had stayed up there and not changed her mind. I would have brought her up a hot dog and potato salad or whatever was still available. But she started down at the last moment. Something about the guard must have brought him in range of the class of hunted beings. M pressed his arm aside.

She was taking her sweet time about it. She hobbled down weakly clutching the wall and placing both feet on each stair before dipping her toe toward the next, embracing herself and clutching her midsection with both arms as though she were pregnant. The red-bearded official bending beside me to grasp the stair must not have noticed M lagging behind at the top, now coming down, taking forever. As I trod the last step onto the cement floor, he didn't look up from his coiled crouch, but the instant I was out of the way, he threw the steps violently upward in un-Christian frustration, M still in the middle. It knocked her off balance and she nearly plunged down.

I realized why he looked familiar. He was my doorman of my own apartment building moonlighting as a guard for the church! (This was one of the affectations of the management where I resided that wouldn't fix a leaky faucet but were always looking for ways to make appearances more pretentious so they could raise the rents—they provided a very seedy doorman.) The recognition occupied me an instant allowing disaster. All I could think was how my uncle from Texas would have known just how to bribe the little guy with a couple bucks and I should have had the smoothness to do the same so M could get something to eat. But you have to have just the right way about you when you bribe someone. It requires style, and anyway now it was too late. Above all it was a matter of timing. She was coming down anyway.

It all happened before I knew it. M lost her balance and toppled onto her bottom and skidded down three or four stairs. With her weight sliding toward him, the wood frame was torn from his hands and came crashing down, smacking the concrete with a sickening and shuddering thud. I thought the wood planks might splinter and the whole contraption collapse. M sat up there groaning, and holding on with both hands, alternatively grabbing her belly. When he saw her, the fury on his face gave way to indecision and alarm, and then red anger once more—at me. But his concern for her quickly returned as he realized his impetuous action might have killed her.

Seeing us both watch her, she finally got up and in a half-sitting posture, with both hands outstretched under her to grab the stairs or cushion her if she fell again, down she came one step at a time. With each step she hesitated, and peered at us, and held herself as if sick. I took the opportunity to give the guy a cursing out. He had recognized me by this time, but his usual authority over the tenants, treating them with the same disdain as management did, forsook him and only added to his confusion.

She was teetering above us and her face had gone white. Something unfortunate was about to happen, and it would lead into a pit of trouble. I regretted having jumped down the stairs when they obviously wanted to close the kitchen—all for a lousy hot dog! I stared at M's queasy, hurtful face and then my eyes fell to where her hands clamped around her stomach, and I saw blood on the hem of her skirt, blood on her hands, drenching through her clothing and running down her legs to her shoes.

The guard (my doorman of all things) saw this too. I saw in the guy's eyes fear of the blood. Perhaps his eyes mirrored my own. All the recent hope of the evening was disappearing in horror. I tried to think about the silver teapot but for the moment it didn't help. Forever something abortive clung about our relationship, Melusina and me, I didn't know why. Anguish, despair, and guilt rose in me, more than was fair. I should have understood the situation at once and taken M someplace else to eat, not forced my way down here. I raced up the steps two planks at a time and took her in my arms. She had passed out.

I stroked her cheek while she lay at the foot of the stairs before the cops came, but it was too late. An exhausting trip to the hospital ensued, and miles of red tape since she was not properly insured, the dark stares of the nurses, and my sense that it could have all been avoided with a little care or the proper magic. I would have her blood on my hands and not only hers. In her silences (and from the whispers of the nurses) came news of a miscarriage, after which she would sneak out of the hospital and disappear before morning. The reason she disappeared was that she was mad at me because I had decided to take a little trip away, arranged by my Uncle from Texas. It was only for a few days, a family reunion, but she made up her mind to be upset about it. She just wanted to be unreasonable and torment me.

"Couldn't you go another time?" she said with dripping sarcasm, while she lay back on the hospital bed.

"It's a family reunion, I mean one time only, people from around the country. I'll be right back!"

"*A FAMILY REUNION!* Sounds like a Charles Adams cartoon or a Stephen King novel!"

"Oh come on, really, you should meet my Uncle sometime. You'd like him. You need to rest up here."

"I'm here dying and you are going to have fun."

"If I thought you were dying—"

"I *am* dying! Maybe I won't be here when you get back."

"No. No you're not. Man, it's not fun exactly. If you knew my Uncle—I need to do this, it's been planned."

"How about us. We just got re-united again, speaking of reunions."

"Well then, it'll survive a couple days."

By now I was missing her already and thinking maybe she was right. I didn't want to leave her even more than she didn't want me to go. It was hard to say who was more upset, we were both irritated, loveless, and raw. But I'd promised my Uncle before she'd showed up again. He was invested in the reunion and bent on my going. M as usual had gotten herself into a scrape and now a snit. I was very sorry about her. I'd be back soon. She would rest. To my surprise I had found I still cared very much about M, in fact I loved that scalawag. I could hardly drag myself away. Had I known she would disappear before I got back I would not have left, I'm sure. Maybe. You would think she could've been patient three or four days if I obliged my Uncle. But not M. I was in for it, but that night in the hospital I had no inkling of this. It was quite a dilemma. In the midst of it I found myself wishing again we hadn't left the goddess and Black Sun Man. The way she looked in that bed you could never have guessed she would have the strength to skip out of the place. I imagined the caregivers and doctors nursing her back to health, and when I got back in a couple of days she would be herself again and I would take her home.

I turned my back, walked out of the hospital, and headed for my apartment in a northside slum. On the way I thought of the solace of the goddess's kitchen. My feet almost turned that way, but instead kept hurrying on. You didn't say no to my Uncle, in fact you didn't want to. He was a fascinating character and I always enjoyed seeing him. But I had M to think about tonight and the memory of the goddess was on my mind too. That was competition enough even for my Uncle. I expected him anytime, maybe even tonight, or certainly the next morning. He always liked showing up early in the day, sometimes so early it was late the night before.

From my window I could see my Uncle from Texas engaged in conversation with the doorman in his black coat and cap on the sidewalk below. It was early in the morning. I had just woken up. The doorman must have just come on duty. He was only there on show during the daytime. The sight of my Uncle was not so strange, as he sometimes blew into town now and then on a whim, or for no reason he cared to tell me about. I don't think it was only to see me. Actually he had called a few days earlier to invite me to the family reunion. So I was expecting him, as I had insisted to M. Even from above I could tell the doorman was impressed by my Uncle with his trademark white Stetson cowboy hat cocked on his head, and had taken a step back. The sight of the two of them in some kind of colloquy had a disturbing effect on me and I felt my stomach knot up.

The appearance one day of a doorman in front of the rundown apartment building I lived in had the sort of comical effect of putting a stovepipe hat on a snowman or scarecrow. It was supposed to add "class." The management intended to raise the rent and they did, high enough now I was going to have to move, unless my luck changed, so I no longer cared about my place and never even bothered to sweep the floor anymore. But we had a doorman.

My Uncle from Texas was a favorite of mine, who had been a sportswriter for a newspaper, a copy writer for an ad agency, a Marine in the Second World War, a ranch hand in Texas, and other romantic things. He still lived in Texas, doing what I did not know. He had endless amusing sports stories and other stories but it was never his conversation but his mere presence. He had a solid, knowing way about him and was at home in any company. He was over seventy, retired, very fit. Somehow he had come into some money, he didn't say how, but now he was a man of independent means and traveled constantly. On his face was always one variation or another of an expression that said he knew the score, and he did know, you soon found out. I admired him a great deal and enjoyed his company. He had a way of talking to people that suggested he knew a great deal more about what was really going on than they did, and they swallowed that always. He was having that compelling effect on my doorman right now, I saw below, who was maybe going to have some respect for me after this.

My Uncle fathomed the backdrop of whatever scene confronted him, the shadows in the field on which we all play and even the little stones and obstacles around our feet. He always knew which way the ball would hop. For me it has never been like this. I'm always surprised by people, and never have the slightest idea what they are going to do or what is going to happen next. Looking straight down on him I couldn't make him out because of the cowboy hat until he cocked his head to the side while he reached into his back pocket. Then I realized what he was up to, although I couldn't imagine why. That white Stetson dipped down conspiratorially while he slipped the doorman some money, not too much. What in the world for? I wasn't sure I could confront my Uncle, but I intended to question the doorman later about what he had ripped my Uncle off for. I guessed my Uncle had reached that stage of life when he enjoyed handing out tips to inconsequential people. But I was sure he was up to something. The truth was I would never ask the doorman, it embarrassed me. I could tell by the way he was nodding his head he was satisfied and impressed by my Uncle.

When he had come up and was seated across from me at my kitchen table, he spoke plainly, "You look bad. A trip away will do you good. Coming to the reunion, aren't you, okay?"

I knew I must look tired out and didn't respond, since I didn't want to get into my life with him directly just now. I hadn't decided about the reunion at first since I wanted to continue working on my novel, and now that M was in the hospital I felt guilty about leaving town. But we both knew I was going. Then it occurred to me he just might mean my nose, which had swollen up ridiculously as soon as M had wound up at the hospital. But he didn't mean my nose exactly.

"You look like you seen a ghost."

This fetched up from me a sigh, for as with all my Uncle's observations, it was quite accurate in its strange way, for M was a kind of ghost as far as I was concerned.

"You afraid of something? I'll tell you about fear. To hell with fear." He now launched into a story, but it wasn't a sports story, but one in his other vein, a war story about his days in Germany in World War Two.

"One time we went out on a night patrol. We were getting ready for a big push, so we were sent out to see what the lay of the land was for the next day. Do you know what the Krauts had waiting for us? We were on a little road through the forest, no more than a path in the woods, peaceful and serene, until we came to a crossroads where they'd hung up two corpses. The day had been hot and the corpses were so rotten they were ready to explode. One was hanging upside down and the other was chopped off at the waist, intestines hanging down. The guts had swollen up like balloons and were swaying in the wind. There

65

was a gusty breeze that night and the corpses were dancing in the wind. But I swear they would have been dancing if the air had been still. They were full of juices and hot air escaping here and there. They were jumping around like puppets on a string. I stared at them and the corpse with no bottom half began to sing a song—I mean the swollen guts were whistling, dancing and singing a song. I was just amazed at the ingenuity and imagination of them Krauts but I knew they meant it and we were in for it tomorrow and they were telling us what we would face. I mean the corpse was singing us a ghastly rhyme. One of its swollen up guts which had been whistling burst with a splutter. Blapppp! Then all was quiet and after a moment we had a good laugh at our own fear."

So by now I knew he read me like an open book. Without knowing just what I'd been going through lately, he knew I had seen something like that leper with no face on the "L" last night that I had seen, and how the Rottweiler of the cops had grabbed the homeless person by the throat and almost killed him and there was no need to tell him about last night, any more than it was in me to mention M being in the hospital.

The night before, on my way home from M in the hospital, I was riding on the "L" to my humble apartment when we passed Wrigley Field and through the black window appeared the orange-pink neon glow of the Cubs logo filling the sky and radiating wholesome and happy vibrations, in spite of the fact that at this time all the baseball players were on strike. Just at this moment up the aisle of the car stumbled one of the homeless beggars who are more and more numerous and freewheeling in all public spaces these days because of the "war on poverty" (most recent version) in spite of the guards in their black jumpsuits who nightly ride the trains with their Rottweilers and German Shepherds. It is at this hour of the night that the beggars come out in numbers enough to get around the guards a little bit. I knew I was about to be hit up for a donation. I saw that in a wave all the passengers' faces were turning away to look out the windows into the pink horizon over Cubs' park in front of me, and I could feel the beggar zeroing in on me, since I was the only one who kept looking at him (I was mesmerized by the sight and couldn't look away), and no doubt my spiritual condition of being on a level with him and a strange brother to him at this time he could probably sense. The way the car was illuminated by the great pink logo of the Chicago Cubs over the beggar's shoulder cast him in shadow and he was a very black man to begin with so he approached in pure black silhouette.

Only as he stood directly in front of me, inches away, did I get a good look into his face and understand why those in front of me, where the position of the lights in the car may have afforded a more convenient glimpse of his features, had turned so violently away. It was an apparition of Biblical dimension, straight up from the subcontinent, but it was a very real Chicagoan. The guy almost did not have a face, no nose, no lips, and on the stumps that wedged a tin can for alms against his chest, no fingers, just pink palms and stubs. It was a case of leprosy—he was a leper such as one might see in Africa, read about in the Bible, here walking the aisles of the elevated trains in the city of Chicago with a begging bowl, the body and face of the fellow dissolving or being eaten up, a deeply shocking sight in America. But I can assure you there are such sights, if you ride the "L" in the middle of the night, and this is no tale, I saw the leper in Chicago, not moments after I had bid M a goodnight in her own precarious condition.

Overcome, I didn't give him a dime but staggered from my seat and up the aisle to the door and got off well before my stop. Maybe among the other scams going nowadays the hustlers are flying lepers over from Africa to beg for them, but I didn't reason it out that way just then. No wonder he had gotten past the guards. A visage to strike terror into any heart—no one would want to incur the bad luck that might come from barring his passage. So down the aisles he roamed tonight among the many sad sights to be seen in the shadows of the city. He had no nose and I too much! (As I mentioned strangely my nose began to swell the moment I got in the ambulance with M and it had acquired an alarming dimension.) Did my own face inspire such fright? Was the leper staring at *me?* A vision of rare cruel horror, and I wondered if it were an omen and my brotherhood with the grimmest creatures of the earth was going to be confirmed and I supposed that it was. If my nose did not stop swelling up and finally proceeded to explode and fall off, if M did not get well and come home, my face might wind up looking like the poor beggar's. My anxiety reached extremes of resignation and I had barely slept last night. I reached up and felt my raw swollen nose like one of those bladders in my Uncle's tale.

Just before I had gotten off the "L" car, at the wrong stop, a drunken homeless person with an antic sense of humor had made a wry face at one of the cops' Rottweilers who were guarding the train in the early hours as they do, and loudly said "Woof! Woof!" at the dog, and the dog had taken umbrage or at least not taken the joke and lunged at him and took him by the throat and gave him a great shaking to the amusement of the cops who let this go on until the train came to a stop. The bum's friends in a panic had clawed their way past me onto the platform in a rush to get away from the cops who were laughing their heads off. So they probably got off at the wrong stop too. The dogs and cops left the leper alone though. Through the window I saw him plying up the aisle with his bowl.

I decided against mentioning any of this to my Uncle, and certainly not anything about Melusina either. He liked to give me advice about women, which it was one of his ideas about me that I needed. Like everything else my Uncle assumed about me it was probably true, but areas in which he could offer me notions for self-improvement were so numerous that I did not feel obliged to add more. He wanted to take me out to breakfast he said, and I was agreeable to that much, but before we went out he gave me a short stern lecture on the appearance of my apartment, which it was true I had completely let go.

"You've got to clean this joint up, and we're going to start now," he cried, and with that he flung open all the windows one after the other and began tossing all manner of things out. Lately

I had been absorbed in working on my novel and had let various domestic tasks slide. I had a number of black garbage bags loaded with trash I hadn't bothered taking out for days or even weeks. These went first. He threw them all straight out the window! He leaned his head out the window, and I saw him wink at the doorman below, who waved back and gathered in each bag as it fell and hauled it around to the dumpster. So I found out what that exchange of money had been all about. I mean I assumed or had actually seen my Uncle hand him a couple of bills. No way otherwise would the little red-bearded guy have hauled away any bags of garbage of mine. He would have called the cops. But my Uncle! My Uncle had a way of preparing for all contingencies and taking care of business. Somehow he had foreseen the need. With my head in the clouds of the writing process I had as usual forgotten all about the normal duties and necessities of life. My Uncle was a very practical character even at the most basic level if necessary.

As each huge distended black bag sailed earthward it seemed to me the heat and swelling in my snoot diminished by a millimeter or a degree. I felt chastened, lighter, and some strength seemed to return to my legs momentarily. I was no longer afraid I had contracted leprosy, and even felt optimistic about M's condition. For sure my place looked a lot spiffier without all the black garbage bags full of trash in every corner. As usual a visit from my Uncle was doing me some good. He didn't point his finger at me or lecture me. He just told a war story or two and started chucking bags out the window.

Later we went out for breakfast and he took my mind off things with some inside gossip about the baseball strike. He knew all about their "dirty business," he confided, players and owners alike, and for once dropped his knowing cynical air and expressed outrage at what he took for their greed.

"Egos!" he exploded. "Swollen bladders!" Then he relaxed and gave me his knowing wink. "Poor bastards, we're all puffed up like that, but imagine having to live with yourself if you were famous for excellence at playing a beautiful game. Professional athletes are all mildly insane, believe me. They take themselves absolutely seriously."

"Yeah, kind of like the rest of us, who don't even have that good of an excuse," I agreed chewing my eggs. Deflated, in the good sense of feeling your feet return to the common ground, chomping breakfast contentedly as a cow, I felt a little power return, a little morale, my nose shrinking by the moment too. In the cheerful presence of my Uncle I forgot about lepers, dogs, guards, and homeless bums, and even Melusina, every thought now concentrated by my Uncle's conversation on that pink ambience cast by the Cubs ballpark sign which last night had been but the lurid backdrop of a sordid encounter.

"Have another cup of coffee. You're looking almost like yourself again. Believe me a trip away to the family reunion is going to fix you up. You have to show up at such things, you know. The interface is important, believe me, take my word."

"Listen, my friend Melusina is in the hospital and we have to swing by and see her on the way home," I countered.

By the time we reached his car again parked about a block away from the breakfast joint my doubts had returned, along with thoughts of M. He was rattling away, but I wasn't listening to what he said, and all I could think about was my fear, my ego, I suppose, my own undeniable puffedupedness and swelling, and M in her hospital chamber. My nose reddened and expanded slightly as if about to take flight. I probably had leprosy. M's child would have a leper for its step-father! I hadn't confirmed the miscarriage yet and was actively hoping against hope and denying it despite all the blood last night. Just before we got into his car, he brought me back to earth again.

"Yeah, you're looking better already and you'll feel a lot better when we finish cleaning out your apartment. Are you becoming a *hoarder?*" He grinned widely at me as if he meant no such thing and it was only a joke. He puffed his cigar. But he had made his point. He was a great guy. That was the wry style of any admonition of his directed my way. He meant me well.

70

"What? No, the opposite. I just forget about things and don't notice them. I don't keep them, I just forget about them."

It was then at the hospital that we learned that M had disappeared from her bed during the night. I began to question the nurses wildly and looked for my Uncle to help me out investigating the situation. But he always took the measure of any scene immediately and would not get involved now. He knew there were laws against them telling me anything, and he must have seen how embarrassed they were that they didn't know anything anyway. He didn't seem to be concerned and apparently was of the opinion it would be fruitless to linger here. Not that he didn't care. He radiated genuine confidence that it would all turn out right in the end later on.

"She'll turn up, believe me, listen to me," he said knowingly. But how could he know?

As well as I knew M, while my confidence in my Uncle was complete, I both believed and disbelieved him at one time. As smoking was forbidden, he had extinguished his cigar but still clenched it between his teeth. His Stetson looked outlandish in the aseptic corridors, but the nurses didn't hold it against him and on the contrary smiled at him fondly like he was their Uncle too. They appreciated his smiles and his calm. They knew he knew the score and was on their side.

"She'll be back before you know it," he repeated, slapping me on the shoulder as we departed for my apartment. He clearly meant this, but I didn't know. If anyone could reassure me it was my Uncle, but I felt M's absence acutely. I was overcome with guilt and felt very lonely. It was possible she was really gone again. It was even likely. Outside her room in the corridor we suddenly ran into her juvenile boyfriend that she had come into the club with last night. He had some of her clothes and other possessions in his arms that I recognized instantly including some bloodstained ones. My shock seeing this guy gave way to extreme offense. As soon as he saw me, he took off running downstairs fast and disappeared into the labyrinth of the hospital. There was no chance to press him on where M had gone to, and I don't think I could have made myself speak to him anyway. I plunged into new depths of anxiety and gloom and was in a kind of trance as we drove away. My Uncle didn't bother trying to cheer me up, and I felt the lonely blues coming on worse and worse every moment.

Upstairs again in my apartment, my Uncle had rolled up his sleeves and drawn a big sinkful of suds and begun throwing glassware, dishes, and pots and pans into it when I saw an amazing sight through one of the open windows, one that lifted me out of myself in a desperate rush and took my breath clean away.

Melusina was standing on a window ledge of the building across the street four stories up in the air, a diaphanous mottled sea-green and turquoise-blue wrapper wound round and round about her, head to toe, as if she had been a fashionable Arabian princess or a suicide bomber with lovely taste. It was just like M to play a prank like that on me, dress up and come up across from my apartment and try to scare me within an inch of my life. She looked like she was about to jump for God's sake. Where had she gotten such a gorgeous gauzy blue robe I wondered, some costume store. She had certainly recovered fast. Maybe she was still ill and completely out of her mind. Outraged as well as very frightened for her I ran to the window, my mind racing. She seemed to gaze down directly and forlornly into the abyss. This was all because I wouldn't wait around and visit her in the hospital but had told her I meant to go to the family reunion. For this crime I would be punished! Hadn't I promised her I would be right back? Wouldn't she have faith in me and see it my way one time? No, she was making a desperate scene, as usual! But I felt terrible about it all. It was all my fault. I was so shocked to see her up there I was paralyzed with fear and apprehension—and grief already. I think I knew she was really going to do it.

Beneath or within her sensational see-through cape or sari shifting in its watery hues as though she had been glimpsed swimming in depths of the sea rather than on heights of air, another, skin-tight, blue-green garment encased her stunning figure—a shining rubber or latex diving suit it looked like, for as a matter of fact she did appear to intend to dive, even though through the air, into the deeps, although it was nothing but cement pavement below. She was going to kill herself! She made her suicidal intentions plain by little pointing or swimming motions of her hands, pressed together at the tips of her fingers, then separating out in surrender, like an Olympian on the diving platform visualizing and practicing the death-defying strike into the water far below.

But there was something comically exaggerated about her movements, and she couldn't help grinning down at the crowd which had begun to gather under her, as if it were a big joke (on me!). When she saw my head poking out of my window, and heard me yell to her, beg her, to get down from there, she waved flutteringly to me, and then pointed at me, gesturing to the crowd below to look at me—the cause of her despair. She pretended to start to dive, then she held her clasped hands up to her eyes and mimed tearful suicidal sorrow, gesturing with her thumb at me for the crowd's benefit, weeping into her fingers through which she suddenly peeped with one eye and looked straight at me and gave me a ludicrous wink.

Beside me the Texan chuckled knowingly, looking from her to me and back again. His confidence in his insight into the scene (whatever it was) this time only exasperated me and I flew into a rage at them both. I didn't know which one of them angered me more, M or my Uncle. He laughed out loud as at a good joke at my expense. How could he?

"Wise up, will you?" he said. "Cool it."

She was standing up on the ledge and laughing at me too. I was beside myself with rage at him, something he did have a way of reducing me to sometimes, and was enraged at M as well. She might really jump—or fall! All of a sudden I had had enough and wished she would. But at once I realized she really might and terror struck. There she was, no doubt about it, trying to embarrass me as she often had. She was appealing to the crowd below, many of whom were staring at me like a lynch

73

mob. What if she did it? She was capable of it just to hurt me, I feared, laughing all the way down.

"Keep your head," said my Uncle. "Keep calm."

The crowd watching her kept turning their heads toward me to check out who was to blame for the unfolding tragedy. I wondered how much farther she was willing to go to thoroughly indict and embarrass me. Would she actually kill herself to spite me? Never, I reassured myself—immediately to remember she was crazy enough to do anything. She was teetering on an old ornamented Chicago apartment building ledge above a busy street. She had dressed to the hilt for the prank. Probably she had gotten those silky sheer turquoise threads that looked to be made of the blue sky or green sea itself over on Devon Avenue where the Indian women bought their saris at the Indian clothing shops. I supposed she had made a special trip to do it. It looked like she could just waft away in her light and airy outfit.

Then she did jump. Without another look back at me, she suddenly stuck out her fingers and dove headfirst and plummeted earthward with her blue-green garment billowing out behind her. I nearly lost my mind. This was no joke and as she fell my heart plunged to the bottom of my soul. I had always known M was wild, unpredictable, vengeful and ready to do anything, if she thought it was called for, or just out of spite. She'd always made it plain I had better look out and be on my toes as far as she was concerned. But this was such incredible and really spectacular horror. She was taking her life in front of my eyes! After all I had been through lately, she was killing—had killed—herself? All because I was taking a few days off to attend a family reunion! Was that it? I was abandoning her? How absurd—and real. As she spilled down through the air it occurred to me maybe she had wanted to go with me and I hadn't thought to ask her to come along. Guilt stabbed me mercilessly in the second or two it took her to hit the concrete with a sickening thud. It was too late. She must be dead.

She was on the ground, splattered on the pavement and the crowd rushing to her side. Though I saw her fall, I couldn't take it in. A soft, final implosion of my spirit brought numbness, lightheadedness. I never actually saw her hit the ground because all the other people who had been watching her up there and waiting for her to do it swarmed to the spot ahead of time to see—but I heard the impact.

I took one accusing look at my Uncle and raced down the stairs and across the street with my Uncle after me and pushed through the crowd to kneel by her side, tears of shock and dismay pouring out of my eyes. Strangely, there was no blood, this was what struck me first, only an alabaster whiteness spread all over the sidewalk where she had exploded into various pale parts. The most uncanny sight presented itself. She was dismembered. Her head had become detached from her body. She lay in white pieces, arms here, legs there, her skull white and shaved, as if she'd been wearing a wig. Yes, there was that black wig in the gutter. M was all disassembled, headless, limbless, like a store mannequin awaiting re-assembly for the next window display or maybe that had met with a warehouse accident or a hurricane, sections of white plastic or wood torso strewn up and down the sidewalk. Even the mermaid's tail lay there cut off in a fat triangular chunk, scaled, blanched of color.

Behind me I felt the crowd shifting and glanced back to see the snout of my Uncle's big car parting the onlookers. As always, the Texan knew just what to do and was master of the situation. Leaving the engine running, he popped open the trunk and piece by piece, chunk by chunk, methodically packed Melusina in. A strange calm overtook me.

Apparently she had manipulated this store dummy hiding behind it or from around the corner of the building. Even more amazing than how she'd managed to pull off the trick of slipping back inside through the window while she pushed a dummy off the ledge was the new mood it left me in. The worst of my paralyzing anxiety had departed. I could feel my nose begin to cool down for good at last and to shrink back to normal. It was back to the ranks of the wretched living for me. I had escaped the very worst. She hadn't done it after all, had she?

"Your building's super can't deal with *this,*" said my Uncle as he drove the three of us away from the scene before any cops arrived. Nobody tried to stop him, since it was clear no real blood had been spilled or actual brains bashed out. Just a store dummy had fallen out a window. This seemed more a crime of the heartless than of the heart. M had played an obscene trick on us. But my Uncle was treating it more seriously, as if it were not quite how it looked, not a dummy after all, but really M all right, despite appearances, who had to be disposed of carefully. You couldn't bribe your way out of this, he seemed to indicate. He was going to have to clean up things in a proper manner. He knew how.

"What are we going to do with her?" I finally asked with dread engulfing me. I didn't see how I could go on a trip with this hanging over me and M busted to pieces like this. "I don't even know what I'm feeling."

"Have to put her together again, of course, but not around here," he said. "Leave it to me." He said a strange thing, "As soon as I put her back together, she'll go away, she'll disappear, just like you thought she already had, but don't worry, she'll be back. As soon as you go to the family reunion, I mean, and forget about her a little." What he could mean by that I didn't know. But he had a lot of mysteries about him that didn't tolerate going into and I didn't care. I was feeling a letdown and a lot of anger and grief at M for having pulled that stunt and caused me such anguish and fear, with a store dummy, as well as new stark loneliness, all coming together in blank confusion.

"You need a break, you need a change of scene, and I know just what the doctor ordered," he admonished me again. "I will meet you at the family reunion on the not–Mississippi River, okay? Lot of folks you haven't seen in a long while and some you never met yet. I have a bus ticket for you." I had made the mistake of mentioning this to M in the hospital, but she was going to find out anyway, so what could I do. Maybe I should have just split and not said anything to her and let her find out for herself. It didn't matter now. It hadn't occurred to me she

76

might want to come too. I didn't want to go anymore, but what was the point of hanging around. There might be some kind of trouble yet, raining down on my head from God if not the law, and I had better follow my Uncle's advice.

Back in my apartment after he had washed a huge stack of a couple weeks' worth of dirty dishes that had been piling up in the sink (with M in segments in the trunk of his car yet), he handed me the bus ticket. Even though it wasn't M exactly (was it?), but some facsimile of her that she had rigged up and talked some friend of hers into placing on that window ledge (I wondered who), I still basically had the feeling my Uncle had a body in his trunk, maybe even M herself after all. Those white chunks of her packed in his trunk took on a lively plasticity in my imagination and I pictured them magically coalescing somehow and her flipping open the trunk lid and stealing away down the alley toward some new misdeed or retribution. The bus ticket had the quality about it that I needed to get out of town for a while till things cooled off, and I took it. Maybe a family reunion would cast a useful perspective on everything.

My Uncle had given me the bus ticket to attend my family reunion on the not–Mississippi River so it was a foregone conclusion. I wouldn't be gone very long. Trying to recall all he had said about how it would rejuvenate me to get away, I had tried to explain it to her. She had not had a good word to say, just feeling sorry for herself and making me feel bad too. The reunion was only a few days, and I would have plenty of time to visit her in the hospital, I'd reassured her. She'd stared at me with a self-indulgent look of betrayal in her eyes, and refused to speak. The nurses said she had "escaped." She'd jumped off a building before my tearful thunderstruck eyes. Now she was in chunks in my Uncle's trunk.

It's terribly true life is a lot stranger than fiction. I had stuck my novel under one of the legs of my kitchen table which was too short where it was useful to keep the table from rocking back and forth. That was where I "stored" it. I was a little paranoid sometimes that somebody (like my doorman) would steal it and make a million dollars selling it to Hollywood. I didn't have a copy of it either. Nobody would steal something that was being used to prop up the kitchen table.

My Uncle departed later in the day. I forced myself not to think of her. I was overcome with a remorseful wonderment that not twenty-four hours before I had been blissfully forgetful and unconscious of M, happily in my world in my favorite hangout. Now I missed her deeply and was in a black hole of loneliness. This rollercoaster ride was not one I would have elected to go on, and it seemed unfair, even cosmically so. A couple days passed. I went through the excruciating process of packing. I hate packing for a trip worse than anything, another domestic duty I find almost unmanageable, even when not in the throes of the creative process or suffering a bad case of the blues. I kept thinking of something else to take, in case I needed it, you know. I even eyed my novel under the table leg, I might find a few moments to work on it. I was only going away for a few days. Finally I had thrown enough stuff back in drawers again to get it all in one bag, and I took off for the bus station, still feeling worried and heartbroken. On the other hand, I began to feel a positive anticipation about the reunion, God knew I was badly in need of a distraction.

Basically I felt too fragile, my accomplishments in life too thin, to be held up to examination by a bunch of distant relatives, but I was going to the reunion on the not-Mississippi anyway. How I missed M, to whom I said anything that struck me. She always understood and much more! Or she didn't understand and said so directly. Riding along I carried her with me in my bruised heart, even if she was in pieces in my Uncle's trunk, although by now I was sure she had got herself together and crawled out.

The South unbelievably is not that far from Chicago (or anywhere else). When I disembarked at the station I was rather impressed to see that an entire section of the waiting area had been roped off with a showy purple-plush cord of a kind that brought back dim memories of old movie theaters. The family name was on a large placard, and behind the cord illumined by the strong afternoon sunlight stood twenty or thirty people I could only suppose must be relatives of mine from various parts of the country, though I didn't know a single one of them. It's an extremely large and far-flung family, numbering in the hundreds, so I was just guessing. The crowd of relatives was difficult to make out individually as the brilliance of the sun on one side of each face left the other deep in shadow and their silhouettes trembled in the heatwaves. After introducing myself to someone, I asked, "Does anybody know what's going on?" Maybe that was an odd way of putting it; at any rate I was stared at briefly and quizzically, and got the reply: "Him. The guide."

I followed the arc of a pointed finger to a spot beside the large station window that was letting through an effusion of burning afternoon southern heat and light that obliterated everything. I pressed through the crowd. The "guide" with his back to the window I could make out clearly if in shadow. He was crowned by an aureola of light that increased his importance for me, given my weariness from the bus ride, and a certain sense of strangeness that was creeping in to be amongst a bunch of relatives I had never met. The crown of light on his head suggested he would explain things and do his job and guide me. I wanted proper introductions and an itinerary. I cleared my throat and opened my mouth to speak openly to him. But as I emerged from the last of the crowd and approached him, the sunlight burst upon me with such radiance that everything went white, and when I had stepped to one side and managed to shield my eyes enough for some vision to come back, he was gone. That was just like it, I thought. I never should have come here but stayed at M's bedside.

All the homesickness I had constantly been feeling for M as I rode down on the bus came to a peak in a rush, and I missed her badly and wondered why I had disappointed her so in her condition in the hospital and agreed to come here, the last place I wished to be. Suddenly I felt in pieces just as much as she had been on the pavement outside my window. I couldn't bear standing in that pointless crowd anymore and I stumbled out of the station lonely but determined not to stand around like a sheep but to see the town for myself which I hadn't seen for a very long time.

Immediately an affably smiling young man wearing an open-necked white shirt with a peculiar badge on it and utilitarian black trousers came hurrying toward me, calling me by name, apologizing for his lateness, and explaining that he would be my guide for the afternoon. Certain visitors who had been away for the longest of anyone in the family (or based on some other criterion I didn't fathom) were to be provided with their own private guides, he explained. That was fine by me, since I hadn't been here since I was six years old, and what little I remembered no doubt would have all changed. Actually I was soon to discover that this was one of those country parts of the States that haven't changed at all in a hundred years let alone a few decades. For all our relentless progress there are many backwoods places like that in America. At any rate I gloated that I had left that crowd of rube relatives of mine back at the station as I had my own private guide as it turned out, as I needed, expected, and deserved.

There is nothing worse than walking around in a pack of people led by some official, but one on one with a guide it's not so bad. I was keeping a pokerface outwardly so as not to reveal my sense of good fortune. I dreaded igniting any jealousy in that faceless crowd behind me. They were something like a lynch mob by now in their itchy discontent of waiting and might take it out on me in spite of being family. I felt the guide had showed up in the nick of time before I became thoroughly addled. I hurried with my "guide" (for some reason he seemed something else than a guide) to his car and shortly we were weaving down Main Street through an opening-day reunion parade. Brass instruments glittered in the sun. Mine was a musical family. At a stoplight the car idled beside a pack of kids who marched in place in mock military fashion, laughing, singing, their faces flushed with pleasure. These must be second or third cousins, I observed, unable to feel much or any relationship with them. The light changed. Full of joyous animal spirits, totally unconscious in an adolescent way, they streamed up the street like young goats in a meadow, like trouts in a brook. Just before we got rolling again, one of them who had a big golden saxophone hung around his neck complained through the open window of the car to me: "I don't have a mouthpiece for this instrument. It fell out someplace!" Sure enough the tip of the handsome horn ended in a gaping black hole—no reed. For lack of this delicate connection he had to march along mute. I sensed his itchy irritation and could imagine how he felt. As we took off, I yelled back at the kid, "Then why are you carrying that heavy thing? Just lay it down someplace." I couldn't imagine why he kept marching along with it. I felt for him and felt somewhat mute myself. He was hoping against hope to find the missing piece.

My guide informed me that later in the week we would visit not-Hannibal to take in not–Mark Twain's birthplace, who had once been a friend of the family (and everyone else on the not-Mississippi), visit one of the big resort areas that have sprung up hereabouts to take in a country and western music festival, and gamble in the casinos or on the riverboats if we wished. He chuckled indulgently, and I muttered that it would be all the same to me. On my ride down here on the bus I had sat next to a very strange guy, a six-and-a-half foot Indian wearing shades, with pomaded hair falling shoulder-length over a buckskin jacket, who'd told me he was an assistant manager in one of the casinos. He'd passed along one or two revelations and some advice to hang onto my money if I came here, and some humorous insight on the business side of casinos, always adding the refrain: "But people have a good time." I thought I heard in this an irony, but he didn't smile. He evidently meant it. The people did have a good time, I was sure of it. He was a tough hombre but wise. It had made me reflect on American history, the tenacity with which Indian culture has hung on, successfully. Just like the white people, hanging onto theirs. For hope of a good time. It made me tentatively sympathetic to my relatives.

My guide took me to my hacienda, as he called it with a straight face, for some reason. But he wasn't kidding, it was a beautiful rambling home on a lush river whose banks were climbing with flowers. It was a tributary to the Mississippi, or it was a not-tributary, as was intimated to me. There was everything green, fertile and lively about it, and the golden lights rose from the water, full of fish, frogs, and turtles, everything to make you very happy. I wanted to rest right there. After a moment I decided I wanted to go down to the water, but the guide prevented me. "You can't go that way," he explained.

Instead he led me around the house down the road to the neighbor, and showed me into somebody else's garden. We took a side path bordering the property down to the beautiful river. It seemed extremely odd to me to have been brought to my hacienda and then told that to get to the river fronting it I had to walk around through the neighbor's land, and what's more there was something surreptitious about it. The vibe from my guide was we were sneaking in, and I felt anxious we might be accosted. We were trespassers and what's more there seemed no point to it. Anyway we found ourselves in this fecund valley, bursting with life and color, rich with resources, something better than the garden of eden, a scene from the New Testament. The river was the "river of life" of which the ancient literatures were full of allusions and promises. And yet we had to sneak into it like thieves, when my very own hacienda abutted these charming waters.

"Why in the world do we have to go around the back way like this when I can step out the door of my hacienda and walk straight down these banks?"

"Don't rush things. Who knows what will be possible when they get to know you and you have learned a thing or two. But first," my guide was going on and on, we had to do "some target practice." Before I had a chance to be astonished at that he slammed the door of the car and we were off again heading into the countryside. Not five minutes later we swung off into the large yard of a white house where several men were firing guns at targets pinned to the clapboards of the old barn, which had been white once too. Huge old oaks and elms added immense charm to the scene. One of the shooters was firing an old black-powder, muzzle-loading rifle, and at once I understood the close ties of the culture hereabouts to the past still intact and deeply felt. City people like me simply had no idea what ideas must motivate the citizenry out in the boondocks here. The smell of gunpowder lingered under the great spreading limbs of the old trees. When the shots went off all their leaves seemed to dance and shake with laughter. The trees were of great antiquity and no doubt had been growing here for a century or two. The shooters had even donned old-fashioned clothes as if this were a Civil War reenactment. Some of them wore blue and some grey, though the Union and Confederacy were elbow to elbow, which seemed hopeful. It occurred to me suddenly they were just their actual everyday clothes. My utter inability to relate to any of it gripped me by the throat and I leaped to ape whatever my guide did, who now went to a sort of armory and came back with two rifles for us. Mine was a museum piece, a splendid artifact with a lot of Masonic-looking graffiti carved into the stock. The sights, concentric circles mounted front and rear, were silver, and the front one I could see at a glance was loose and swung to the right. My guide fixed it for me and we proceeded to blow off a few rounds. Though my gun was a decorative and splendid old piece, it was still modern enough that I could load it up with nine shells at a time. It was great fun and I began to feel less self-conscious, although I can't say I had hit any of the targets yet. I did hit the barn I think but was not sure. The tiny silver circle on the end of the muzzle kept coming loose and swinging to the right, which didn't help, but at least I was playing the game. I was relieved no money was involved.

One of the Civil War veterans passed close by me and I again had the queer sensation that he was in no costume but wore those clothes all the time, for they fitted him too well and had an exceedingly comfortable and well-worn look to them. He moved in his antiquated duds as though he had never worn any other sort of clothing, and the way he laid his rifle back on his shoulder in a practiced gesture made me think he'd been doing that every day of his life. History lingered on in the remotest parts of the country, didn't it. You couldn't have said what side he was on for the color of his musty outfit was a dark hue halfway between blue and grey as though either the blue had faded or the grey had stained and muddied with age. So some kind of rapprochement had occurred over time. Or maybe no war had occurred at all and the "sides" were only in my educated head, the thought struck me. He was a small but well-made man who sauntered over to me with the grace of a cat, and throwing back his pointed black beard suggested that I take a few steps back as it would be more sporting. I had barely hit the barn at this distance. I noticed that this made everybody smile all around, but he seemed dead serious, if not downright malicious. He was wearing a strange golden hat with a rolled up brim that seemed to have little to do with the North or the South. Since I wasn't sure I'd even hit the barn yet let alone the target I imagined I was the butt of some joke, but I took it in good spirit, and stepped a few paces back so that now I was firing through the green leaves of some low hanging branches. I was afraid I'd kill somebody and I could barely see the barn.

I suddenly realized it was a lynch mob. They were just "funning" with me. I was a "liberal" from the city, kind of a carpetbagger to them I thought. A very short veteran, almost a dwarf, with a hunchback, wearing bright blue Union cloth, came up behind me and fired at my head. Hey, I was on the Union side! Somehow he missed. Even the Union side was after me. He reminded me of something but I had no time to mull it over. I broke forward at a run. Passing the armory, a long box on wheels like a chifforobe, I reached between slightly parted canvas curtains (as on a miniature stage) and located a handgun, which I found loaded, and, casting aside my rifle, began firing the revolver from my hip at the barn as I raced toward it. I found myself standing directly in front of the grey wall of the barn with the target's black circle on a white square so close I could have touched it, and into it I poured round after round. When my ammunition and emotion were spent, I turned and walked back toward the silent, observant shooters and veterans. I hoped the dwarf had seen my violent display. Somebody remarked, "He can hit a barn after all!" to much laughter. You know, for country people there is no North or South anymore.

My guide took the opportunity to spirit us out of the glen, and we soon caught up to the parade, which we followed at a dignified pace, occasionally waving out the windows at well-wishers, small boys, and the kinds of idlers who gather in a small town when they hear that a reunion and a parade is to take place down Main Street. We were now part of the parade ourselves, I thought with relief, well hidden in the happy commotion. The brass band, the cheers and huzzahs, peels of laughter from adolescent girls, barking dogs, honking horns, all the festive sounds and sights had a pleasantly reassuring and comfortingly soporific effect on me as did the afterglow of my exertions, but I could still hear the whistle of the little guy's bullet as it sailed past my head, and I knew that unaccountably, mystifyingly, and terrifyingly, I was a hunted man. Sunlight gleaming almost painfully from the valves of piccolos and the balloon rims of the tubas. A boy on a roof waving a state flag. Girls on a pink corner diving their hands into one box of crackerjack among them. Some white hairy goats were cavorting along. When one turned its head, I saw it had a human face.

The farther we got from the target shooters at the old farm the more I relished the experience after all, which had been very exciting and energizing. It was good to plink at targets with guns, something I hadn't done since I was a kid on vacations in these woods. One felt renewed, focused, and altogether clearer after a good target shoot, the sharp aroma of gunsmoke in one's nostrils. In the end I had managed to carry it off in good style, I decided. Fortunately there had been no need to make small talk with that crew. I knew quite a lot about the Civil War and gratefully there had been no opportunity for me to spout out any of it and make a fool of myself among those veterans. I basked in the reflected light of a semi-martial experience the moreso as we put some distance on it. What good fun it had been. Especially blasting that barn dead on, ha ha! I had the odd but satisfying feeling that something had been put in order or that I was making progress in some way or in some sense. My Uncle had been right, this family reunion was doing me good on the whole. My guide even seemed satisfied too by my performance so far.

"That was good practice," agreed my guide nodding over his shoulder as if reading my thoughts. As before for some reason I sat in the back seat. He insisted on it for professional reasons, something about the insurance. It was pleasant enough and not something I was accustomed to. I found myself on the edge of straying into small talk, which I viewed much as I would indulging in a few steps into quicksand. I never knew what people were going to say next, always the most bizarre things, under cover of the commonplace, and before I knew it I would be in over my head, and I would be questioning everything they held dear. Especially this must be so on the not-Mississippi.

"Hey, it was fun. Thanks for taking me! I feel just great, although I think there was one guy who had some problem with me, I wonder why that was." I hoped my guide would pick up on that and venture his opinion so as to give me some indication who might be after me, but he didn't.

"One should always practice at small arms," opined my guide, gripping the wheel with both hands and training his attention on the heels of the last pack of revelers. "You'll be grateful later. Listen, the next stop is—well you have to figure out your relations—General MacPherson's great grandson's widow. I don't know how she is related to you but she's a very important person in town, and so forth, okay?"

I believed a general of that name had been with the Union, but it was a common enough name, and he had died young, so it could be another. But I hoped not. Even though a Union veteran had taken a potshot at me I still felt safer on the Union side, even if in reality there are no sides anymore.

We swung out of the parade and pulled onto a side street. Are we in the Union or the Confederacy? I wondered pointlessly. I thought better of asking. By the look of the guy with the golden hat in his grey-blue uniform it was neither one.

"See that big white house? That's where we're going."

It was certainly a big white house, giving me a feeling of comfort and affluence and at the same time strangeness and unease. Both sides had big white houses. A well-to-do and fashionable part of town set on a hillside, the homes were big and spaced far apart and looked like a million dollars. In the distance one could just see the leafy tops of the big trees along the edge of the great river. A quite colossal old tree ornamented the front of the house. Or surely it was the other way around, the tree wore the air of having been here first, with a girth of extraordinary gnarly dimension, and some of its higher, smaller limbs the size of the trunks of your usual suburban trees. It dominated the whole scene, an ancient tree that must have been here when there were no white people in these parts yet, to say nothing of the War, or this house. It towered over the house.

A glance at the white house suggested to me it was quite old, or the main part of it was, maybe a big farm house onto which expensive additions had been built as time went by. But "old" in this part of the country might be only a hundred years or so, and yet it seemed far older than that. The tree was far older. The wealth and solidity of the neighborhood paled and began to look very insubstantial as I gazed up into the dense green thicket of the upper limbs of the magnificent tree. Dozens of birds and squirrels flitted and leapt in its embrace ignoring all structure except as their feet found it useful, there was so much tree to land on. In fact, there was a life being led up there lost from view that had nothing to do with what was happening on the ground, ignored it, and it was impossible to say what creatures might be harbored up there, it seemed to me demons and spirits from the times of the pioneers could easily still be alive up there, since though the white man had mowed down all the prairie and cut down all the trees except those he chose to let live around his homesteads to shade and ornament them, he had no control of what went on in the tops of the trees, and life of another order abounded there. I would have been happy staring into the top of this incredible spreading tree forever rather than go into General MacPherson's great grandson's widow's house.

To accommodate the old tree, the cement sidewalk when it had been poured had made a detour around it—a semicircle of cement skirting the monstrous trunk. I found this all very charming until as I walked up to the tree and then progressed around it I saw and felt the immense power and strangeness of its huge roots that had moved the slabs of cement sidewalk into the air, so that not only did the pavement make a circle here around the tree but its planes went up and down as much as a foot and were full of cracks through which the grass grew. One felt that soon the tree would obliterate the sidewalk, throw it aside, grind it to dust, and its monstrous roots would begin to shift even the foundations of the house, whose walls would fall down. Above my head the amazing and perverse shapes and patterns of the limbs looked like a nest of vipers sidling through the Spanish moss, a diabolical plumbing, thrusting every which way in the centuries-old search for light and sagging into weird veers and clumps under such accumulated masses of heavy wood, grey moss, and thick black bark. Such a fabulous old shaggy green beast, struggling up under its own hoary weight, must have been thought of as a nice old shade tree by the neighbors who had never bothered to look up into it and notice something as strange as the Amazonian canopy to say nothing of imagining the gigantic and far-reaching root system that writhed underfoot. As I traversed the broken pavement that rose and fell on the tree's great tentacles as they searched for food, I seemed to sense the presence of all the roots of life, my own included, that went out and back from one into the past and underground, fleshy bloody roots of one's personal life that disappeared but no less certainly drew sustenance from the ages, with all their convolutions and combinations, on which one stood unwittingly, inescapably, painfully, on lost forms that had gone before. Well, that is the point of family reunions, isn't it?

My guide nudged me and pointed to some outbuildings visible through the trees as we moved up the front walk. "We'll visit the pleasant stables," he said. I had a glimpse of horses and stablehands before the looming plantation house cut off the view. In the doorway, he took my arm, pointed at the threshold, told me to watch my step, raised the brass knocker, and rapped heartily. "Think of this as a duty, a necessary social call, after which you'll have the run of the place, if we get away from here alive," he muttered as the door opened.

A strawberry blonde maid in a white uniform with a black apron stood back to let us enter. Her expression was as blank as her bleached blouse. In her outstretched hands were two green wooden bowls, one for each of us, containing water. My guide gave me a look that said to do as he did and have a sip. He bent his head and put his lips to his green bowl shaped like a half of a melon scooped hollow. It was very strange and not what I had expected at all. The attitude of the maid was impassive and unreadable as if she were controlled and well paid by some awesome force. She seemed to be floating in the air politely. Maybe she wasn't the maid, and something told me she was a "cousin" just helping out. I leaned down my face to the bowl or large half of a gourd and had a long sip of the water as I was thirsty, after which I felt eager to follow the maid wherever she wanted me to go. The water was strange and listless. My mind seemed to dissolve, my strength to waver dramatically. I regretted the sip of not-water I'd taken, some drug or poison. I had lost my volition and even if she were to lead me over a cliff I'd follow. By the look of her she wouldn't have noticed or cared if I had drunk or not, and it was a pure formality, but the effect on me was different. At the same time she had become extremely attractive. I looked around for the guide in order to give him a dirty look, but the drink had affected him the same way, or at least he had collapsed into a chair and was staring at the ceiling. The social procedure which had to be undergone here had begun, I had to follow the maid, and there was no way back.

As long as I followed behind the blonde maid in her white uniform, I felt okay, the fear diminished, I seemed to be able to think, and my legs functioned. But the minute I thought of escaping and running out of the place, a sense of despair overwhelmed me that I associated with the worst and most insoluble problems I'd ever faced in my life, because I would not be able to escape. This strawberry blonde servant, cousin or not, represented some ethereal authority and she was more wistful and lovely by the moment, especially viewed from behind. I felt like an adolescent faced with all the sexy mysteries of life for which there is no key. I followed behind her as she seemed to float in the slight breeze that drifted through the open windows.

There was a party going on in the back of the house. I felt very uneasy about it since I'd probably have to make small talk. Through the walls I could hear shouts and laughter. Even before she pushed open a door and led me onto a porch and then to the side of an almost Olympic-sized swimming pool, I could hear the splashing about of a couple of dozen cavorting guests. Light playing off the water and nearly naked bodies cheered me up. A very large handsome black-haired woman sitting in a tall deck chair with her legs crossed beguilingly had her eyes fixed on me, and I suddenly realized where the spell that had enervated me was emanating from. That is, she was the paymaster of the maid. Her seat was ten feet high. Next to her was a giant pool toy—an inflated rubber cat. She had the kind of eyes which seem to fasten on you no matter where you turn, and I could feel my energy draining straight out of me and going into her eyes. This must be my hostess, the widow, I surmised, she must own the place. She sat above the pool surveying it like a lifeguard on her pedestal, but you didn't get the feeling she would actually ever rescue anyone. In case anyone drowned she would have a good view though of events. Her reaction to such an accident would be hard to predict I felt. For one thing she had a tall drink in her hand she was pouring down her throat and might be drunk.

Out of the expected courtesy I must display, I walked over to introduce myself and murmur a greeting, which nearly undid me as she seemed to sense my whole struggle to move and speak and peered down at me overbearingly. I was still loggy from the not-water in the gourd and accidentally hit the rubber cat with my elbow and it rocked back and forth, thrusting its round head again and again at me. The widow never took her eyes off me. She wasn't fat, she was just large, probably six foot two, but proportioned handsomely, with a fine blue-black mane. She must be the queen of society around here, a doyenne, by all appearances, more like a dictator. After what seemed to me a long pause, she merely smiled and asked me if I'd like to swim and invited me to a dressing room. Her eyes were very liquid and fine. The maid who had been hovering in the air nearby showed me to a small bathroom and handed me a swimming suit.

At the edge of the pool I noticed several things I hadn't seen before, probably because I had been magnetized by the woman's eyes. First of all the water was almost black. This was maybe because it was so deep in the pool that no light reached the bottom. Yet it didn't begin till an initial drop of twenty feet over the side. I mean the water started twenty feet down—a twenty foot drop to the water to begin with, and after that blue-black depths. There were no stairs, but instead ladders made of iron chains down which the swimmers descended, swinging and clanking. This was not so appealing as at first it had seemed. The echoes of the clanking chains reminded me of a dungeon and the tortures conducted therein. I was just contemplating how to go about getting down to the extremely deep water, since the chain ladders struck me as looking painful to the feet, when the blue-haired queen called me over and explained that it was extremely dangerous and that I'd better attach myself first to the safety ropes. This was the second thing I had not seen: all the swimmers were harnessed up to ropes which trailed up over the sides of the pool, wound around the deck, and found their way to the ankles of the queen, the widow. That way, she explained, she could prevent people from drowning. She could pull them out if they were in trouble. I doubted this would work though. There was something oddly familiar, and also extremely attractive about the widow. I didn't mind obeying her even though I had lost interest in swimming.

The fun in the pool that I had for a moment anticipated was somewhat diminished by this arrangement with the chains and ropes. It would make swimming rather onerous. Still I was a very good swimmer and could probably manage it. I was basically here for a "social call," I remembered the guide explaining, and when in Rome, and so forth, so I attached the ropes around my waist as she showed me how to do and jumped in. It was a ways down before I hit the water.

Just as I did so, a black waiter passing by with a tray of empty glasses and a wry and knowing air about him, muttered to me out of the side of his mouth, "That lady turned Death Valley into a desert!" I was sure I had seen the waiter somewhere before.

With that preposterous—and I felt extremely telling—remark in my ear, after a lengthy drop, I hit the water hard, and was instantly glad to have the life rope, for it was deep and dark as a well down here and one couldn't see as high as the high rim of the pool, because of a sudden mist, and the water was cold and seemed to have a property of sucking you down. I had to swim very hard, turning the purple water to a froth, to keep afloat and make my slow progress toward the other end, which I assumed and hoped was shallower. By now I was glad to know the society lady up there could pull me out again if I started to drown although I wasn't sure she would. Over the rim of the pool I could hear her arguing with one of the waiters, telling him he had to go down into the pool and help one of the guests learn to swim. Then the high-pitched voice of a guest, who wanted to be left alone. I didn't blame him. But shortly the two of them were lowered over the side, and the attendant held the guest up as he paddled hard to keep from going under, so it was just as well. The dark water might have sucked him down into the vortex like a cork if he didn't swim hard and wasn't held afloat. The widow queen suddenly peered down over the edge of the deep well, calling to me to ask if I was doing okay or wanted an attendant to come and help me, too.

No, no, definitely not, I shouted back, wanting to be left alone, but maybe I did, as the water kept sucking me down. But I waved to her that things were okay and kept flailing and swimming. When I managed to reach the surface and grab a breath, by now she was sitting in a real lifeguard's chair on the top of a white wooden tower, with a whistle poised between her lips that she took out to talk. Still, she was a dynamite looking lady, only big as an ox. Suddenly her pool toy bounded from her side and took off running and to my amazement I saw it was a live cat not a toy, a monster, that cat must have gone thirty or forty pounds, and around the deck it romped nearly running guests over.

With a great, almost heroic, effort I kept going and eventually saw the shape of the end of the blue pool loom up before me out of the fog like the side of an ocean liner. Strangely the water seemed higher at this end too as if I had been swimming uphill. As soon as I got there though, it wasn't twenty feet up to the deck either but things were a normal pool level over here. The ropes soaked with water were by now an unbearably heavy burden. They were cutting into my waist painfully and had become wound around one arm somehow. I saw a man hanging at the edge of the pool happily kicking his legs with no ropes attached to him. He had his elbows hooked over the edge of the pool and was smoking a small cigar. The pleasant grin on his face or something else about him drew me to him, and I wanted to get up near him where I could hang onto the edge of the pool as he was doing with my elbows. He had the air of someone you might like to chat with. I saw it was my Uncle from Texas! I couldn't get my elbows over the rim of the pool because of the heavy ropes which were chafing badly.

"Look at you, you know how to swim, get rid of that stuff," he said waving his cigar at my ropes, and sticking out a foot he kicked the rope off my shoulder. "So you made it."

"Hey, you made it too!" I was so happy to see him. It was an incredible relief to get the ropes off, I didn't know how I had swum here with that awkward weight on me.

"I never miss a party."

No sooner had I met up with my Uncle than mild blue water began gushing in the pool from pipes along the sides and in a minute the water filled up the pool to the very top and was sloshing over, pearly blue as it lapped over the tiles. Without the ropes to encumber me I did a few laps with ease, and there was nothing to it, and the water and everything was approaching normal. The exercise was doing me good and blowing away the cobwebs and paranoia. But the towering widow began blowing her whistle at something. The level of the water began to drop again. "No smoking!" she shouted at my Uncle. She was extremely attractive and wore a sleek black bathing suit over her striking figure like Wonder Woman in a wet suit.

"Hop out and get dressed," said my Uncle, ignoring her and puffing away on his cigar all the more. "Let's look around." He flicked a short cylinder of ash into the pool water, and we left.

I rather hated to leave the very attractive if overbearing widow. I almost wished to take up smoking in order to get yelled at by her. Shortly I joined him behind the main house in a corral where kids were riding donkeys and horses, and stablehands were saddling and unsaddling the animals. It was so good to be standing out in the sunshine with the kids, horses, stablehands, beautiful dirt, horse, and hay smells, and all the pretty animals, chickens, dogs. Around the circle galloped one stablehand on a beautiful black pony. It was the same guy who had made that remark to me about the Death Valley, now having doffed his waiter's costume and put on riding gear. He was waving his hat and laughing at something. My Uncle stuck out his cigar and signaled with the glowing ember, and the stablehand on the pony came to a quivering halt in front of him. Like everybody else the stablehand who seemed an impertinent character responded to my Uncle's wishes with alacrity. It seemed to me he had been riding such a small pony much too hard, yet the animal didn't seem to be the worse for it, and when the stablehand got off, it stood there quivering, with its nostrils wide and its flanks heaving, full of vibrant life and arching its glossy black neck.

"C'mere," said my Uncle and took my arm and we walked up to the black pony which stood nervously but without bolting though the stablehand had released the reins and backed off watching my Uncle approach. In the eyes of the pony there was a look of trust as they focused on my Uncle.

"Here," he said to me. "She's yours." The pony raised one hoof and pawed the air a little. It pranced in front of me. "She's your reward for making it to the party."

What I wanted with a pony I couldn't imagine, but I didn't bother worrying about it because it was the prettiest little pony and it had positively taken a fancy to me and seemed to have confidence in me and I fell in love with it instantly. Everything worthwhile in life seemed concentrated in its charming form and I was like a child at Christmas. After all the awkward vibes and lunatic small talk I had been subjected to at this reunion, I felt loved and rewarded by my Uncle's gesture, and the mute affection of the black pony. Like a dog almost, the pony rubbed its side against my leg and chest. It raised its little hoof again as if to salute me and pranced and danced. Beyond words we had an instant rapport. My Uncle had said it was mine, and I was unaccountably charmed and enamored by something I wouldn't have dreamed of. I thought the pony had been meant for me and felt inseparable from it already.

"She's yours to enjoy since, in the end, you didn't drown in that pool, I guess."

"What's her name?"

"Smoky," the smiling stablehand volunteered, who was still in attendance, and immediately coughed on the back of his hand.

It had a jagged white mark on its forehead like a bolt of lightning. I loved it a lot, and I could tell that against every probability it loved me too.

"What am I going to do with a pony?" I asked my Uncle uncertainly.

"She's *yours,* as I said. She'll be waiting for you. Come back any time and get her, in case you can't take her with you."

So a pony had entered my life. But how I was going to come in here and get—steal was more like it—this pony I didn't know. I would have to deal with the widow some more first to do it. Her coat was the same glossy blue-black as the bangs of the widow and I sensed a secret identity between them though their personalities could not have been more diametrically different. I didn't think I could take Smoky back to Chicago on the bus.

"I can't take her just now."

"Well, it's probably impractical, isn't it? You're just riding around in a car, aren't you? It's always impractical for you, isn't it? Anyway, there's something we have to do now. Where did you leave that guide of yours?"

So no sooner than having met Smoky I would have to leave her again. I vowed to myself that no matter how arduous the effort with the large woman I'd get her again. Smoky meant everything to me all of a sudden mysteriously. She just called up affection in me, she was so cute. In the meantime I was uneasy that she would be left in the charge of the stablehand who seemed a very unstable stablehand to me, who had ridden her rather cruelly. There was something about him that struck me as familiar in an evil and uncanny way but I couldn't place him. That is, the way he eyed me I had the sense that he thought he had my number in some inexplicable way and I didn't like it. We had to leave now, and I was ready to turn away so as not to have to watch him jump back onto Smoky, but the next thing that happened was a very well-built strawberry blonde girl in a sleeveless white shirt and riding jodhpurs came out of a barn and walked straight toward us. She regarded me curiously, as if wondering who I was, but ignored my Uncle as if she knew him well, who slightly bared his teeth at her. She seemed ready to say something, there was a moment of strange tension, and my Uncle held his peace, although he seemed about to laugh. At the last second she turned and sidled up to the stablehand, and said, "Hello, darling, want a ride tonight?"

The gloating glance he gave her reminded me of something. There was far more to this stablehand than met the eye. He had grotesquely large shoulders. The blonde was the widow's daughter apparently, I heard someone say, as well as being a cousin of mine I deduced. She was very handsome and built like a red barn. She was in charge around here in back of the place in the stables. I wondered if she realized I was now the owner of Smoky and whether I would have to deal with her too. I wouldn't mind but I was overawed by her sex appeal. She seemed her mother's daughter all right.

I stared at her, mulling over the possibility she might be M turned up in this unlikely spot to make trouble. Not only would she have had to get out of her hospital bed, but put herself back together in one piece. She didn't seem to be M, thankfully, but you never knew. Anyway, I was relieved they were going off together, and my pony would be spared any more cruel workouts today, and I would be left out of it.

Bravely I walked past the blonde and the stablehand and up to Smoky for a farewell that would be only temporary and looked fondly into her big limpid black eyes. I say bravely because of bidding farewell to Smoky. All the wonder and magic of life stared back at me from her eyes. I felt in love with life again and I was trembling with joy. Smoky suddenly seemed to understand that I was leaving her. At this she drew up and rose back slightly off her little hoofs, in disappointment, I felt. The widow's daughter did not seem to notice any of these subtleties. She kept staring at me over her shoulder as if wondering if there were any way she could possibly mess with my mind. The grotesque stablehand smirked at us, biding his time.

Slowly, Smoky arched back and floated into the air. How troubled I was by this. I watched helplessly as I realized there was no tether or rope attached to her to keep her connected to earth. Where was the society queen with her safety ropes now? Smoky was four feet off the ground and rising. Up the pony floated without so much as moving one hoof again. Higher and ever higher Smoky soared, catching a breeze so helplessly and wistfully like a kite that has broken its string. She whinnied once pitifully before going out of earshot. It seemed she would blow away far into the sky. Already she was no more than a speck with toothpick legs on the horizon. The clouds engulfed her. My loss was so sudden and profound I was temporarily paralyzed with grief. I started for the stablehand. I was going to kill him, for some reason, as if he had something to do with it. He had a strange staff in his hands that he held out as if to stave me off.

My Uncle intervened with his good sense. "Where did you say your guide was again?" asked my Uncle striking me on the shoulder with a pair of gloves as I passed him. I stopped and tried to remember. Still parked right in front of the house, I supposed. My Uncle reached out and took me by the arm.

"Hey, we gotta get going if we're going to catch her!"

The guide had been having a palaver with some other drivers or guides under the shade of the monstrous old tree but he came charging after us when he saw my Uncle striding determinedly toward his car.

"Let's go!" cried my Uncle, and in a moment we were tearing off down the roadways crisscrossing the territory chasing after Smoky barely visible, just a tiny black dot now above the distant treetops.

We had passed my guide slumped under the tree smoking a cigarette waiting with some other guides. An ugly circle of butts haloed their feet. Seeing us he threw down his fresh cigarette and trotted to catch up with us, his expression reflecting annoyance that something was obviously afoot that had nothing to do with his job or his plans, but on the other hand my Uncle was a man of authority and some mystery. My guide's air had changed from the self-possessed authority he exuded with me since that would not go over anymore with my Uncle. He no longer seemed so eager and at first wheeled his car perfunctorily. He was obliged to take orders now. In a minute or two my Uncle had managed to charm him, however, or intimidate him. It took him another minute to absorb the fact that we were chasing a horse about a thousand feet in the air, but when he did he understood the urgency and somewhat got in the spirit of the adventure. By now Smoky must be gliding over the river.

We rolled down from the hilly part of town where the big mansions were, block by block, barely pausing at stop signs, and entered wide boulevards that connected the old money part of town with suburban vistas. Suddenly we caught a glimpse of Smoky but for an instant as again she floated out of sight over the horizon beyond some cornfields through which there were no paths let alone roads. Thinking quickly, my Uncle grabbed the guide's shoulder and indicated for him to abandon the chase in this direction, and to head back the way we had come. He instructed the guide to head back to a road that ran along the river and from which we might gain a new vantage and catch up to her. But we never did see her again. It was excruciating to backtrack but then we were on the river road and hoping against hope. The excitement of the chase began to wear off, first for the guide, then my Uncle who was reluctant to give up but could see it was useless, lastly for me, for I was in a state of panic and wanted to keep going no matter what. The situation was very disturbing, my dear pony floating away helplessly into the sky. By now we had no idea where she might be.

The guide was morose, as he was no longer in charge, my Uncle setting the course. I got the impression that our new route, "down by the river," would not have been on the scheduled itinerary. We departed town on a highway that eventually curved through low hills and scrub woods that flanked the big river. Coming around a blind curve we nearly crashed head on into a red sports car coming straight at us in our lane. The guide swerved onto the ragged shoulder barely threading between the errant car and the forest, letting out a yelp and a curse, and as the sports car whizzed by, I was amazed to catch a whole line of speech from its driver, who rattled out the following, which must have been part of a diatribe he was delivering to himself for the fun of it because he was alone in his car:

"The highest order of reality is that gratitude which steals upon you when you realize that every day every year every minute you have found yourself once again where it had already been intended you should already have been long ago so there you are again a little realer once again for being where you might as well have been the first time around—"

The voice extinguished in the wind was an old geezer's wearing a jaunty cap flapping his gums rapidfire to deliver such a speech. I was aghast that a red sports car should be driven so wildly by an ancient rascal like that spouting such nonsense, who had nearly killed us. Suddenly the guide stamped the brake and staring dead into the rearview mirror announced, "He went over the cliff!"

We screeched to a halt and he executed a neat U-turn raising the hair on my neck as I looked off into the air over what was really a very sharp drop on that side down to the river and we raced back up the road to the point where the red car had left the road. I saw tire marks on the gritty shoulder, then over the edge the sports car in a muddy pool at the base of the cliff, submerged up to the tops of its windows. The three of us scrambled down the steep embankment into the brush. But it had taken us perhaps ten minutes already and it was far too late. He must have been dead on impact. Our brave guide struck out into the water and waded out to the car, managed to open the door and pull the old man out and haul him to the muddy shore, but he was dead, doubly dead from concussion and drowning it looked like. The guide administered CPR and mouth to mouth revival efforts. Perhaps he admired such a racy old driver, or knew who he was, or he was just a decent soul. He did his best to resuscitate him without success, in spite of almost having been run off the road by him.

A deep bloody gash puckered his forehead and river water ran out of his gills. He still had the goofiest smirk on his face, as if he were just sure he was the best driver and wisest old fool around. Even dead he looked smug and his driving cap was still stuck to his head somehow. That must have been his final expression as if he never knew what hit him. The effect was ridiculous on top of devastating and alarming since he'd almost killed us too. I wondered what he thought now about the circle life had taken him on and the place he'd woken up in and if it was real enough for him. The starkly cruel irony of the philosophizing old fool's being cut off in mid-nonsense made the silence around us shocking as though life itself were amazed at pontificators and philosophers.

My guide was chain-smoking in a daze and staring at the lifeless body whose resistance to his attempts at resuscitating him seemed mystifying to him.

"He nearly kills us coming around that curve, and now he's dead himself," he mumbled wonderingly.

My Uncle, who had not spoken a word during the whole episode, though his jaws had worked as though he were swallowing various things down, glanced at the guide as if at last he had said something barely worthwhile, before some words finally emerged from himself, a few practical ones. Perhaps seeing that the guide was hardly in shape to do much more driving for us, and that someone ought to stay on the scene, he said, "Sit down right here and wait here for the cops," and the two of us climbed back up the bank. Saying he wanted to show me "another part of town," he took the wheel and we drove on. Nothing passed between us for a while.

The sudden horror of the accident lent an edge to my dismay about my pony flying away. The disappearance into the ether of Smoky had left me very sad, of course, even shaken, but now it seemed threatening. My Uncle, though he didn't say as much, seemed to suspect it was another one of her tricks. He knew something about her, he had his opinions about her, from the few words he let escape. I was quite weirded out with her flying away, I missed her and my hopes were dim, so I was overjoyed to hear him say, "We have to take a new approach to our day, I mean from a completely new angle. There's no other way to catch her." So he wasn't giving up the chase. "We have to retreat and take a broader view. She'll turn up again, you don't have to worry about that!"

This would involve a detour unbearable to me, had not it been my Uncle in the lead. What impressed me about my Uncle was how he had extracted us from a maudlin scene on the riverbank, to which we had only a fortuitous connection, where we could have easily spent the balance of the day mired in shock, dismay, and police bureaucratic red tape, while in no sense were we running out on our responsibilities for he had gotten rid of our driver at one stroke and the main witness of the tragedy was waiting for the cops at the scene.

"At least we got rid of that bozo," he agreed.

About ten miles farther the pavement ended and a dirt washboard road commenced, now nearly at a level with the river and affording long glimpses through tall grass of the wide green waters. We rambled over this road for several miles until all traces of the town had vanished and my Uncle decided to stop at a spot that looked no different from any other, except that the grass was thicker, behind a tall clump of which he parked the car carefully, as if he were hiding it. He took out a pair of binoculars from his briefcase and we got out of the car and pushed through the grass toward the water but not all the way there. We sat down behind a last stand of brush and grass behind which we were somewhat concealed—that seemed to be his idea—but through which we had a view of a wide span of the river. I contemplated the treeline for Smoky as she was all I could think of. I thought we must have stopped here because it must be advantageous somehow in our search for my darling pony. My Uncle handed me the glasses and pointed at something across the water.

What I did instead was to point the glasses into the sky and scan every horizon for Smoky. Her absence was a hole in my heart that was not diminishing. I had no idea what my Uncle was up to now along the river, it didn't concern me, and figured we must be waiting for her to appear in the atmosphere. My Uncle didn't object, but finally put his hand on my arm to redirect my attention, saying as he did so drily, "Don't worry, I said she'll turn up. You'd have to try pretty hard for her not to, if you know what I mean." I didn't know what he meant actually. There was a limit to what we could do, however, and she had flown away. I allowed my gaze to be diverted as he wished and it was easy to be absorbed in the powerful new vistas of the river. The day had been so strange, and now the bright sun on the grass stirred up scents from my childhood and the childhood of the planet itself, and strange old states of mind passed over me indistinctly but pleasantly. Smells are such powerful associators but what they bring back may be as nameless and traceless as they are evocative. The afternoon light dazzled the water. Strong odors as of turtles and catfish and mud wafted across the bank to us. It was the hot part of the afternoon and the great watery stillness engulfed our personal silence profoundly.

From our right around a distant bend a flatboat suddenly appeared on which stood a very large orange farmer's tractor. Slowly the flatboat bearing this equipment was being poled along by two men, one in the bow and one in the stern. They were hugging the shore where it must be shallow. Their clothing, almost rags, was so brown, mudcaked, and primitive as to suggest a long bygone era. They poled in unison and in silence and little by little, with the help of the current, came nearer to us until at last they were directly in front of us. What was profoundly unusual about this sight was that the boat and its occupants had but two dimensions, up and down, right and left, perfectly flat, no depth to them at all.

I squeezed my eyes shut to try to conjure up some perspective on the scene and when I opened them examined the thick grass, my inscrutable Uncle, and the bright blue sky (all possessing the usual coordinates) before turning back to the oppressively flat flatboat which was finally about to pass out of our view to the left like a tableau. The brownclothed men poling along, the orange tractor, and the boat were uncannily without substance but vividly real for all that, as if their reality had been heightened by being squeezed thin as a pancake by a steamroller. Everything in them had been brought to the expressive surface, as it were, like prisoners holding onto the bars of their cage, excruciatingly painful for the observer. The effect was to deepen the river silence to an immense stillness, and the sense of being lost in some mysterious distant past clicked up another notch. The vision was striking, alien, and vaguely terrifying, and I must have squirmed about or made a move to get up because my Uncle put his hand on my shoulder and said, "Look." The boat was no longer visible. What did he want me to see?

With the boat passed out of sight there was nothing on the river before us any longer to look at and so my line of sight took me far away over to the opposite shoreline where in the shadows under the bank I could barely make out a little dilapidated pier and some evidences of what might have been a fishing camp. This must have been what he wanted me to look at all along. At the tip of the pier I thought I could see the tarnished chains of live nets or stringers or some other equipment hanging over the edges of the planks. Over the misty top of the brush on the riverbank were low roofs of some shacks of a camp. There was no activity to be witnessed and the scene had an overgrown and sleepy, if not abandoned, look.

After a while I put down the glasses, thinking I had seen everything there was to see and it wasn't much, but my Uncle raised them again to my eyes with the back of his hand and nodded again at the far shore that I had been studying. So I looked again and now I saw something odd that I hadn't noticed at first, but I had no idea what it was. Right next to the pier in the water and almost lost in shadow was a long, strange-looking box. The way it was floating about two-thirds of it was submerged and the top third of it bobbing in the air. I might not have been able to see it at all except, like the tractor, it was painted orange. It wasn't a true orange but a very faded red and I wondered if the tractor hadn't been painted with the very same faded paint. Time and the waves had stained the box's wooden sides, and there was the depth of everyday three-dimensional reality to this floating box unlike the flatboat and tractor, and everything else across the river looked normal enough, though with an air of abandonment, radiant of a feeling of time interrupted.

Now through the field glasses I took a careful look at the long box next to the little pier, for it had excited my interest, as much as I could make it out through the glasses at the distance, which were pretty strong. It was not regular, or generally rectangular (like a coffin) at all, as at first I had supposed, but somewhat triangular shaped, the far end or apex shorter than the stained red bottom of it pointing in my direction. Furthermore the two long sides were subtly curved inward in the middle and then rounded at the top where they joined each other, or perhaps they just sagged inward with age and the effects of the water, so the box when viewed end-on seemed almost bell-shaped. I studied the box, fascinated, as apparently my Uncle expected me to do, while it bobbed gently and imperceptibly in the water alongside the pier. It was about six or eight feet long and three feet deep maybe. But it was only a guess how much of it was under water.

"What is it? What's *in* it?" I finally asked my Uncle, since it was he who had called my attention to it.

"That's for you to find out, isn't it?"

I knew just what he meant, for it was already in my heart as an ungovernable impulse to find out. I stood up, the better to search the near shoreline for some conveyance to get me over there. "What's in it for me," I said.

"It's sort of an old trap, you know," said my Uncle.

Yes, like a fish trap or crab trap, but something valuable for me was caught in it, far more than any fish or crabs. *Something that would help me was in the trap.* Without another word from him, or a sign from him or anything else, I knew that something of mine was in that trap and I must go over there and get it, and I would go right now. It suddenly occurred to me that *trap* spelled backward was *part*. A part of me was in that trap and I must retrieve it.

Another flatboat passed slowly by, this one much larger, with a crowd of men on it, who appeared to be hobos, or poor rivermen on the way to work perhaps, standing or lying stretched out on the long deck, still, patient, watchful, smoking, slouched and coiled like snakes, perfectly silent and resigned, on a journey from one part of the deep woods to another, or from some other time to our present one. Again this boat and these men had no depth, no third dimension, but were intensely present (and past) on one pressed plane only, as if they had been an apparition playing across some magical canvas in the air, now about to disappear on my left where some tall trees cut off the view of the river. It was as if a painting were moving along in front of us from right to left, but a painting has illusions of depth and from this painting the artist had masterfully obliterated any such hints of "reality," and an uncanny flatness exuded from the flatboat and its motionless occupants, all the more vividly real for that.

All that was solid and even eternal in these men and their boat had been compressed into an impossible nonexistence as on a screen, and was the more intensely alive for being under this powerful restraint, as if something caged and hidden would spring forth. Alive but lost, they were prisoners lashed to a barge wide as necessary to hold their exact shapes but squashed zero inches thick for extra precaution. I had the feeling that they wouldn't have been able to see us for we were in another world. They were profoundly absent from time as well as having no depth. So you could say two of our four dimensions were absent. This made what was left of them all the more striking, and infinitely sad. The something missing was poignant, dangerous, evocative of what I didn't know. The way a silence might be evocative of an explosion if you knew a fuse had been lit out of sight someplace and you had only a little while to find it before the damage would be done.

With no breeze stirring, the expanse of the river itself was so flat. As they passed by, they flattened out the air, water, mud, and all vegetation some distance ahead of them releasing it again behind them as if the scene were passing through their flatness. Out of sight they sailed beyond us right to left along the smooth plane of the river out of our field of vision into another realm, another time that was able to touch ours but keep its own integrity as if time were like the surface line of the river from below which, out of which, astonishing anythings might emerge, flatboats full of rivermen from other ages, or whatever you liked. I realized there was a connection between the compressed riverboats and the long box or trap tied to the pier across the way that made me even more eager to cross the river and spring the trap.

107

What was missing from the flattened, caged and oppressive scene was caught in that strange bell-shaped trap across the water bobbing next to the pier, I conjectured, like the key to a lock that would spring everything loose at once. I was thrilled by the challenge of how to get across the river and open the trap, let out its mystery, and carry it back to this side! If I could do it, maybe the rivermen would come to normal 3-D existence and be free, maybe I'd find Smoky again, M would get herself together, and the riddle of life be answered. The goddess might appear again or something unimaginable would happen.

"I've got to get over there," I said to my Uncle.

"Of course. Go on," he encouraged me, settling back as if for a wait.

I found myself by the edge of the water, searching for a johnboat, a canoe, or even a piece of timber on which I could paddle across the river. I forgot everything else. I had only one aim. I wanted to show my Uncle I was man enough to do it, rescue whatever it was of mine that was in the trap. Yes, I knew it was mine. I had my feet at water's edge. I took off my shoes. I couldn't see any old rowboat or even a plank to float across on and I figured I would have to swim for the far shore. I was a good swimmer, though I hadn't swum in a while, but I had just recently gotten in the swing of it back in the widow's crazy pool that kept changing depth. Maybe it had been good practice to do a lap on that pool! My guide had been right. The not–Mississippi River wasn't all that wide at this place, maybe a mile it looked like.

Just then, one more old boat swung into view, this one poled by black men dressed as you might have imagined the slaves had been, in this part of the country, short-sleeved tatters of shirts the color of sweat and mud, baggy trousers patched and practically in ribbons, above bare feet. On this flatboat their load was some kind of huge threshing machine, the same sullen rust color which kept appearing on all the machines that were the freight of these barges that were anachronistically and mysteriously passing by. The threshing machine the slaves were poling to somewhere or other seemed oddly modern, then I noticed this flatboat had a motor. The slaves poling were really only steering and keeping the thing on course. Why did I think of them as slaves I wondered? They had an outboard motor. Suddenly a white man on a black pony cantered out from behind the great thresher and laid a whip on their backs with appalling violence, and I had my answer. To think that things were still going on like that in this part of the country in our modern age. But I can assure you they are.

Slowly this flatboat floated from right to left like the others, having appeared round one bend in the river, and ready to depart from sight beyond the next. The great thresher machine fixed my attention as I realized I was about to lose sight of it. It must have been very valuable if there was a slave overseer on a horse with a whip providing security for it and driving the fieldhands to keep it on course down the river. The thresher looked like the sort of rude contraption dust-bowl farmers would have been trying to keep running with string and baling wire. Strange appurtenances hung off it or stuck up in the air from its back. You would have had to know something about farming in this part of the country to have begun to imagine what all its blades, forks, rakes, and wheels could be meant to be used for— probably simple enough for those in the know.

Several of the slaves were sitting around it and gazing up at it with adulation as if it were more of a god than a machine. I guess not only their livelihoods but their very lives depended on their getting it safely to its destination. Strewn about its high blades were circles of flowering vines, colorful green garlands studded with large yellow blooms like festoons on a Maypole, like sweet wreaths on the neck of a Hindu god in a religious parade. The thresher god stayed in my view for a long time since I had walked along the water's edge to a wider angle on the river, while at the same time I combed the shoreline for any pieces of wood I might strap one to another to make a raft. I didn't find anything useable. I waved and shouted at the slaves and overseer without thinking. But they were in another world.

Finally I gave up looking for anything to float on and just stripped off my clothes and as the thresher god went out of sight up the river, I swam. It was a calm day. I struck out at a sharp angle upstream. I didn't have any doubts about making it. As far as swimming was concerned, back in the widow woman's pool if I could swim in those purple and sucking waters I could swim anywhere. A mile on the not–Mississippi River would be nothing. I felt light as a feather and propelled myself along effortlessly. I must have swum for three-quarters of an hour as the current took me slightly off course but it seemed to me I was there in no time at all, so eager was I to get there, so happy and dauntless at my task. Stroke after stroke, instinctively heading into the current, to get a close look at the trap and find out what it held. All the aimlessness and confusion of my life had come to a focus in this particular mystery and challenge, and I can't remember a more blessed or satisfying swim, a more bracing or renewing effort, such as now culminated, in a flash, in my standing dripping on the old wooden pier, in my undershorts, listening to the somnolence of the river and the rapture of the trees, cocking an ear for any sign of life in the fishing camp, and hearing only the trickle of water as it ran off my legs and ticked on the dry wood planking.

The bell-shaped red trap was even larger than I had imagined it. It ran half the length of the pier. It could be holding giant catfish or for that matter a couple of alligators it was so big. What did they need such a large trap for? Why its triangular shape? What would be inside it? There must be a gate or hatch hinged conveniently somewhere on it you could throw back and get at your haul. In its looming presence so suddenly, I momentarily shied away. I didn't know how to approach the imposing old thing with its faded-red, chipped and warped, bell-shaped wooden boards.

I wondered if I was being watched. I walked up the dock and peered through the grass at the shacks, whose occupants must be out on the river fishing or who knew where. Maybe someone was napping up there though. I was afraid of being

surprised. There were no boats about and so all the denizens of
the camp must be away I assured myself. Maybe it was off
season for the camp. Only slightly relieved having drawn this
conclusion, I studied the shacks which were mostly obscured in
shadow as it was very late in the afternoon.

I killed a little more time and procrastinated further by
hauling up one of the chain stringers that hung from rusty nails
off the end of the pier. At the end of the stringer was a single
round fish. The sight of this fish affected me deeply. I felt a lump
of affection for it in my throat, and it seemed to me a clever and
important fish, and about the cutest fish I had ever seen if rather
ungainly—certainly the roundest fish. It was a very strange fish
and not at all what I might have expected on the not-Mississippi.
It looked like no other fish I had ever seen before. I lowered it
back into the water carefully. I wanted it to stay alive at all costs.
I wondered if I should let it go. I would have liked to, but
apparently it belonged to whoever hung out at this camp, and I
didn't want to offend them. If they were holding fish on stringers
they must be around here someplace. The slavemaster on his
horse watching over the threshing god and the slaves suggested a
ferocity in the people around here I would rather personally not
encounter. Having lowered the round fish back into the river, I
stared down at it and could see its gills moving reassuringly.
Finally, almost shaking with expectancy, I leaned over the end of
the bell-shaped red trap to look for a latch on a trapdoor.

In the wooden end-piece or bottom of the bell near my feet,
I saw just such a small door as I had expected there would be,
latched by a big hook at the water-line. It was relatively small
given the great proportions of the whole trap. The trap door was
only about six inches by six inches. It would be awkward to
reach inside. Just like that, I reached down and caught the hook
on my fingertip. It wouldn't budge as if it were rusted to the
metal eye, welded to it by the ages. It was going to take more
than my fingertip to pry it loose, and I looked about for a
screwdriver or crowbar.

Instead came the sound of footsteps creaking on the pier! I almost fell into the water in fright. A tall shadow loomed over me. I glanced up at a tough character wearing a black bell-shaped battered old-time country boy's hat, glowering down at me with a corncob pipe in the teeth of his widely grimacing mouth. He was barefoot and stood just at the other end of the trap. His pantslegs were rolled up over his bony white hairy shins and huge feet. I still had my finger on the latch of the trapdoor, and had to crane my neck back to look up at him, who was well over six feet tall. The top of his black hat made him closer to eight feet. He and I faced each other just over the trap. He held a rifle which he slowly raised and pointed at my heart.

Paralyzed and hunched over by fear the first instant, I straightened up and jumped back in the next. I was about to dive into the water and swim for it when he swung his rifle away from me and walked back up the planks the way he had come. Seeing him go, with a burst of bravery I dove at the trap again and fumbled for the latch hook, but my move brought him back over me in a split second. He drove a bullet into the breech of his gun with a loud well-oiled mechanical crash and I thought I was done for. Again I leapt back, and again like an automaton commanded by my own motions, he departed halfway toward the camp on shore. Apparently if I didn't mess with the trap he'd go away. He didn't seem to care if I just stood on his pier.

The way he came and went on the plank rails so perfunctorily as if he were on wheels connected by a secret mechanism to my subtlest intentions had me speculating whether I could think of something far away to send him to and distract him while under cover of my thoughts I could open the door of the trap. But no, a third try made it certain he was here expressly to keep me from springing the latch. I wondered whether a bullet of his would actually kill me, but I didn't want to try it. He looked the serious and vengeful sort of rascal you could imagine guarding a corn-liquor still in the backwoods. Could it be they had ingeniously thought of hiding gallons of stump whiskey under water in what for all intents and purposes looked like a big fish trap?

It was now or never, the moment of truth. I was on the verge of giving in to my impulse of courage and opening the trap, gun or no gun, right under his nose, and gun, and trying to make a run for it, when I saw an even more gigantic pantsleg and black-and-white-checked shirt tail the size of a house glimpsed through a watery mist up the shore. Coming down from the camp, rising up to an imponderable height, was another guy, who looked just like the first except that he was thirty or more feet tall, and made of a smoky substance so that his limbs had an elastic hot quality that could have stretched across the river to get at me let alone on a small pier, and he carried a gun like a cannon. This infinitely menacing figure never said a word, and his head was in the clouds, all I could see was his giant torso and checked shirt, but I understood pretty well that he too hoped I would not open the trap—or actually maybe he hoped I would just try it!

Panicked, when I took several quick steps back from the trap toward the corner of the pier, the ordinary-sized rifleman moved several yards backward too, toward the shore as usual, and then the giant cousin merely faded away like a passing cloud, or fogbank. I also seemed to almost control him by my intentions like his partner and they were both supersensitive to my moves. As he disappeared though, he gained size rapidly so that in a moment he hovered over the whole region like a vast storm from which a violent and deadly rain might fall. The entire atmosphere was threatening. The warning was clear. What might happen if I suddenly tripped the latch on the trap might be the end of me. The whole region was flashing unmistakable signs that I was not welcome here.

I had thought the fish camp abandoned but it was filled with bad dudes. It occurred to me that I was not going to open the trap today, well guarded as it was, and that to do so I would even have to come back with a gun of my own another day. I knew my Uncle carried one and wished I had brought it with me. But I

113

don't know how I could have swum across with it. Maybe there was a bridge over the river somewhere nearby and we could come back at the camp by land from another direction and well enough armed to hold off these guys until I could see what was inside the trap. After all it was something of mine. We could pick up some guns at the armory on the shooting range. I congratulated myself that I had recently taken target practice. My Uncle had an old silver .44 made by a company I had never heard of. On its handle was etched Post Co. Old No. 10. He had intimated it packed a mean punch. I saw what the guide had meant about the importance of taking target practice and decided he wasn't so bad a guide at that. But I yearned to try something right now. I couldn't just retreat without giving it a try, could I?

I stood on the end of the pier in the growing shadows of evening with my back to the river. Standing tiptoe on the balls of my feet with my heels over the water kept the moonshine boys halfway back to their camp. I could have just fallen backward and struck out for the far shore where no doubt my Uncle was keeping an eye on me, with the tantalizing unknown contents of the trap almost at my feet, but completely out of my reach. I was frightened out of my wits, making me gasp for breath, but I felt so close to the secret it seemed to lift me up. The awful powers of the rifleman and the giant behind him though they were ranged against me and even threatened my life seemed to give me ecstatic life, as if secretly they were on my side, against all evidence. I thought they were wishing for me to succeed but ready to blow me away if I took a false step. What was in the trap must be a great treasure.

By their being on my side, I mean I must overcome them. My Uncle was watching curiously to see if I could. If I had ever understood anything in my futile life so far I understood this challenge. But I must be smart about it if I was going to do it. Turning around, I stood on the very last inch of the pier, my toes curling over the edge, thinking hard, and gazed on the vast and ancient river as purple shadows swept down and promised dark night in another hour. The awareness of the coming nightfall and of the terrific expanse of the water in front of me between me and my Uncle made me shiver with freedom and terror. I could open the trap, could get myself killed, could make a discovery, or could swim back and retreat to plan how I would steal the treasure on another day. Dim silhouettes of more passing flat-boats reminded me I was on the frontier of some new or very old land. On the frontier there is always another day. But maybe there wasn't. It was time to swim back and explain things to my Uncle, but I couldn't do it yet. Maybe there wouldn't be a second chance at something like this. It seemed I ought to try something desperate. I racked my brain for the answer. I waited for an angel to descend, and blow his horn into my ear.

On the horizon approaching very fast came something new all right—what appeared to be the bow of a tall ship, no flatboat this time, but something even more primitive and far grander, a slave galleon rowed by a hundred pairs of flashing oars, heralded by a great snake's head on its prow piercing the twilight with fiery breath. Did they have these back in the Confederacy? I was a little vague on my history but I doubted it. They had a submarine. Who knows, but this outfit seemed to belong to many centuries earlier. The galleon flew toward me two hundred feet long and the oars broke the water in unison. My breath was sucked out of me by the appalling dark majesty of such a primordial rig driven at such a high speed by a pack of chained rowers straight at me. The dragon on the bow spoke of powers from the strange unknowable depths of time.

But this sudden sight was coming far too fast for any boat, it was galumphing through the water, undulating like a giant otter—no, it had changed into a monstrous river snake two hundred feet long, with a fat body like a hippo which exploded the water in huge waves as it swam toward me hungrily. Following it were two others of its kind, three of them, like nothing I thought still existed on this earth. Suddenly I saw a huge wake of water sent out by the first swimming reptile coming straight at me and I hit the deck and held onto the pier for dear life as the monumental wall of water tumbled violently over me and entirely submerged me nearly ripping me loose into the torrents. Three times the huge waves hit as the three snakes dove past and the last one finally tore the boards of the pier clear apart and I lost my grip and I found myself under water, turning over and over in the middle of the river in the violent upheavals following in the churning wakes of the reptiles.

As the profound turbulence of the river subsided a bit, so I hoped to use my hands to propel myself, but before I could find my way and float to the surface again, I felt something smooth slide against me and in a panic thinking it was one of the great snakes come to devour me, I opened my eyes and saw the round fish which had been freed from its stringer. It bumped against me again and again and opened its mouth in a friendly pout. It softly slithered around and against me, and then swam in front of me, looking back to see that I understood to follow. I finally pushed my head above water and took a mighty gasp of air, ducking down again instantly in fear of losing sight of the round fish, and there was the round fish right in front of me almost seeming to wait for me. Yes, it was waiting for me. When it saw I had needed air, it had come back and waited.

Then slowly and easily it began to swim off and I could follow it, because the violence of the giant snakes' waves had subsided. But the commotion of the waters had turned me around so completely and washed me so far from shore that I had lost all sense of direction and had no idea of which way I should be swimming, unless the round fish should guide me. So I had no choice and was so grateful to the fish for finding me. Night was coming down very fast and I could no longer see the shore which I had abandoned, let alone the opposite one I probably ought to head for. It was up to the fish to lead me.

There was nothing to do but follow the wonderful round fish. We swam and swam. It was now deep night. I got tired and cold but the events of the day had been so strange and exciting the adrenaline was pumping through me and I felt I could swim all the rest of the long night. The moon came out and its round cold light made me think the fish had swum up into the sky to

116

give us light to see by. Eventually we passed near an island. There were many small boats and piers on the shoreline of this island suggesting we had reached safety at last. But the round fish did not swim toward the island but made a circle around it. On the far side the fish edged closer and I followed. There was some sort of camp or small village on this end of the island, where fires and artificial lamplight made halos in the dark. I could hear the hum of gasoline-powered generators. Then I began to hear the most horrible cries and moans above the motors. The fish paused and stuck its little head above water for a look and I treaded water and looked, too. Spotlights made a circle under which uniformed guards were torturing prisoners gruesomely. The prisoners lay in the dirt or were draped over sawhorses. Happily I was far enough away to be spared seeing the details. It was more than enough to hear the terrifying shouts of protest and surrender. I knew there was a hell on the island beyond any conception of it. As if there were not water enough all about us my eyes ran with tears.

The round fish looked at me, its eyes sad too, and said, "The night is very different from the day. Terrible tortures take place beneath the circle."

It didn't occur to me to be amazed the round fish could talk, for the sights and sounds of the prison camp had overcome me, danger surrounded us, the night was fathomless, and I depended entirely on the intelligent round fish to guide me.

Around the perimeter of the camp scene spotlights made a glowing circle in the sky, like some wild mirage cast off by the moon hanging independently in the blackness sending off showers of light, guard towers it must be, so none might escape. We must stay outside that circle I knew. Above the hum of the generators came a rising beat of soldiers' drums, a grim and horrid tattoo, perhaps signaling an execution. The round fish turned and swam on with a wriggle of its powerful little tail. It had only stopped here to give me some sort of lesson I thought. We came to yet another black silhouette of some other island rising slowly out of the river before us. On this one were no lights, no signs of human habitation, no boats, no little wooden docks, but there was something else, the heads of hundreds of snakes poking out of the water in a circle clear around the island, smaller versions of the great beasts that had beat the water to a frenzy and nearly drowned me. The phalanxes of snakes guarded the island. Each one with its hindquarters wedged in the mud faced outward into the river. Had I not had the fish with me I would have swum away from the place at top speed if I had been a hundred times as tired as I was, and I was dead tired. But the fish led me straight toward the snakes and then straight amongst them, and the snakes were so close together I could feel their scales brush my elbows. The fish swam into the shallows as far as it could go, and I stumbled onto shore. This was a propitious island, I believed, and what was better, uninhabited. I was completely worn out and didn't think I could have swum another stroke. I understood the snakes were protecting us here, and I had got to shore alive specifically on the word of the round fish.

I didn't make it twenty feet up the bank before I collapsed and I thought I'd just rest a while, but must have fallen asleep straightaway. The next thing I knew the morning light was cooking me and the sun was fairly high up in the heavens. The snakes stood their watch. They looked even more dangerous than they had at night, with their grey dinosaur heads and long necks as thick as tree limbs. These animals were not hostile to me in the least, but would have instantly killed anything that had moved toward me while I slept. My guide, the round fish, had hipped them I was a friend to be looked out for.

It seemed to me I was almost happy for the first time in my life, but not quite. By about eleven o'clock, or as the sun rose medium-high in the sky, the snakes one by one began disappearing as if they didn't like the heat. Like ducks down they dove and must have swum for the cool depths of a shady hollow. As it got hotter the wind began to rise. It blew straight off the water onto the piece of shore where I sat, first carrying a sense of moisture that was fresh and welcome but finally picking up hot sand and even small sticks and pebbles until I felt I was enduring a sandstorm in the desert. The wind began to whistle. It snaked over the water whipping up the water and whole big drops were raining on me mixed in with the twigs and stones. I had to bury my face between my hands cupped against the earth, and I found it increasingly hard to breathe. Finally the vortex of the gale was sucking fish right out of the river and small perch and catfish flew past my head and slapped down on me and writhed and jumped everywhere on the shore. It was a rain of fishes.

When it finally died down the shore was pitted by the hard raindrops and littered with small leaping dying fish. I thought I would throw any that were still alive back into the river. I strolled around searching for live ones, but they all seemed to be dead. The only two lives ones I saw made a peculiar sight. Black and golden, this pair might have been handsome except that they were headless; I guess the wind had just snatched their heads straight off. But in spite of this they were still alive and writhed together in a commotion in the sand, frightening and repelling me. I ran away from them. A little farther on I spotted a live fish with its gills moving slowly. When I picked it up the side of it that had faced the sun was baked hard and dry but the other was still moist and in spite of its injury it was definitely alive. I was going to carry it to the river's edge when it suddenly piped up and said, "Take me to the center!"

It seemed a strange thing to be running away from the water (with a fish) toward the center of the little island, but I obeyed the fish's command without a moment's delay. It was a far stranger thing that fish had begun to talk to me lately. I accepted it as a favorable development, and something I absorbed with ease, which usually I would not have, resisting every hint the universe liked to give me. Finally I had started learning something, I thought. I won't bother trying to justify my point of view beyond observing that in this world if something satisfies, refreshes, intrigues, and seems to guide you, making life seem more real and less pointless, plus it gets you out of some immediate danger, no matter how weird it is, wouldn't you be the worst kind of fool to reject it on account of a cultural prejudice in favor of so-called reasonability?

So I carried the wounded fish away from the water it had come out of and toward the dry (I imagined) inner part of the island. As it was just a tiny island in mid-river, we reached what was more or less the center of it in a minute or two, and there in a grove of trees was a pool of clear and delicious water. The water lapped the bases of the trees, some of which stood right in the pool, in whose depths their roots grew. I saw the fish knew what it was talking about, and when it exclaimed, "There!" I knelt down and in my cupped hands inserted it into the pool, which is what it wanted me to do. For a few moments it worked its gills and caught its breath. Against my thumb I could feel the hard dry crimp in its right side loosen up and grow flexible and vibrant, and in a flick of its tail it escaped my hands and disappeared into the pool down into the roots of the trees. As I was thirsty, I lay down and took a drink of the clear water which bubbled up from great depths. I sat beneath the shade of the trees to think of the red bell-shaped trap some more. Everybody must be missing a *part* of something, lost to a *trap*. It seemed to me the first island I had come to last night was where those went who had given up or lost their faith—however little their faith in their search! The island I was on now, well guarded by the snakes, was a haven for those in mid-journey toward springing some sort of trap. I noticed that I was sitting on an old stump, and at my feet was a hive full of beautiful combs of honey, to which I helped myself liberally. I rinsed off my sticky hand and strolled back to the beach refreshed. It was a good sign I had been forgiven for not opening the trap on my first try, so long as my motive remained pure. No more than fifty feet offshore my Uncle was drifting past the island in a small rowboat.

I dashed straight into the water and swam out to him, and he helped me haul myself into the boat. He told me there was going to be a big fishfry that afternoon to celebrate the climax of the family reunion, and that all the men had gone out this morning to catch a slew of catfish, and so had he. Nevertheless, although he had a fishing pole on the boatseat next to him, its hook was bare and dry, and he wasn't fishing at all. His statement had the air of a threadbare excuse for his being out here, and I assumed he was being delicate on the subject of my never having returned to where he'd been waiting for me last night. I felt rather sheepish that he must be out looking for me and was overcome with gratitude. But that wasn't it at all.

He picked up the oars and began to row us toward the center of the river. I'd assumed that he had been out searching for me, but in fact he had greeted me only matter of factly, or even absentmindedly. He was completely casual toward me and didn't even ask where I had been all night or what had happened to me. Once he'd hauled me aboard, he seemed to forget about me. His eyes kept flicking back to shore. When he found a current out past the island, he let the boat drift but kept his eyes on the island and on the shoreline until, so it appeared to me, he felt the island had blocked off the view of the shore. Then he reached under his boatseat and hauled out a dead man by his shirt collar, who all the time had been curled up beneath him.

"The nice thing about a reunion, you can even a score or two," he muttered as he struggled with the body. I was about to help him, but my Uncle was strong, though in his seventies, and didn't want any help. He manhandled the body up onto the gunwale, where he sat the fellow upright for a moment, took a good look into his face, and tipped him into the drink. A big anchor was tied round and round the ankles of the dead man, who went down into the deep fast. "An old acquaintance of mine," allowed my Uncle in a wry tone out of the corner of his mouth as he studied the bubbles rising to the surface. The profound silence of the river rang in my ears. Over the water came voices as if they were nearby, but that's how voices carry on the river and we were quite alone. Staring down into the water, my Uncle muttered, "Some people expand and heal you, not him." I didn't really want to know more about it. I had enough on my mind.

121

My Uncle turned around to me, causing the boat to rock. He dusted his hands off with a whack. He gave a muted war whoop. His chest puffed out and his eyes blazed.

"No, an old man don't sing life!" he boomed. "An old man don't sing life! No, no! Ha ha ha!"

Laughing with triumph until he had to wipe the tears away, he swelled in size, got bigger and bigger, until his end of the boat was nearly submerged and I was sailing along five feet in the air in the other end. He got so big that I imagined he would sink us, and I thought to myself that if we crossed the river he would be a match for the giant back at the fishing camp, for real, and so he might, but at the moment I was a little afraid to speak about it to him. My Uncle was the swellest guy, but this murder—that splash! followed by bubbles—was something that had to sink in, no pun intended. I decided life was for singing, it was all for the very best! It was okay. I sang a little myself.

Finally he decided to return to approximately his usual size and began to row again. "Say, fish! We have to bring back some catfish!" He thrust the rod at me and kicked a can of worms my way. I baited the hook and lowered it into the water and settled down to wait. After about ten minutes I got a bite and shortly I had a big one on the line. It fought violently and we were sure it was a monstrous catfish, and so it was but when we had netted it and had it in the bottom of the boat, we saw there was something wrong with it. It had been skinned all along its back and its flesh was red and white there. While we watched it a tiny golden catfish swam out of its mouth and lay in the bottom of the boat breathing hard.

"This fish is wounded and has to get well," said my Uncle tossing the big fish overboard, "and this nice one is too little and has to grow some, you might say it's our very soul." With that he threw the little golden one back in too.

I put another worm on my hook and began to wait again. After another ten minutes I had another one on, and this one pulled hard but not at all as violently as the other one had done. When we finally got it up, my Uncle's mouth fell open, and undoubtedly it was one of the weirdest fish I had ever seen too. Except that it was very fat-bodied and thick across the middle, it looked like a huge angel fish but it had not two feathery fins top and bottom but hundreds of them like hairs or tendrils growing out from it at all angles. It reminded me oddly but not reassuringly of the Black Sun Man, if he had gone on a drunken self-destructive tear, and alarmed me to look at it, so human looking with the hair on its head, and it seemed to even worry my implacable Uncle a bit.

Hurriedly tossing the big furry fish overboard, my Uncle remarked, "Son, you are catching some crazy fish today," and took the rod out of my hands. "Give me that."

"You don't know the half of it," I mumbled in awe. I was busy thanking God that we hadn't inadvertently caught the round fish on a hook which I trusted to keep swimming nearby till I could catch up to it again one day. But maybe it had dived to imponderable depths by now.

"You row. I'll fish." Soon enough he had hauled aboard nine or ten nice catfish, and we headed back to shore and town for the fishfry. The family reunion wound up with not only a handsome fishfry, but a big old-fashioned square dance. The next morning my Uncle took me aside.

"So what happened on the opposite shore?" he asked.

I told him about the old boy with the gun who had appeared from out of the empty camp and faced me on the pier the moment I went to unlatch the trap door.

"If you'd opened it, he would have just vanished."

"Oh yeah?"

"Probably shot ya first, ha ha."

I told him about the round fish that had saved me and my long swim to the islands.

"Oh yeah, maybe there was no need if the fish had already escaped." My Uncle gave me a penetrating look that restored all my faith in him.

"By the way I saw your friend again—all in one piece. She was sitting on the hood of my car filing her nails when I got

123

back. She told me she was closing a big deal and was going to Europe on the proceeds, so to tell you she'd see you when she got back. She says, 'Tell him I'll see him when I see him.' If I were you, I'd forget about that one."

With that, my feelings about him became very ambiguous again.

Back in Chicago I found myself at the hospital hoping to get some lead from the administration on where she would have gone when she left the place. As much as I admired my Uncle, he was capable of telling some tall tales, and he didn't know anything about M, I thought. Anyway, he couldn't, for he didn't love her like I did. I didn't buy that story of her having gone to Europe. I bugged the nurses and tried to argue them into telling me. Once I got back to town, somewhat to my surprise, I badly missed M, more than ever, especially since it was a mystery where she'd gone to and I couldn't find her. It was as if my whole peace of mind rested with her again like in the old days. All I could think of was her, and all I wanted to do was look for her. This should have been amazing if I had stopped to think about it, because recently, the night she came into the club, she was the last person in the world I was thinking about or ever wanted to see. At the family reunion my thoughts had shifted so I had completely forgotten all about her for a day or two. Now she was the only thing on my mind.

How could this be, a woman whose main object was to torment me? My Uncle had tried to get her off my mind or at least help me see through her. I had been so upset by the incident at the church fair that night caused by my desire for a bratwurst sandwich that I couldn't bring myself to ask whose baby this one had been anyway. By now I had put two and two together and figured it had been a miscarriage. Only later was I able to bring myself to ask her, and when she replied, "Mayor Daley's" (the son), I was sorry I asked. For the moment she had left no trace, and the nurses were under some legal obligation not to give out anything they might know. She had walked out while the night nurses were busy with things. She'd disappeared without checking out, so maybe they really didn't know anything. Naturally they didn't want to talk about it. It sounded ominous to me. I looked all around town for her and called people who knew her. What was I expecting? I had sort of hoped my experiences at the family reunion, especially my long swim with the round fish, would have changed the picture somehow.

For the interlude when I had swum with the round fish I had lost all worries that anything might be missing, least of all M. I forgot about her and even couldn't remember that she had vanished. I forgot that Smoky had risen in the air and drifted over the horizon. While I followed behind it, the round fish had absorbed every ounce of my attention promising fulfillment of some sort. All seemed well or on the verge of becoming so as long as I had the round fish in sight. So when I got back, I kind of expected to mysteriously find M waiting for me. Of course, M made her appearances when it suited her. Maybe she really was in Europe like my Uncle said she had told him.

The trail was cold. Now that I was back in Chicago again it was this reality that took hold. She seemed to have floated off into the air like Smoky leaving everything flat and listless. I wondered how long she would stay in Europe. It occurred to me that since she had looked me up once recently in that club I liked to hang out in on Clark Street, maybe she would again. She would know where to find me, in case she was not in Europe. It was the only chance I had to locate her it seemed. This was strange because I used to go there to avoid her. Well, I had seen what happened to people who forgot their journey on the hellish island in the river. The memory of that island added impetus to my somewhat frantic search for M at this time.

The visit to the underground (as it now turned out to be) nightclub, my old favorite haunt, only deepened my awareness of the disconnection to M and with her, everything else. This is not what I would have expected having slipped that fish into its pool on the island in the not–Mississippi River and felt such reward. I did not feel closer to "life" or anything of the sort back in Chi-town. I seemed to have taken a step backward without noticing it during the reunion. This thought depressed and disoriented me the more as M had warned me not to go. I found the club while walking home along Clark Street from the hospital. I say "found" not because I'd forgotten where it was but because I was thinking of something else, Melusina mostly, as I walked, and it slipped up on me, and also something about it had profoundly changed while I was gone and it seemed like a completely different place.

I liked to walk and stretch my legs, not take the bus or a cab and just "get there," wherever. I liked to think about things and mingle with the people on the street and stay out in the air. Passing a club I had never seen before, glancing through the front door out of the corner of my eye, I saw stairs descending from street level, in an L-shape, down and to the left. But this was not what I had expected. I was sure this was the club I used to visit but it was not familiar. I was at the right address, how could I forget it? I did a double take and checked its neighbors to be sure I was at the right spot. I was, but things had changed. Some remodeling appeared to have been done since I'd last visited.

You used to go straight into the joint, but now some stairs led down to another level. This brought up the unpleasant memory of the stairs M had tripped on in the church basement. On the theory that two wrongs sometimes do make a right, and that poison cures poison, it occurred to me that if M's injuries and my despair had resulted from a descent down such a set of stairs, I ought to attempt another, bratwurst or no bratwurst. I was confirmed in my decision when I heard a voice say authoritatively, "You can't go up until you go down, you know that." I jumped at that, and looked around, but nobody was there, and I felt I had good reason to go down these stairs.

But the littered concrete set of descending stairs confronting me not only made me uneasy but filled me with distaste, because they were dark, filthy, dank, and nearly worn away as if by countless footsteps of despair. These steps bore the imprint of thousands of searching feet. It was one ugly subterranean joint by the look of its entrance downward. Idly I kicked an empty cigarette pack from the topmost step and thought twice about it.

Finally I descended as far as where the stairs made their turn to the left. I thought I would go down that far and decide. At the bottom of the well a neon beer logo beckoned in the gloom pinkly. It wasn't the same old familiar joint like home. What was different was these stairs. I didn't remember the beer sign either. The neon beer sign radiated a warm pink light by which I could see dimly that the steps were built into the side of a hill. Not that this added any natural beauty, the ugliness was even increased by a glimpse of a raw bare dirt embankment, the kind of urban soil in which are embedded broken bottles, beer can tabs, used condoms, and bits of chewing gum wrappers. The construction of this subterranean establishment, though it had obviously taken place long ago, had never been quite completed but certain aspects left roughed out. The dirt sides had never been covered over. In the dirt hill I saw the remains of a broken culvert that had run along the side of Clark Street in days long gone by. A quick glance revealed that this must be a much older building than most on this street, maybe one of the first built here. I was entering down into the bowels of the city, a kind of urban archaeology of Chicago. You could say that such basements are sort of commonplace museums of the city, and I thought it was probably only a matter of time until entrepreneurs, clever curators, and artists began selling tickets—just to what is there, not having to change anything, well, maybe polish a pipe or two.

But in the meantime life must go on and these places are put to use for storage, as dwellings for immigrants and the really poor, and what have you. Now that the city has grown and every cranny been filled up and put to commercial use and space is at a premium, the rambling foundation levels, the basements of such old structures, with their rusty pipes and boilers, sometimes with rude dirt floors not even cemented in, from which strange artifacts protrude, are called into service, and become churches of foreign or syncretistic sects, foodstores for recently arrived ethnic groups, basement apartments for students, and cheap nightclubs like this one.

A ray of late afternoon sun poured weakly over my shoulder from the street above, recalling a dubious normality I could still return to on my desultory walk home. Below, the weak glow of the pink neon beer sign reflected off what looked like a hideous mud puddle at the bottom of the stairs, seepage from broken city pipes or natural effluences of the Chicago River. I hesitated, for in either direction the "above" and "below" looked pretty dismal and there was nothing much to break the spell and decide me either way, other than that voice in the air I had heard. I thought of M and knew I had to keep going down.

Curiously, and adding an antic, fanciful air, sunk into the dirt embankment several old lawn ornaments stared at me, southern coachboys, with red beanies, black stable slaves, common until (unbelievably from the point of view of average white people) they became politically incorrect, and had to become white coachboys, crouching or bending the knee to present a ring, with plump black (now overpainted white) cheeks, brightly painted exaggerated red lips. These figurines were in their original unreconstructed state, American arcana offensive in any society to the left of the KKK. Well, somebody had tossed them in the culvert, and they had sunk into the clay years ago. I paused to gaze more closely, and I saw it was not so, it was rather worse and more peculiar. The figures were not in their usual happy servile poses at all, but their arms were raised in horror, and their faces were twisted in anguish, at something they had seen, or maybe at being sunk into the ground as they were, up to their waists, up to their chests, but still the demented racist artistic touches, bright red mouths, eyes like cueballs wide with fright. The fact that for political reasons one had a white skin lent them a most peculiar and confused effect. Then I had a very bad moment when I suspected that these were not cast-iron figurines or repainted coachboys at all, but short dead winos who had sunk down here and been forgotten, half-preserved in a bog. The stretched-out finality of hard pain in their grimacing faces was so real. I leaned over and examined them more closely, and it was so. I almost fell down the stairs at the horror of seeing the shrunken faces and dead bodies of fairly young homeless children dressed up in this strange way embalmed in the clay. Their final anguish and the questions in their rolled-up eyes, their twisted features and parchment skins were gruesome. Perhaps this nightclub had burrowed under a graveyard.

This horrifying sight sent me straight downward the last flight in a panic to escape. I raced down and had reached the bottom of the cement steps. To my surprise I saw that in front of me another set of stairs ascended again immediately. I mean, accessing the door to the barroom, two approaches and egresses, two sets of stairs, an outlandish superfluity for such a tavern. For what purpose? In such a joint? I had made a descent into history. What had this joint once been long ago in Chicago's storied past? The new staircase was a far cry from the grim concrete one I had come down. As I seemed to have reached the bottom of a pit, the second set of stairs immediately before me opened up a new and more charming vista, with a vaulted polished ceiling carved with Moorish figures like garish 1920s' speakeasy embellishments. My sharp unease and claustrophobia were replaced with wonder that this basement hideaway featured such an openness of architecture, a double set of stairs, coming down left and right, then a moment of airy grandeur under Moroccan arches carved from sandalwood. Imagine the cost! I might have woken up in Tunis or old New Orleans, or Al Capone's Chicago. A heavy, impersonal nostalgia filled my nostrils, clanged in my ears, overwhelmed my heart with nameless dread and longing as if struck by a half-remembered musical phrase. Once upon a time somebody had built such flamboyant steps in Chicago, some northlander with too much schnaaps or Schlitz in his veins circulating these steps in a vision of a poor man's Alhambra now peopled with lawn ornaments and demented howling buried children from the screaming hell of an era of mayhem that Americans have sentimentalized and actually don't believe ever happened, but soon will be able to buy tickets and revisit.

To my right was the door of the club and that was obviously the direction I had to take. The voice had intimated that I should keep going down, it was too soon to go up yet I thought. I felt I was in the antechamber of something. I wondered what was inside, so I turned right, pushed through the door, and headed for the bar, where a woman served me a parsimonious shot of something over a couple of cubes of cloudy-looking ice. She was a new bartender whom I didn't recognize. The place was actually vaguely familiar, and just about empty, not surprising as it was only about one o'clock in the afternoon. The strangest thing happened when I went to pay the bartender, for instead of green money, four pages of the novel I had recently been sweating so gloriously over appeared in my fingers as I removed what I thought were bills from my wallet. With a dry gulp, I understood that whatever I had written there on those pages was now lost, because I had made no copy, but that seemed to be the price of the shot, and one well worth paying, the whole book if it had to be! She tore the pages up deliberately and delicately dusted off her fingers as the torn pieces of manuscript fluttered down to the barroom floor. I was overcome by a mischievous impulse to speak to the only other patron at the bar this time of the afternoon, a rather scrawny, pathetic-looking woman dressed in a way to make her appear wild, glamorous and young. I could easily imagine her pathetic business here, nevertheless somehow it seemed to me I should make myself welcome in this place that seemed completely new to me or at least justify my existence by gallantly making a pass at this woman, whose eyes were glued to the TV set softly chattering overhead.

The bartender was a woman of "a certain age," as I think such competent looking women who appear to have seen it all, or at least a great deal, are described, with plenty of wrinkles and knowing lines about the mouth evincing a grim view of life but still not all that bad looking. Both women struck me as tough customers, suddenly, with depths of worldly wisdom, and I realized I was on the verge of making a fool of myself, or no, I already had done so, but maybe not irreparably. I had only said something inappropriate but not criminal, which could be interpreted different ways. Both women were looking at me very strangely with deep misgivings. Well I used to be well known and familiar around here, somebody nobody would look twice at, and I was just trying to reestablish that air of freedom and pleasant authority and anonymity and so forth. I was just having fun, trying to take my mind off things, and I'd meant it as a compliment, but it was not received well. Everything was different and out of joint.

One of the eternal poolshooters came out of the back room and, smiling to himself, with a glance in my direction, cried, "Oh, the vile and despised life!" Where did he get such language? Even poolshooters must read old books in moments of awe or despair. Maybe he was writing a novel too. He leaned on his pool stick and laughed in a wondering sort of way. Then he placed his stick against the wall and sat down at the bar. In spite of this, there was everything about the guy that said he enjoyed life very much, and only didn't get enough of it. Either hope is irrational and we are all half-insane, which seems a strange premise, or else ultimately hope refers to something. Saint Paul said as much. Having been raised in the church I had some sense of these things. He had a beer (the poolshooter I mean). Before returning to his game, beer in hand, the pool player cried, "Oh the rejected stone!"

So be it, I thought, I must be in the middle of a strange dream. I pinched myself and seemed to be wide awake though. In the middle of the barroom a well-dressed younger woman in a black gown that accentuated her figure and pinched her waist stood behind a table on which stood rows of glittering punchglasses and a blue vase with flowers in it. A moment ago this charming tableau and this attractive woman would have aroused my curiosity, but now I brushed by awkwardly and hurriedly intending not to make a further spectacle of myself and say something foolish to her, and escaped into the poolroom.

The overhead light picked out the green baize of the table and made it glimmer with excitement and a sense of heraldry as much as the floodlights at a baseball stadium switched on for a night game. As they took their shots the players' arms under this spotlight became momentous; no other games were in progress and the other tablelights were off and the room retreated in shadow from the glow of two guys' play. Since they were fairly good players, I stood and watched for a while. Like the barroom behind me this poolroom had changed a lot since my last visit here, but while the club on the whole had fallen into disrepair and become very bare and unattractive, the poolroom section of it was elaborate and vibrant. The vividly colored balls in motion suggested the ceaseless permutations of the high life. This was why people loved sports. It gave you the feeling you could participate in this life and even bet on it. At my feet the pool of light from the table stopped. The other tables were shrouded in darkness as a theater goes dark as the drama begins. The balls that were in play on the lighted stage sparkled like jewels accidentally dropped in the gutter, rare stones forming secretly in the earth. Big money hung on the next shot. A red-and-white ball received the impact of the ivory cueball and whirred to the corner pocket where it fell off the edge with a solid victorious plunk. A master of ceremonies in a tuxedo walked up and handed the winner a check and lights flashed. Life glowed commonly and resourcefully in the spotlight. "Nice," I said. This poolroom certainly had a grandeur about it that it had never had before. But I no longer felt I belonged here, and I couldn't have just relaxed here, for some reason.

So I progressed on across the gleaming floor past the brilliant tables and through a far door into a very peculiar sort of back storage room or cellar with a dirt floor. What was peculiar about it was there was nothing in it but a few big crates in a corner and one square pillar in the middle of the room with a black guy leaning forlornly on it. I had never been aware of this backroom before, let alone gone into it. Unlike the other rooms in this establishment including the barroom, none of which had windows, this back cellar had a window set very high up in the far wall with a patch of blue sky showing through it. This gave the cellar in spite of its barrenness and gloom a unique hint of hope. I felt rewarded for having walked in here. At the same time the window accentuated and contrasted the doom and charmlessness of the dirt-floored backroom. Depended which way you took it I guess. The window was about three feet wide, but only about six or eight inches high. So there was no feeling of the great vault of the heavens as a tall window would have afforded, but just a yearning glimpse of them through a slit. The sunny blue shaft of light from outside seemed very hopeful though, and I yearned for it, as did the guy leaning against the square white post too apparently, who stared and stared at the window forlornly. You could forget where you were, what sort of room you were in, because of that little window. There was something strange about this character next to the post, who did not move.

The dirt floor revealed all too crudely the status of this whole underground palace as no more than a basement, a foundations, before it had been turned into a "nightclub." Either they had not yet gotten around to reclaiming this section of it or they were never going to bother. Then my distinct feeling was that I had accidentally wandered down into the "dungeon." The blue window was of the kind in a prison affording a view without hope of redemption, the slash of a window that tortures the view with longing and the involuntary impulse of hope

133

enough to torture the inmate into living one more day. The slave was longingly gazing at it. That's how I took him now. He was a prisoner or even a *slave,* I realized, noticing the chains around his body that fastened him to the post. I drew close to him and glanced into his eyes which held an expression of agonized wistfulness as he stared through the tiny window into the blue light. Where the post was sunk into the dirt a rise or mound in the earth we stood on brought us up a foot or so, enough to get a better view through the window and I was surprised to see beneath the blue sky yet more blue, this of small waves glittering in the sunlight. I hadn't realized we were so close to the Great Lake here, but we were.

The eyes of my companion (as I now conceived him), whose hands clasped the post against which his forehead rested in deepest disconsolateness, were fastened on the line where at the distant horizon blue of sky and blue of water joined imperceptibly. So desperately still and silent was this figure that with a pang of alarm I suddenly wondered if he were not a live man at all but a withered corpse like the "lawn ornaments" sunk into the embankment outside the front door. This would have been too weird, because unaccountably I had formed an empathetic bond with the guy because of his way of staring at the pretty square of blue as if he were yearning so hard to be free, and I was driven to test this hypothesis of his being a dead "ornament" and observe closely once again, to glance wildly out of the corners of my eyes into his eyes, at which he fetched up a sigh like a sob, and hung more heavily on the pillar, his eyes refocusing on some distant and unreachable hope of his out there in the blue on blue. Startled, I understood he was a live slave, a live prisoner here. Suddenly he lamented, "In Africa is my treasure hidden."

No matter that it was not the salt water of the Atlantic but the murky blue of Lake Michigan, still he was staring in the right direction, east. First to cross the Great Lake, then another haul overland, and then only the Atlantic to cross to get home! His seemed a living death, no less complete than the tortured men

134

sticking out of the ground outside, a raw and irrevocable fate redeemed only by a wisp of promise, a trace of vapor in the blue, that fixed his eyes on the improbable, impossible, unspeakable horizon—home. For the first time since I'd walked into this favorite haunt of mine (completely different in every respect), I felt somehow I recognized something, felt a kinship to a kindred spirit, chained to the post. I knew just how he felt.

Down deep I empathized with the homesick African bound to the white pillar. The thing was I understood him completely, and at the bottom we all share this yearning feeling I am sure, whether consciously or not. "Home" was far away. A wave of loneliness and homesickness welled up from deep inside me. Some vital connection was missing, had been severed. For the companion it was Africa. I envied him that he even knew what it was, for him. I couldn't have put a name on the star that was missing from my constellation. But standing next to this strange anguished character, a lost dimension of my being became dimly conscious to me. I too yearned to seek it.

Without being aware of how I had moved there, I found myself again in the center of the main barroom peering with curiosity at the girl with her bowls of flowers and rows of punchglasses ready to be filled. They must expect a big crowd tonight, but there was no sign of any such thing yet. The joint was empty in a barren desultory urban afteroon. By contrast her presence was classical, rich and alluring. The girl was wearing a black velvet short-sleeved jacket, with the sleeves pushed back to her elbows, over a long tan skirt. It seemed to me she had dressed with the idea of creating a dignified impression, and given the extremely funky reality of the bar, there was pathos and mystery in this. No telling what illusions of high times and even opulence would be woven out of thin air when a drunken crowd rolled in here later tonight. But if this is what I saw, it was hard to imagine what the girl herself saw, gently returning my gaze.

I grew more and more self-conscious, posturing and unwelcome way too early for the fabled night, far from home, next to this alluring girl, with her mythical air, preparing her refreshments that promised satisfaction and comfort. Suddenly I realized it was a poster! I had been staring into a print of an old impressionist painting from the nineteenth century, you probably know the painting, that had improbably been pinned to the barroom wall. No wonder the girl with the rows of sparkling glasses and banks of flowers never moved. Seeing this, amazed at the optical illusion I had succumbed to, I almost came to myself and left, but I couldn't.

The girl in the print with her sandy-brown hair reminded me of a favorite cousin of mine, who unfortunately had not been at the family reunion. There was a gentle acceptance in her eyes. This was the impression that the painter had sought to create and had created. Nothing that had used to comfort me in this club had the least appeal to me anymore, except a poster on the wall that hadn't been there before, and a slave in the backroom I hadn't imagined existed in a lockup in the basement. The poolroom itself had become a major league sports franchise that I could admire but not dream of myself playing in. Above all, Melusina was not here and I knew that tonight she would not walk in. The joint was just echoing with the dry reverberations of this dead certainty. In fact, everything that was wrong and missing could be precisely summed up in the shape of her not being here and never going to be here tonight or maybe ever again if I wasn't mistaken. Only the girl in the poster offered consolation. Every now and then I glanced at her out of the corner of my eye to see if I could catch her moving, in case it was M after all.

At this I couldn't help remembering her breaking up into white chunks when she had hit the pavement after jumping out the apartment window. A wave of the astonished fearful loss I had felt at that moment raced through me. My Uncle had assured me she would be back in one piece "before I knew it" or at least when I got back from the reunion. Before we parted he'd hinted that he'd even seen her sitting on the hood of his car, but I wasn't sure whether to believe this as he said all sorts of things.

At one level it was just another of her pranks, but it was highly suspicious. Something about my Uncle's tone of voice had not been reassuring as if he had been far from predicting happiness for me in any case.

If my hopes were up when I got back to town, and had reached a peak when I'd walked in this club, they were absolutely dashed by now. I began to get the sense that she was gone, really gone, at least for a while. The place for me had achieved an air of abandonment polished and burnished to a hideous luster. I felt myself vacating my body, I was so lonely, hovering in the air, in a doomed attempt to escape. I levitated into the air about six or seven inches probably. That was as far as I got. And the smell of wet charcoal permeated everything once again. Apparently it was their practice just to build fires and incinerate unwanted items in this bar. This was one thing that had not changed about this joint. Something was smoldering on the floor and a poolroom bum had come out to throw water on the remains, releasing a stench. You would have needed a good pair of boots to wade through the drenched pyre, and even though I couldn't believe it, I noticed I was wearing a pair of white suede shoes. Where had they come from? I didn't know I owned such shoes. They were sort of cool, now I paused to admire them. But they were out of place in a joint like this, even before they had doused the fire and left the floor awash with sodden ashes. They had put out the remnants of a cookout, or had just cremated rats.

The hiss of the water hitting the embers and acrid odor hit me like a slap in the face and I awoke from a reverie. I saw next to the rows of glittering glasses on the table of the girl in the black velvet in the painting a small elegantly handwritten sign: **SHOTS $3.75.**

The hour must have arrived, because people started coming in, mostly young guys off from work who sat at the bar or sauntered back to the pool tables. Then the exquisite slim hand of the girl reached out and adjusted the placement of yet another sign in front of her glassware, this one also in tasteful black letters. She seemed to set it up for me, to tilt it so that I could see it. She glanced my way.

YOU MUST GO TO A FAR COUNTRY

Really? I had just gotten back from the not-Mississippi. I was tired of traveling. I no longer belonged in this night club, where I had once lingered thoughtless and familiar. I had to get out of here. A "far country" sounded like the ticket if I could get there, the farther the better. Where was it? How would I get there? I needed a rest. Something had changed while I was at the reunion, and my Uncle must have known this would happen but thought it would be good for me. Maybe it was, but I couldn't find M. I had only come here in case M wanted to find me. All of my recent troubles and discontent, I now reflected, had been caused by the reappearance of M in my life—right here in this club. I had to get out of here at once, comfortable as these surroundings had once been to me. Would M be in the far country if I got there? The girl was watching me covertly. She was standing square behind the little sign. It was real and not just an idea in my head. I was about to get up and head for that "Far Country." So I hoped and resolved, not having the least idea though. I was tired out and a bit discouraged but apparently it was meant that I do it. She nodded at me encouragingly and smiled. I studied her closely for a moment to see if she might just be M playing one of her games.

The slave, who had somehow unlocked himself from his square white pillar and thrown off his chains, sat down at the bar and ordered a Miller High Life. He was right at my elbow, he facing the bar and me looking away from it toward the girl, our elbows, pointing in opposite directions, almost touching. "In Africa," he repeated, patted my arm, and hung his head. I pitied him and certainly wished him well. I thought I understood his condition, in fact my own didn't seem all that much different somehow. There was something about the rather handsome bartender that reminded me of someone but I couldn't quite place it. That wry glint of a smile on her lips which instantly faded. Then dismissing me she looked away sadly and most seriously while one hand dug out a small gold crucifix from her blouse which she raised to her lips and kissed swiftly before returning it to her bosom. For her it held all meaning, whatever was troubling her momentarily. The gleam from the crucifix hurt my eyes and I leapt up.

Just as I left to walk up the Moroccan staircase a voice in the air declaimed, "I am the door!" Startled, I almost laughed because I was going through the barroom door at that very moment. Being of a Christian background, I cut off my laugh for "the door" held every significance to me, but I didn't dwell on it just now. It was important to get out of here and I took a long stride. The rude tavern door cut in the dirt hillside partook in some way of that sacred and eternal one we hear of in the Bible. The door opened onto the beautifully crafted stairs, the opposite ones to those I had come down earlier.

While I was standing there lost in time and wondering at it all, down the Tunisian staircase came a young man naked above the waist wearing a kind of Arabian skirt below and barefooted, and as soon as he hit bottom, right before where I stood, he fell face first into the black pool of water there and pressed his breast into it mumbling prayers, then turning and ascending the stairs back to the Chicago street and whatever business he purveyed up there. This religious act of his took about a minute or two and overwhelmed me with its seriousness and sincerity. It was almost as if I had performed the profound act and done the praying myself. I was affected by the humility of it and partook deeply of it. It was the moment of hitting bottom that did it. The celebrant had not hesitated to throw himself headlong into the pool. After this there was nowhere to go but up. But this was only because of the absolute surrender before God that had been conducted. Now things might be right with the world. Wherever I was headed, and whoever I was by now, I took the steps at a gallop and full of anticipation hit the street.

I passed an old city church familiar to me, in fact the church which had sponsored that festival recently, to which I had taken Melusina's kid (or dwarf) to entertain him. A big stone church with massive steps and that somnolent and touching look of unkempt sanctity and perennial good cheer old churches in rundown neighborhoods have, the crowds it had attracted that night, the acrobats with their "wings" or kites, the games and booths and food vendors were all gone and it seemed bereft. Greenish spire seeking the heavens, slablike wood doors closed protectively on whatever community of old ladies, clerics, and illegal immigrant kids were thriving within, at the foot of the worn steps the usual soda and beer cans, cigarette packs and litter, oddly redeemed if not recycled, an old church like this sent a happy shudder of unlikely peace through me, and the sense of having walked out of a harsh light of the urban jungle into a cool shadow of repose just by looking at it. In fact, I now intended to cut through its modest gardens, and be consoled there, as it shaved a half-block off my journey home and there was an improbable stone fountain bordered by banks of flowers in the shade of a monstrous old oak tree I had sometimes glimpsed though I'd never walked by it. I was hot and wanted to throw some water from the fountain on my face perhaps. Though I'd never done that before, the fountain always bubbled.

Just before I stepped into the narrow sheltered lane between the church and nextdoor building that led to the fountain, I noticed out of the corner of my eye a strange tall character with a square crewcut carrying a crudely hand-lettered sign pacing in front of the church steps. The church was being *picketed*—by one lone picketer! He had come to the end of his circuit, or I should like to say tether, and now he approached me shoving his sign at me through the air like a spear he'd bring down on my head. His face held the snoutish expression of the zealot, ignorant of any saving doubt or grace, bug-eyed with determination to enforce his half-truth whatever it might be. I would have thought this harasser was one of the "pro-lifers," had this not been unlikely in front of a church, but you never knew. Anyway this was his wild-eyed boy scout from hell appearance, whose position if stated modestly you certainly might have felt some understanding of but which thrust at you as bare dogma on a pole had the effect of withering all sympathy. When I saw one of these people, though I joined in their horror at taking life myself, all other things equal, I wanted to grab his sign and yell, "No, *you* get a life!" I mean, if I were the unborn, would I want the kind of "life" a zany guy like that offered me? I'd rather just be done with it. The sign in blood-red block letters clutched in his white-knuckled fingers above his crew-cut dome said: ONE SPECIES OF THE SET (GENUS) MUST DIE TO BRING TOTALITY INTO NATURE. That wasn't quite what I had expected. I was puzzled but eager to go into the garden and get away from him.

Behind the church Nature needed no improvement, in the shadows of the old stone Gothic structure, lushly green and slightly overrun, the fountain with a stone angel on its lip, bubbling gently. In the limp scorched air I stuck my head under the trickle of water. I noticed a metal cup lying in the basin. If it was slightly green there was no question of its deep cleanliness for I felt the spirit of the Ancient of Days alive here. The fancy struck me that this was the garden of a very old and wise man with flowing white hair, even wiser than my Uncle (who liked to walk here in the garden on his visits, so he'd once told me). As I held the cup out to be filled by the slight stream of water, I caught something of M's playful spirit peeping out through the eyes of the stone angel, who seemed to stretch her wings on the fountain's brim. The cup had a strange shape, like a chalice on a thin stem. I knew Melusina was around here somewhere. She might be hiding in the depths of the garden peeping out at me and having a laugh. I felt I was someplace I was supposed to be though.

At this moment two old people, a man and a woman, came out the back door of the church and gazed at me. They had extremely large heads, which seemed to swell and pulse. They appeared to wonder if I was a trespasser. The man called, "Are you a member of the congregation?" How unChristian of them. I was being invited out of the garden! Well, they didn't want any atheistic loiterers up to no good hanging around. Maybe they associated me with the picketer. They glared at me as though I had been having very presumptuous and big-headed thoughts in their church garden. But it was their heads that were very big and peculiar and maybe they were the species that must die? The thought sent a violent convulsion through me as I realized it was blasphemous and incorrect. To the contrary, they were the holy people, the saved. I hoped they would let me join them.

The stone fountain was in the shape of a flower, a dark purple flower. It put me in mind of the flowers on the table of the girl in the painting. The cup was overflowing and I raised its clear nectar to my lips. With a violent sob of resignation, the big-headed old woman called out, "Yes! Drink it down!" There was something momentous about it I didn't entirely appreciate and I was amazed that she, a bystander, apparently did. We're ever inverting the true structure of things for of course she was the insider and I was a mere passerby. As soon as I drank from the cup, their misgivings fled and they invited me to sit on a stone bench with them. I didn't mind doing so as everything had changed and I wished for their company. They nodded their approval, and asked me how I had come to stroll through their garden. It was hard to respond, since though I lived around here, I'd never taken the shortcut through the garden before. It had seemed too cloistered and private. "I believe that I must go to a 'far country,'" I mused aloud, with emotion, but I did not know what to say to them. They couldn't agree more, and nodded all the harder, as though I were quite right, more than I knew. They began to chat pleasantly with me. Of all things it turned out they were travel agents, by occupation, when they were not at the church, that was their day job, and they told me about a package for students who wished to visit Africa. Well, they said, that was "far." It occurred to me that M might as well be in Africa as anywhere. Knowing her, she just might.

The big-headed old couple were missionaries of some sort. I remembered the slave under the nightclub, and wondered if I should tell them about him. I thought to myself that indeed Africa might be "far" enough all right. There was one seat available as a student missionary had canceled out, they said. The irony that it would be me heading to Africa and not the slave didn't trouble me as stranger things happen every day. Probably he'd wish me well. I would be leaving M again in Chicago, I thought uneasily, wherever she might be, but maybe the trip away would help me forget her. Then hope struck again and I thought she might as well be in the "far country," she might have set out for there already, why not.

Shortly I was on a jet full of pilgrims, some of whom had changed from Western suits and jeans to traditional gowns, and some of whom hadn't, who filled the aisle to takes turns touching their foreheads to a symbolic earth. Some were returning from vacations and shopping trips in the States and the bins overhead were stuffed with their toys and fashionable purchases. A few mzungus like myself were inserted here and there deeply absorbed in new novels by authors from Iran and China. The actual Iranians and Chinese on the plane were reading *The New Yorker* and *People* magazine. I thought I saw M through the crowd toward the front of the aircraft, near the pilots. I hoped she wasn't going to cause us to crash. The fact that millions or billions of people suppose they are going to go to heaven can make only one impression on the unprejudiced observer, namely, they might be right. I looked around for some of the students I was supposed to be flying with in the missionary or school group but didn't see any. However there was a tour group in the back of the plane to which I attached myself without any trouble at customs.

The plane landed and the tour group had hired a bus and so before I knew it I was crammed onto a yellow bus with other mzungus and amateur photographers careening through the green hills. Such peaceful scenery abounded outside the smudged windows, thatch and tin roofed villages, women in long colorful gowns with babies on their backs tending garden plots, barefooted stragglers along the shoulders of the road every foot of the way. Every time a monkey hanging from a tree limb grinned at the tourists they cackled and gesticulated like baboons. Then we came to a border crossing and the bus pulled off the road into the parking lot of the border post. It hadn't occurred to me we were going to cross any borders or travel to another country so soon. Actually I did not know what country we were leaving either. No matter, the European colonists invented all these borders and countries, something the local police take advantage of and the people just ignore to this day. I assumed the bus driver or the tour guide would take care of the appropriate baksheesh or whatever.

I got down from the bus to stretch. All my pre-trip weariness with the search for meaning had vanished and I found myself excited and energized. The adventure had refreshed me and I couldn't wait to see what would happen next. The fact that I had no plan, no expectation, no itinerary, and no guide struck me as perfect. Whatever transpired would come about from the infinite resources of mystery. What was astounding was to run into friends of mine suddenly, who had been up at the front of the bus so I hadn't noticed them till now. The coincidence of finding them on the same tour group was uncanny but very pleasant. It was comforting, even though one was an ex-girlfriend. But bygones were bygones under the circumstances. In Africa we even looked at each other with new eyes, as if enchantment could well up from a stone. Every rock and pebble on the road and at the edge of the hills held an ancient and even sacred grace, such was the force of these timeless hills. The other friend was an elderly lady, wife of a teacher of mine, deceased, a very good and kindly lady. So feeling myself almost with sister and mother, as it were, so forceful was the familiarity in the strange land, in we all went to get our papers stamped.

The border post complex consisted of two white buildings, one very neat and official and the other a kind of marketplace and hostel combined, before whose doors people mostly males pressed together and milled about, crowds of migrant workers in tattered clothing, child hawkers of food and drinks, and some families huddled together, and students sporting new suits or new Western jeans. We were heading for the smaller house, where the paperwork got done. From the buzz of my fellow tourists and then from the lips of the bus driver I was appalled to learn that this was as far as he would take us. From here a short "walking tour" would progress and we could ride back with him in an hour to wherever we had started from. The walking tour would take any pilgrims through the green hills at the edge of the new country, not-Benin. The guide pointed out that any of us who didn't feel up to the walk could still get an hour's glimpse of the lovely hill country from a vantage point a little ways beyond here where a big hill descended to a valley. The two women were uncertain what they wanted to do but I intended to go ahead. We all walked into the customs house and produced our passports which were duly stamped, all bribes having been included in the original tour fee apparently.

Bus after bus was pulling in, mostly carrying not-Beninian workers, students, and pilgrims. Our group was the only mzungus, I observed approvingly. If you want to hang out with white people you may as well stay in the States, the northern and western parts of it. I certainly didn't want to see any white people, in Africa, with the exception of my old girlfriend and teacher, to whom an unexpected warmth and magic clung. I was glad to see them and uncannily they fit perfectly in the scene. Old memories sloughed away and they were transformed in the unfamiliar environment. All the not-Beninians smiled at them.

The African arrivals bypassed the small house and made their way directly through the yard into the big main building, or simply streamed over the hill and out of sight into not-Benin forgoing any formalities. The odd thing was that no buses seemed to come out of not-Benin in the other direction and none entered the country but turned around and returned the direction we had come. An official told us we could get not-Beninian currency, food, extra clothing, anything we wanted in the native domain in the other building and we set off for it, picking our way through the crowd, whose chatter in not-Beninian and other languages, high spirits, and colorful vagabond dress gave me the most wonderful thrill of reality. The two women were enjoying themselves, smiling at everything, muttering small comments about the sights to each other, stopping to examine some fabric a woman was selling, slowly heading through the huge yard with me, although in a thoughtless way, still not having decided to take the walking tour. I was resolved on being a pilgrim though. At different moments each of the women gave me the very peculiar feeling that I didn't really know them, or they were not whom I had taken them for, a doubly disturbing thought fraught with melancholy that made me feel quite crazy and fragile with longing. Our bus would shortly leave to return to the city probably taking the two women with it, whoever they were. I was afraid I would feel quite lonely because I had just run into them and they exerted a peculiar fascination on me.

But then they announced that they were coming with me, as far as the hill, maybe more. So we walked ahead to the second and much larger building to stock up with some refreshments if possible. This was nothing more than a huge concrete block shed painted white with a cement floor, looming and open on the side that faced us, with walled-in areas and corridors where a variety of activities were going on—a bazaar. People drifted in and out the doors and stood in knots laughing and arguing in the concrete byways heaped with vegetable produce, smoked and barbecued monkeys dangling from strings, live chickens for sale. Games of chance being played by boys in the corners exploded in jokes

146

and fights. Chickens were slaughtered, plucked, and set out for sale in one cubicle. Second-hand and novelty clothing (many articles embellished with the misspelled names of U.S. rock bands and sports teams) and sundry toiletries were heaped on tables. The two women, my ex-girlfriend and the widow of my teacher, bought black T-shirts with *not-BENIN* in white lettering on them. The money changer occupied the largest and most central cubicle. To my surprise, he printed the currency to order, from a small hand-rolled press, and when I told him how much I wanted, he started up the old black printing press, and cranked it hard with a loud whir and clatter of gears and rollers. Off came a block of crisp green bills in various denominations embellished with pictures of fruit and politicians which he inserted into another machine that separated them or sliced them apart into denominations, and he formed a small stack of bills with his deft fingers and passed them to me, taking my dollars in return. The money seemed to have been produced for a certain limited purpose, like gambling chips in a casino, unreal and yet all very real. "You take that money over the border," said a man at my elbow helpfully. So I got the idea it would not be good anywhere else, but for use in not-Benin only. I mean there would be no trading it back into dollars later I suspected so I got ready to spend freely, why not. Neither of the women changed any money. So I saw they were going only so far with me, just to the hill for the view. It was just as well for the whole point was to have an adventure with God in a far country, not hang around with old friends. They seemed to take the whole scene with a grain of salt and hold themselves very much within themselves. They put on their *not-BENIN* T-shirts though. As women usually do, they understood what was appropriate and the limit of things. There was beautiful country just up ahead, over the hill, to gander at. They were all for setting off for it at once, a few minutes' hike up the road. I was spellbound by the scene here in the indoor market. But they had only an hour to linger until the bus departed.

147

Things were weirder than they seemed, but the women didn't even notice it—or they just took this for granted! I didn't know how to take the women's attitude, to feel contempt for their shortcomings or indeed a slight awe at feminine wisdom. For instance, these chickens that were being beheaded and plucked, bleeding all over the grey cement floors of two or three of the cubicles, were not merely being set out for people to buy and make into stews. This was the end product, but the killing was a ritual I saw when I stopped and watched for a while. Priests stood by the slaughterers, either to bless the process with a few incantations and a pinch of some invisible powder sent into the air, or it was the other way around and the killing was a religious sacrifice, and the dead birds were being set out on the counter just so as not to waste good meat or because after the magic the birds were not something to be wasted. This wasn't a butcher shop but an inner sanctum. It seemed that religion was blended right into the market scene all around, the sacred was not held aloof from everyday life as it was in more "advanced" and alienated societies. This appealed to me and seemed worth thinking about. So I supposed anyway, as really I didn't have a clue about it. My ignorance I experienced as a state of grace for which I congratulated myself. The two women however were not impressed or interested, maybe because it was men everywhere running the show in this market and/or temple.

Then it didn't surprise me to see a stairway going down to an underground level. One thing I've noticed is that there are always far more stairways going down than one could have ever imagined. Take my old club on Clark Street for instance. It had sprouted not one but two staircases going underground while I had been away at the reunion. For that matter, many people in Chicago do not realize that there is another level entirely of the Loop underground, streets, shops, services, the "Lower City," even though one constantly hears references to it, to "Lower Wacker" and so forth. Few Chicagoans ever go down there and only people with business there routinely go down to the lower level. I believe there is a tavern down there sportswriters favor.

148

So it is almost everyplace. There are always stairs going down to someplace else. And I always take them, eventually. They almost always lead to something. The women said they would walk ahead. They felt no need of going down the stairs. It was getting late in the afternoon, and they wanted to see the valley in the light. Their bus would be leaving soon. Remembering what had befallen M on the stairs down to the hotdog stand outside the church I could understand their reluctance to go down the stairs in the market. My old teacher pulled out a camera and announced her intention of taking some photos of the bazaar though, at the last second. While she did so I decided to peek down the stairs just for a minute.

Down here under the marketplace were bathing and sleeping quarters on a large scale. Numbers of workers were asleep on their bedrolls elbow to elbow on the floor. They all had bright blue or yellow blankets making a vivid scene oddly in contrast to the chorus of snores. The lights were on; everything was brightly illuminated, but that didn't keep tired men from sleeping. There were big shower rooms where dozens could bathe at one time. If worse came to worst, I could camp out here later on my way back from not-Benin. Against one of the walls in the shower room were dozens of battered suitcases and bedrolls seemingly just abandoned there. They were just out of range of the water and only got a little wet. People had just left their possessions here amazingly enough, trustingly. It struck me as odd that in this region where bribery, theft, and corruption were so common people would sleep soundly confident that their possessions would remain safe. My own knapsack was getting a little heavy and I was tempted to drop it with the others. I was inspired by their confidence that it would be here on my return. People just left their things anywhere. Nobody would steal them. What prevented me from doing so, I didn't know how far I was going to travel or if or when I'd ever get back this way. There was nothing to keep me from going a long way and staying as long as I wished, so I'd need my things. I was heading to the far country, I reminded myself.

Outside, above ground, I saw the thin silhouettes of the women, shimmering in the late light on the top of a hill a quarter mile ahead and I hurried to catch up with them. I was so charmed to have run into them in this unlikely spot, and I was so attracted to them both, in different ways. The sun was falling, and the air was getting slightly cool. There were no trees on the hilltop but low bushes of a vivid waxy green showing through a covering of yellow dust. The mists and shadows of evening were making everything craggy and purple-black and mysterious. It was a green country but in the late light green turned to black. The long view ahead and below was worth the hike and we stood speechless and breathless for minutes, turning our heads from left to right and taking in the majestic valley. A very small village of five or six huts could be seen far away, seeming impossibly remote and lonely. I just couldn't imagine what life would be like in such a tiny hamlet so deep in the black-green hills far from a road, far from everything. Some of the other people from the bus joined us on the hilltop, and conversation turned to where exactly the border was and where below the country of not-Benin might really begin. Everybody agreed the next hill on the horizon was definitely well inside not-Benin, but that might be twenty miles away. Somewhere below was the unmarked border. In a political sense we were already in the country because we'd passed through the customs house. People said there was no post right on the border. One just crossed it without knowing where it was exactly. In short, not-Benin was too poor to have its own border post. The exact geographic as opposed to political boundary was no more marked on the wild forest floor than it had been a thousand years ago. The tourists in this sense were reassured they were not there yet and could hop on their bus home with no problem. Thus they lingered contentedly. But they could be wrong, I thought.

As a hint of darkness insinuated itself over the vista, the women said they were going back. They must have overstayed already, although they hadn't the least fear the bus would leave without the likes of themselves. At that my sensations of ease and grace got ripped. An unexpected overpowering loneliness overwhelmed me and I couldn't deny I was still halfway in love with my old girl friend and even though I had just accidentally run into her by happenstance, I would miss her a lot more than I liked. I was drawn to go with them and wondered if it was the thing I ought to do. Not go to the far country? I had been secretly hoping they would accompany me, an absurd proposition. More than an hour had passed and I wondered if the bus was still waiting. I hoped it had left them behind. They were not concerned about that, being of the sort for whom the bus always waits. They were the smartest pair, arm in arm, all smiles. If it had been me who was bailing out of an adventure I would have been apologizing and excusing myself no end, and wondering if I was doing the right thing, but from them not a word. Going back was the sensible and obvious thing to do. There was a pack of mzungus around us, so no doubt the bus was waiting for them all, paying customers. Schedules meant little in this part of the world. No bus would be leaving till it was packed with paying palefaces.

The women were delighted to have seen me again, they said, and it had been fun. I secretly hoped my girlfriend would decide to stay with me, at the same time relieved when she didn't as their presence had become suffocating. I was suffering with disjointed feelings going in opposite directions. She just gave me a mildly disappointed sort of hug, rather an all-knowing one, maybe false. I did hope one of them wasn't M because they were leaving. They began to walk back the way we had come with a light swinging stride, heartbreakingly sexy and athletic, even the widow, who was rather young, confident of catching the bus, in the way of women of the world. They'd seen ahead into not-Benin and that was what they had come for. It had been grand, but enough. They knew how to keep things in proper bounds. They made it clear that naturally they could understand I wanted to push on ahead a little farther and wished me luck with smiles. I had my sleeping bag with me and could sleep anywhere in the valley below. I caught up with them and walked back with them part way out of politeness. It was hard, the feelings I had watching the women leave. What was below in the valley didn't concern them but to me the two of them were as strange as the wide valley. They would never have denied that very interesting things might be witnessed ahead. It was just that interesting things would certainly go on whether they witnessed them or not and they knew how to put an end. In some profound way they would be no less affected by whatever it was ahead if they went back and never saw it. They had a sensible attitude, but I didn't. It was somewhat exasperating, as women are. Finally I turned away from them. My girlfriend gave me a searing little wave that blew my mind for a minute. An image of her slim naked body which I remembered so well flickered before my eyes, sinking in and burning.

Once the bus was in sight, we paused for our farewells and the other tourists kept going. I was suddenly struck by how beautiful my ex-girlfriend was and by how soft her neck looked. I decided to throw discretion to the winds and tell her so. She smiled ironically, "What are you doing here anyway?"

"What are *you* doing here," I countered.

"We've been planning our safari for months."

"I'm heading for a 'far country,'" I admitted, rather proud of myself.

"Don't take any wooden nickels." Her comment struck her as hilarious, and she tittered melodiously, after making it, and strangely to me too it seemed pointed and apt as for some reason I had my wad of not-Beninian bills in my hand (I was ready in case I wanted to buy something).

The widow added wittily, "Don't spend it all in one place!" smiling radiantly and benignly, and they both laughed good-naturedly, irritating me. I could tell they both liked me as much as they ever had probably but didn't take me seriously, which was galling. They certainly more or less hoped I wouldn't get killed or disappear in the jungle and were keeping the tone light to hide that distasteful possibility. But that was as far as it went. They had no idea what I thought I was up to and didn't hide it. I

152

felt lonely and lovelorn contemplating their departure, I missed them already as I watched them turn and head for their bus. It seemed to me I didn't know them at all, they were complete strangers I had formed a fatuous attraction to. The mind-blowing conviction came to me that it was very likely M had disguised herself as my old girl friend.

Suddenly, she turned back and gave me a wry and knowing look that left no doubt. But then frowning and smiling at once, she called to me, "Be serious, aren't you coming?" She meant it and unexpectedly had the air of calling my bluff. Her allure was very compelling and promised fun. She drew me and for a second my plans were up in the air. At this moment, a very pretty African girl walked past, her nose in the air, a sort of satchel balanced on her head, the effect being that pert and perfect posture of such girls, bearing things on their heads, causing her breasts to rise and tremble. I couldn't help observing her for just a moment.

"Well, ok then," smiled my old girl friend, arm in arm again with the widow. At the same time I had the sure feeling that by leaving they were clearing my path, setting the stage for things to come. Not that I wanted this. I felt on the edge of an abyss of the soul without her, not a valley. But no, I shook my head, I wasn't coming with her. I was honor bound to fulfill my commitment to head into the valley beyond. I backed away with a confident wave of my hand (which she didn't see as she was marching off), which ended being an awkward salute to the "far country" ahead of me I was inexorably seeking.

I grabbed my bedroll from the underground station, and when I came up again the bus still had not left, waiting for some wayward mzungus apparently or the bribe had not yet been negotiated. From the dusty bus window, M gave me a cunning look that went clear through me, knife of unrequited lust, or some other useless elusive emotion, and then she yelled something to the driver, who revved the engine, and the bus lurched off in a cloud of exhaust. Involuntarily I took off running after the bus but after a few steps gave up. What was I doing? It was too late now. I knew it had been M all along. We were meant to part and I was satisfied with it. I turned and headed into the beautiful, lonely valley.

Before setting off into it I stared for a long time down into the lustrous, green-black valley. The vast quietude, darkness, and emptiness down there concealed a profound life, a secret life. On the horizon, misty hills undulated depth on depth into the plum-colored sky against which I glimpsed thin plumes of smoke denoting far distant cookfires. If I had spotted the outskirts of a remote village a moment ago, I could no longer find it, as it had gotten too dark. Behind me a motor rattled, perhaps the bus cresting a hill, but so faintly the effect was to throw the stark silence into vaster relief and to open up new unimaginable realms of sky and forest, revealing as well something towering and spacious in my soul. A walk of a mile and all that chaos and lost love at the customs point had been swallowed up in the night. In the solitary peacefulness I caught something strange and sad, even dangerous, ahead, apprehension of which kept me rooted to the high ground for a minute longer. I grasped for a fleeting instant the absolute unknown. Excitement of the journey overwhelmed me and lifted me onto my toes.

I took my first step down into the valley with anxiety but also relief that I was finally heading toward something unlike anything I had ever known before. This was what I wanted, no matter what it might be. My conviction was it would be both real and good. I had the feeling that Africa had loomed across the sea to greet me, that the plane ride had been no more than a metaphor of some kind, as if space was an illusory convention of the mind next to which the developing meaning of one's journey toward the far country was a reality harder than iron.

The purple scrub blazoning the descent came toward me gently, revealed itself to me step by step. Suddenly I was in Africa beyond my paltry ambitions. I was heading into the forest on a trip which could not possibly have been my own doing except in the most superficial sense. Still, it's impossible to get rid of the ego as we are all pathetically aware (or unaware), and I wished certain old school friends of mine could see me now!

A few stragglers passed me by marching toward the border post, heading for the city for work or adventure. The last light of the vanished sun streamed into their dusty, sweaty faces, illuminating expressions of weary hope and aspiration. Pain mixed with joy in their faces, which must have mirrored my own though we were heading in opposite directions, they struggling outward to the "known" and some goal, I walking toward the unknown to be discovered.

I had been following a dirt track downhill when I came to a narrow forest path leaving the track to my left that I had been sure would appear because I thought the village had been off this way someplace and the villagers had to have some access to the trail. Reassured, I set off down the slender path that at times nearly disappeared. No more than an hour of the last twilight remained, at best, little enough of which filtered in here. The sky was clear, a deep black azure. The red starlight came straight down through the trees and was already strong.

I didn't hazard a guess to myself how far ahead the village I had glimpsed from the hilltop would turn out to be. It might have been a mirage, but the beauty of it was I no longer cared. The path gently ribboned through the bush, one hillock like the next, in deep silence except for the eternal chirping of crickets and frogs, the rhythmic silence at the beginning of all things.

If for one moment I had dreamed this up for myself, I would have wilted with fear on the spot, tripped on the roots and creepers, which I was picking my way over with ease, and blinked blindly at the darkness coming down, which seemed not to increase as more and more stars popped out. My great awe at being here was tempered by the dead certainty that I could not possibly have planned *this*. It had the rightness of a fatality. That big-headed old couple behind the church must have been tipped off by the hostess in the painting that I needed a break. I felt grateful to God to thus be on my way. It seemed no time at all had passed since I had purchased that mysterious drink from the girl in the nightclub.

Each moment now passing disappeared into a time that was no longer of the clock. Suddenly I came out into a big clearing, and I was in the middle of the village. The yellow thatched roofs of a circle of huts glistened dimly in the starlight. An elderly man wearing a white gown and skullcap came out of one of the huts and approached me, and said plain out, "Give me your money." I reached into my pocket and pulled out my wad of new not-Beninian bills, but hesitated in handing the whole bundle over to him. I started to peel off a few bills, assuming the man was the next sort of self-appointed tour guide if not one of the outright thieves usually found lurking about. His advanced age however did not reassure me he would be an appropriate person to bribe, as he seemed to exude some sort of wisdom or real know-how. It seemed the wrong footing to be on. I didn't know what to do. There was certainly nothing here that I would care to buy, influence or favors least of all, not even for another moment of life itself if it wasn't meant for me. Whatever I was here for surely had no price. On the other hand, there was always the matter of adjusting yourself to reality. What did he want of me?

I wondered what M would have said, or done, and for a moment communed with her in my heart. She whispered to me that I was always making problems for myself, but that in any case I was in for a surprise. At this, I prepared to part with a substantial sum, simply because it had been asked of me. The old man was staring at me solemnly, and it struck me that he was very ancient and very dignified, moreso than somebody like me could begin to discern. I felt a horrible moment of confusion and anguish, more or less how you feel wondering how much you can get away with tipping a waiter multiplied four or five thousand times in intensity—ignoble moment!

He solved the whole problem by forthrightly demanding, "The whole thing!" in an exasperated voice and reached out a calloused and very powerful hand to rip my whole wad away from me. Thereupon he proceeded to tear the bills in two, making short work of them, letting them flutter to the earth.

"Holy cow!" I muttered, impressed in spite of myself (recalling what had happened to the pages of my novel earlier maybe), but feeling naked without my money (as we always are of course), amazed that a poor man would tear up money.

"Cows are holy here, yes, but everything is holy here," he remarked with a humorous twinkle in his eyes.

"They gave me that money back at the border post. That's real not-Beninian money."

"There are two not-Benins. You're in the other one."

At that he spat on the ground, on the money, with emphasis, a sort of blessing. A kind of pensive chanting started up beyond the thatched roofs, over low insistent drumming.

"Oh, like two tribes, eh?" I said thoughtlessly, instantly realizing my mistake since I knew very well from conversations with African friends back home that Africans hated above all else to be accused of tribalism, not that it wasn't a sinister fact of life in Africa, like everywhere else—but whites loved to point to African "tribalism" to avoid seeing their own ample and ubiquitous tribalism, and what was worse, endemic, miserable, wildly destructive, and unrootable white tribalism. Trying to make amends, and mixing up eras, probably, as well as tribes, if not bribes, I muttered desperately, "Colonial money, like that?"

Seeing my floundering, he said in a soft and kindly voice, "No, just useless here."

157

"But what if I go to the other not-Benin?" I couldn't let go of it, and kept looking at all my money torn in bits on the earth. A pile of your torn-up money is a sight, especially when you are far from home.

"Your money doesn't exist," he said flatly with ample evidence and began walking away from the center of the village. He was right, because when I glanced down, it was not only torn up, but vanished. A breeze must have blown it away. There was no longer a trace of the money. As I followed along behind him I kept looking back at the empty ground with no shred of my money to be seen.

"What is the difference between the two not-Benins?" I asked catching up to him. I thought I had him there. I had asked not only a clever question but the crucial one, I thought. At that everything speeded up. We were both striding quite fast.

"You're in *this* one, that's the difference."

I hadn't imagined I could walk this fast. Our feet were flying, at times not even touching the ground. I felt myself entering again and again into the unknown, into different colors of night, following him toward something, and helpless without my money. I couldn't get over the fact I was not in the *other* not-Benin, but in *this* one, Even though his answer implied he had said all there was to be said on the subject I mulled it over. Yes, most certainly I was here, and nowhere else, with no money.

"Do you mean like an objective not-Benin, and a subjective one—the real country, and the facade you fix up for the tourists to spend money?"

"I don't know how you got here, friend, but much as you'd like to be, you'll never be a tourist again."

We were passing by huts very fast through whose open doors I could sense eyes watching. Behind the huts cookfires sent up smoke toward the stars. The village circle was much bigger than I had first thought and the huts extended back and back into the dark forest.

"The question is whether having ceased to be one thing you'll succeed in becoming another, or just languish in the middle, and die," he added generously, it seemed, or at least informatively. He gave a slight knowing laugh.

I did not like the sound of that even if he was being real and helpful. But I was glad to have the facts on the table, anyway, for the first time in a while. I wanted to hear of success and certainty ahead in the deep forest. I had abandoned my own plans, I thought I deserved greater things, and now he'd torn up my money. He implied some effort was expected of me but what, or to what end, I did not know. Or maybe he meant it was a matter of fate, as they probably liked to say around here, even worse for a westerner like me, lost in the other not-Benin.

The old fellow spoke impeccable English, with the lilting African emphasis. If he was a tour guide in another dimension, he was an honest one, I had to believe. He could have just told me what he thought I wanted to hear like most Africans and non-tourists in general do, just to be done with it. If I had ceased to be an unbeliever and an infidel, I didn't know what I did believe in as yet. Ominously, I was "in the middle," as he had put it. Yes, I hoped I wouldn't die here. The widow, my old friend, had wished me much the same thing. But she had known I had to make the trip, and so did this old man.

I had only hope to go on now. There was nothing to do but to follow the village chief or wizard who was leading me through the village. My money was gone, having ceased to be a tourist, I would become something else, what I didn't know. The village rolled on and on ahead of us into the night endlessly. Suddenly out of a hut lurched a scraggly old white man wearing dirty khaki pants and, as he fell in stride with us, adjusting a battered pith helmet on his head, an etiolated insignia of rank rather than protection from the soft radiance that fell from the heavens. What a relic! He stank too. It was some hangover from colonial times. He had forgotten to leave or something. It gave me the creeps having him walk beside me, because if I had been a tourist, I had never been a colonist, while out of his mouth now poured a lot of moaning and groaning about the good old days when the country was a productive part of the empire, pretty to look at, well organized, and reverent toward the proper gods. Now the Chinese were taking over, he said. I wondered which not-Benin he lived in anyway. As he spoke I saw a vision of African villagers in chains, convicts and tax-evaders with their heads shaved, being marched off to forced labor—but well organized! Those were the days. This picture came off him like his tawdry smell. I gulped in fear, but everything had returned to normal and as we passed the people were no longer hiding timorously, but sitting happily around the cookfires, and the women were peering at us curiously from their doorways.

Abruptly my unwelcome companion shifted gears, clutched my elbow, and hit me up for a "loan" as a fellow "white man." How appalling and disgusting. I informed him that not only did I find that gambit offensive, I was not white in that sense. I suddenly had a feeling about this sad man that like those on the first island the fish had shown me, he had not lived up to some vision he had once been blessed with and that was why he was lost and forsaken here. That might have been a compliment to this one to have imagined he had ever had a vision, but the empire had its vision, to which it had been true by leaving. We all have a vision, but few pursue it. I told him I had yielded up all my not-Beninian currency which had been torn to pieces and was as broke as he was, if not at his level spiritually.

His gaze flickered toward my guide striding calmly and silently in his long gown a few steps ahead of us, who was ignoring all this as inconsequential palaver between dubious white people, and the colonial must have understood instantly, as he stopped walking. "Oh, he took all your money too!" he cried forlornly, falling back, and cackled a knowing laugh that seemed to say I was in for it now and good luck. He peeled off, and I glanced back at him in horror. His face was covered with scabs showing grimly through his long hair. He didn't speak again but just grinned evilly after us as he watched us go out of sight. This was what became of one when the goal was lost sight of and the quest flagged. This "old hand" did not so much have even a shred of irony about his disheveled self.

Next thing a white kid dressed for hiking or exploring in a bush style with high boots and khaki shorts and shirt, on his head a cap with the handsome logo of some South African or Zimbabwean outfitter, slipped out of a hut and I marveled that Africa could be still so full of mzungus, more all the time apparently. This one was the new variety, but ever ready to make a buck out of Afrika. His boots were expensive and a huge pair of German binoculars hung from his neck, and I saw he was a self-styled or more than likely gainfully employed safari guide who assumed I had come to see the gorillas, and he confirmed my suspicion by quoting me a price for an expedition, which would leave next morning early. But when he learned I hadn't one not-Beninian note or American dollar on me, he too appeared disgusted that his luck should be so, penniless tourists coming around, and as he didn't have time to waste, time being money, he also peeled off and faded behind us. This one might have a vision to pursue in the wilderness but it was a misguided one and I was relieved to see him depart.

We were moving deeper and deeper into the village, and the huts were bunched more and more closely next to each other. It seemed we were coming near to the outskirts of things. An African youth wearing a gold chain and chomping on a toothpick came out from behind a hut and fell in beside me and after gossiping about this and that insinuated I was a CIA spy. This almost struck me reassuringly as more how things ought to be, and in any case understandable. We Americans were worse than the old colonists with our behind-the-scenes enrichment and arming of ever worse dictators than the Europeans, so at least it made sense. I was downcast to hear this, however, directed at me, I mean, as I knew the truth of it, and assured him I saw it his way, but I was no spy. Or was I? Doubts entered my head and my sentiments did not carry much weight when he too learned that I had no money for a bribe. He expostulated and ranted a bit and allowed that he didn't believe me for an instant. A glance from the elder in the white gown who was leading me onward convinced him to drop the matter.

I took this moment to ask a question that was obviously on my mind and would have rightly been on anybody's, so I asked, "Where are we heading anyway?"

"You arrive here without warning and ask me who spend all my days here, where do we go? If you were not here, do you think I would be going there?"

That made me think, but did not satisfy me either. "Well, I mean, you know where we're at and what's over there, I mean, in the direction where we're heading—you're sort of leading the way, aren't you?"

"My friend, dear sir, it is not that we are heading any which way, but I go my way and you go yours, it is not we, but you and I find ourselves on a path together, but for how long, and to what end, it is for you to determine by and by, as it is for me, too. It is true, I feel compelled to show you something. Something is to be revealed, but we are not going there, or anyplace, see?"

Not able to sustain this longer, instead I thought about Africa, poor grand Africa, the real one, so to speak. Where I was in some ordinary sense, which was not why I was here or where I was headed, but objectively existed in spite of me and even my guide, bless him. In just a gratuitous and spontaneous train of thought I had a vision of an Africa to come, a rich and fertile Africa with vast farmlands under cultivation—cotton, legumes, money-making fruits and vegetables, millions of acres of red, yellow, and purple tomatoes and corn and so forth, all for the people to profit from, dictators and crooked cops no more, when Africa had grown out of the present era. I spoke about this glowingly to my guide, who listened a while, then stopped and looked at me and said in a voice that seemed to ring from the hills that surrounded this valley: "Very well, and mighty nice, and so it shall be, one day—but not very soon, unless the laws of the rise and fall of men and nations have been repealed, which is hardly likely. *But that doesn't concern you because you are in another not-Benin altogether!*"

So that was how it was. Didn't concern me. My goodwill was superfluous. I couldn't help being offended. I kept not being able to catch on, try as I might. I wasn't in Africa, I wasn't even in not-Benin. Nothing surprised me anymore.

"I might ask, however, what *you* think you are doing here," muttered the old man irritably.

Well, I was told to go to a far country, and so I came, I thought to myself self-righteously, and here I am. But I said no more so as not to provoke him further needlessly.

At once the sounds of singing and drumming ahead leapt up louder and louder and became very beautiful and very strange. The earth beneath my feet, the waves of hypnotic music, the air pushing against my skin had a body and fragrance which created the impression and finally produced the thought that, yes, all this was *real*. I suddenly understood something at last. A marvelous eternal life pressed on me indifferent to my preferences and whims. Yet it supported me and I was nourished by it. I was going to say something to my elderly guide about this, but I knew very well by now he didn't want to give me any credit.

But I was soon to find out, no matter our proximity was contingent and ephemeral, he was to be a wise and good friend—for no reason at all. A great celebration was taking place outside the village. That's how I would describe it, but I'm sure my leader would have disagreed. He would have probably said it was nothing special or unusual, so I didn't ask, but I was soon to find out, as strange as it seemed, it was nothing unusual or special indeed. As we came nearer to it, we passed a new type of huts or houses that beggared the imagination, and I knew I could never have dreamed such a thing. They were perfect spheres, amber or honey-colored huts, like paper lanterns come down from great antiquity, round bubbles that had floated down to earth and come to rest here. So delicately and naturally did they sit amidst their gardens that I wondered what prevented them from wafting away again on the next breeze. They seemed no more substantial than thoughts, from a very exotic and high order of intelligence. Buckminster Fuller would have fallen on his knees at the sight. There is nothing new under the sun, and such sights as the world has seen beggar the imagination.

163

The music and singing had a delirious effect on me. I knew that they belonged in this valley as the rocks and the trees did, as the stars shining down did. I apprehended it all emotionally, namelessly. If I had had to give words to it, the celebration struck me as tragic and courageous at one time. It made me feel happy and sad at once. Such was the harmony of the choir of voices, melancholy and delightful, and the pulse of the drums, inexorable yet soaring, and the motions of the dancers, leaping and resigned, all those feet moving as one. We were getting closer and closer and it was overwhelming every sense. There was a delicious smell in the air of unknown spices mixed with sweat and the warm leather of the drums. That there should be a unitary, transcendent reality and that the dancers were dancing toward it and creating it, electrified me with a strange alternating current of hope and fear, despair and excitement.

Then as we finally came close to the circle of dancers, the unitary effect, the single note, for me was horror. Around the dancers was a high circular fence and they couldn't get out! They were *prisoners* as well as celebrants. Occasionally one of them broke out of line, and as if to escape, climbed the wires, which were elastic, giving beneath his fingers and feet, unable to reach the top for the mesh kept giving way, and peered out, sightlessly staring through the mesh into a void. It was as if the would-be escapee had had second thoughts about leaving, realizing he belonged here, and couldn't anyway. The fence was made of an organic material like seaweed or coral, or flesh itself. The longer I stared I realized they were not trying to escape at all, for they all leapt up now and again and made contact as if drawing energy or comfort from the fence. What it was made of I couldn't imagine.

Drawn to the dance, I took a closer look at the fence and realized it too was *alive*—alive as a coral reef is alive or the nervous system of the body as it dimly or brightly lives. The amber strands of the web were protoplasmic, the dancers who leapt upon them and stared about trying to get through them found they were being supported by them and drew sustenance

164

from them. Held back and in by the criss-crossing tentacles of the fence, something of substance passed into the dancers, who momentarily became one with it. Brownish, organic in nature, the net suggested symmetry and order, the mesh set on a diamond pattern, thousands upon thousands of living diamonds. It too was imperceptibly, minutely vibrating and dancing! In subtle waves it undulated to the music and took part in it. The uncanny thought struck me that this was how the music "looked," and this was the "body" of the music. As I watched the occasional dancer leaping against it, I realized nobody was attempting to escape at all. That is what *I* would be doing, not *them*. They seemed almost to caress it, made intimate connection with it, seemed to respect even worship it with their hands, and continuously drew nourishment from it.

To have discerned that the dancers were within a living net, that they had no overwhelming desire to escape (but even if they did, only an easily resisted impulse) appalled me, and yet made me wonder if it didn't ultimately lend a fateful meaning to the scene, even if it was beyond me to appreciate it. I regarded it with awe, as if seeing the beginning and end and boundary of things. If the dancers were *not* inside the netting, then where exactly would they *be?* Was it a doom, as it really seemed to me, or was it some preternaturalness superior to the febrile, fleeting spell we called consciousness, freedom, or even happiness? It was their place and their roots, it supported them more than anything, it was where they were meant to be at. Above all the net as the music that supported them must not be broken or disturbed. To have broken out of it might had meant despair or even death, as likely as freedom.

One can't help being who one is, and as I listened to the beautiful and haunting but monotonous and mesmeric music, and as I gazed into those expressionless eyes and unsmiling faces, it seemed to me that the dancers must be brought outside the net, helped to escape. But I had to allow that maybe the net gave the dancers meaning, as round and round they went. Maybe they knew something I didn't know, and I was wrong, it was easy enough to believe that, too. But I wished I could help them fly free, and when one leapt onto the net, I imagined a momentary glimpse of liberty flitting across the mind.

As they danced episodically in their circle, they chanted a single phrase over and over: "Ah-li-vet! . . ."

Ah-li-vet! . . . Ah-li-vet! . . . Ah-li-vet! . . .

I would have discussed all this with my guide except that I didn't want to present him ultimate proof of my foolishness. You didn't arrive in a foreign country and immediately begin asking a lot of dumb questions about why they did things. I knew that much, but I couldn't help thinking that according to the Constitution and the Bill of Rights and probably the charter of the United Nations, the poor imprisoned dancers ought to be aided to escape. And what would happen to them then? What would the dancers ever do outside their fence? Let folks be who they are for heaven's sake. It was enough to see a thing like this and let it be. Yet as events were to progress, it began to seem that there was some basis for my ambivalence, even by the lights of the "not-Beninians" themselves, or at least the old man, my guide, who regarded the dancers with a tragic light in his eyes, which unexpectedly seemed to mirror my own feelings.

He seemed to be touched with some kind of pity as he regarded the dancing. Having stood by my side silently, while for a moment I had forgotten him, he touched my elbow now and called my attention to a small boy bearing a meager meal for me on a tray. It was only a cup of sweetened milky tea and a bowl of rice flavored with coconut, but it reminded me I was famished, and it soon filled me. The boy waited for me to finish, watching my progress. I wasn't long about it as I was hungry, and scooped up the rice African fashion in my fingers and slurped down the tea. The old man laughed seeing me eat the rice with my fingers, which was easy because it was sticky and held together in clumps. He nodded approval, as if amazed by this minor feat of the mzungu. The small boy gave me a bowl of water to wash my fingers. The old man beamed, proud of me, and smiled as if I were making progress indeed, or maybe just that I was an amusing character.

The old man made dipping motions with his fingers and with a frown of concern on his face waited till I had thoroughly dipped the tips of mine in the water and wiped them on the boy's towel, then said, "Now you must witness something."

He led me to a hut, one like the others, perhaps for a rest, I hoped. But it wasn't so. He meant what he said. More demonstrations would be forthcoming. With no premonition, without fanfare, he showed me another miracle, miracle of miracles!

"An animal is to be made right now!" he asserted, and stepped back.

In the middle of the hut with its neatly swept floor there was a large porcelain bowl set on a wooden stand about waist high. In this white bowl was a mass of bloody fur and flesh that looked like roadkill, but worse than that, a mashed-up pulp of discombobulated remains—or *anticipations!* For a voice rang out—and it was the voices of all the dancers rising together in one voice, on a single note, in a single word. *"Ah-li-vet!"* Their chanting grew louder and louder as they repeated it over and over. The word or phrase sounded oddly French to me and I wondered if this was formerly French colonial Africa. But then I thought how foolish, it was a word never before heard in any language, not a word at all maybe. And now the transformation occurred. They sang, and chanted it over and over, the tune or rhythm now so catchy, seductive, hypnotic, danceable, it made you tap your feet, and yet something more ominous. Who would wish to live without music like that? Or else you could imagine it being sung by a chain gang guarded by an overseer on horseback with a shotgun on a plantation in old Dixie.

Ah-li-vet! . . . Ah-li-vet! . . . Ah-li-vet!

At this, the mass of fur and flesh in the bowl began to move and turn over and over on itself, taking unrecognizable form, brimming with heat and energy, and then out of the bowl jumped a little furry dog, who immediately came over to me. It was the

167

brightest-eyed little dog I had ever seen, and so wild I instantly called it a "ferret" to myself, because it was not exactly a dog, it was too wild—yet it seemed to love me. Its hair stood on end as if electrified and its blue eye bore in. But I have no idea to this day what a ferret is, and have never seen one, so I don't know if it was exactly ferret-like, but I wanted to say that it wasn't entirely a dog-like creature. It was so vital, so bright, so strong, so alert, so sleek, so loving, vicious, and feral. Its eyes were blue-black beads. There it sat between my hands and delighted in having its fur stroked. It called to mind a little dog I had once had and nearly brought me to tears, for I had fallen in love with it instantly. But it was an animal the likes of which I had never seen, so primitive and deadly, I would say, I knew it could kill a snake, and I didn't know what else it could kill. It was a killer, but I found it snuggly too. It snuggled to *me*. And the way it stayed with me from this moment on showed it liked me and suggested it always would be loyal to me and would protect me. "Ferret" suggested its deadly instinct, but over and above was its interest in me, which caused me to think of it as my little dog.

"Ah-li-vet!" chanted the voices over and over on their uncanny sing-song rhythm. I didn't know what this meant and I kept wondering what it could mean. It took me minutes of listening to it to get past the African accent. At first I had thought it was an African expression, and then French. "What are they chanting?" I stroked my new dog, who didn't answer.

The old man explained to me that the little dog whose birth I had witnessed from a mass of dead matter was now mine— something that was more than happily apparent to me—and that it was a responsibility to have a pet. I might have been a boy again so much was I enjoying petting its lustrous black and silver fur—and getting this parental advice. You know, if I might put it like this, it seemed to me that there was no difference between pressing the fur of this vibrant little beast and the highest thought I will ever have. God forgive me any unintentional blasphemy in saying it seemed a kind of prayer to something holy sent through my delighted hands. But of course in those days there were a lot of things I didn't understand yet. Meanwhile, like a father talking to a child, the old man reminded me that a certain commitment was involved.

The old man informed me of a task that came with the dog. The owner of the dog—and I was the owner—had to take it to the North Pole, for it relished the snows and had only been born here at the Equator, it wasn't intended to live here forever. I reeled at such a demand since I had only just gotten to Africa by the most unimaginable luck and circumstance. How the heck would I get to the North Pole, but I had to admit anything was possible by now. I just said, "Okay," nonchalantly.

That got to my guide, who smiled sheepishly like he was being successful in my education maybe beyond what he could have expected, but had his doubts. At this point I realized that he might be the main elder around here, my guide and leader, and one wise old man, but there were others above him, way above him. "It will take a tremendous effort," insisted the old man. I imagined so. I didn't know what that could mean, but I was so happy with my little dog I didn't inquire. That little dog was so energetic, vibrant, happy and vicious, one could see at a glance, it could probably run and bite its way all the way to the North Pole and through all the snow in between on its own. I didn't intend to falter on my quest. I hoped it might be postponed somewhat. Everything that had been happening to me lately was so overwhelming, I was not able to focus on any side trips, although fleetingly I did wonder if the North Pole might be the aforementioned "far country" and not Africa after all. What mattered was the little dog belonged to me. To me the dog gave a feeling of knowing where I was and who I might be, which is what love does for you.

"Think of it constantly," meaning the North Pole, the old man repeated enigmatically in his spicily accented intonation.

I spent my time the next few days caring for my little dog, getting to know it, stroking its fur, and finding food for it. To sit with it, hold it in my lap, and look into its gleaming eye was all I wanted to do. That it would let me hold it and stroke it was a wonder. Nobody else ever tried to do it, not even the old man. They kept some distance from it like it might take a bite of their hand. It would sever a finger in a flash, its teeth were sharp as knives. Had it wanted to, it could have run away, chewed the hand off anyone who tried to stop it, or leapt straight over them. It was a very strange animal and seemed to belong to me in a way in which no creature, man, woman, child, or beast, ever had. It was also the most profoundly beautiful creature I had ever been close to. There was no way to encompass my feelings, my love and gratitude, which had no end, to say nothing of my awe, for I had witnessed its creation.

I got to know some hunters who supplied the villagers with small game, rabbits and deer, and bought meat from them for my dog. It also had an appetite for large insects and rodents, and I acquired these from some boys who made a business of trapping the huge grasshoppers, field rats, and so on that some villagers fancied. Without being told, I did not trust the dog out of my sight. Not that I could have stopped its doing whatever it wanted, but I expressed my affection every moment. I had once owned a dog which I had been in the habit of allowing to run, since I assumed and could plainly see that this was in its nature to love to do. But one day it never came back, and I never found out what happened to it, a grief that I will probably always have as long as I live, and I wasn't taking any chances with my new dog. But its loyalty to me and seeming curiosity about my every move suggested it would stick close. It never left my side in fact. When anyone came around it kept its eyes on them.

Over two days when for some reason I couldn't get any food from my sources for my dog, I noticed it didn't seem to mind or be any hungrier than usual. It seemed to accept food from me and let me feed it while it had its own way of getting food, too, without my knowing about it, or else it was used to going hungry for periods in the wild. Had it become hungry enough, or any time it cared to, it could have just burst out of my hands and crashed through the door of the hut and gone into the forest and killed a snake or a rabbit, but it liked to hang around

170

me. As I say, it wasn't exactly a dog, or that's not all it was, a representative of that from which dogs, ferrets, wolves, jackals all come, I would say, the original stock. In its eye flickered an ancient and implacable light. Into that one light and one instinct a myriad of noble aptitudes, such as love, hope, loyalty, viciousness, inviolability, energy, protectiveness, certainty, purity, self-sufficiency, murder, and eternity, all came together and burned in that strange little animal.

I had witnessed the miraculous birth of my little dog or ferret from next to nothing, and at that time I thought if I never saw another astounding thing in my life this would have been enough, though now I know it is insufficient. Whenever I think of him, let alone stroke his vibrant fur or look into his electric eye, awe and gratitude overwhelm me and tears come to my eyes, and my spirit expands, for when I got him in the way I did I imagined I had seen something beyond all religion and all science. Reasonably acquiescent to the wishes and wisdom of my guide and mentor, as it behooved me to be, I gave some thought to the North Pole now and then, inconclusively. But all thoughts of this duty were pushed aside by an alarming turn of events, after which I forgot all about it, and no more mention of the North Pole came from the old man either for a while, as his attention, and mine, shifted to meet an unexpected challenge.

One morning, very early, a lot of commotion broke loose in the village. While it was still dark, men with torches ran through the lanes as if searching for someone. All morning there was harried movement and anxious shouting. The old man came and told me that the king's son had been kidnapped during the night.

At first it was thought he was being held someplace in the village, thus the search parties. By the next day it had become apparent that outsiders had come in and removed the boy. The old man's advice to me was to lie low. Suspicion sometimes fell on foreigners. I had certainly never seen the king or his son, nor even heard much of them before, not the son anyway. The political structure of the village and its relationship to its neighbors or enemies was nothing I had considered, not being

171

ambitious, or an anthropologist, just a pet owner. Nor have I ever been political personally, politics striking me as froth on the wave. But sometimes you find yourself in the middle of it anyway. It was easy to feel the fear and disturbance in the people. The hysteria in the air the old man with a word and a frown helped me to interpret as grave personal danger to me, the mzungu of recent arrival. Whether the king knew about me, or had been curious about me before this, I didn't know. I almost got the impression from the old man that he had. Under the circumstances every unusual detail would be raked up by his spies now, and eventually I might fall under suspicion, as would any other strange factors around the place, since the enemies could never have slipped into the village unnoticed and kidnapped his son without the help of dark sorcery or sheer expertise, and I was at best an unknown.

More than ever, in this danger, and unable to go out and walk around, I doted on my dog. If anyone came to hurt me, he would know it and kill the first few of them anyway before they killed him. I even wondered if he could be killed. The spirit in him seemed eternal. I had seen his birth, and everything mortal comes to an end, so I guess it's true of him too as an individual ferret dog. But before they got him he would do a lot of damage with his razor-sharp teeth and supersonic attack speed. It seemed to me, perhaps superstitiously, just his presence in the hut with me protected me and pushed the danger away.

That was the least of it. He helped me with the boredom of the wait, amused me, relaxed me, and gave me joy of ownership just to contemplate and stroke him. Not that you could own such a magical creature. So I spent several days inside contentedly enough at first. As time went by my dog provided me ever more vital companionship while things grew increasingly strange and the people as I glimpsed them through the door of my hut (which I cracked just for a stir of the air) began to look demented, haunted, and royally disturbed. All normal life in the village seemed to have been replaced by a consternated and aimless search and movement.

The disappearance of the king's son could be no ordinary crime. It upset the whole order of things around here and put everything up for grabs until he could be returned. The old man, my guide, was not royalty, but he had a certain usefulness to the king and his court, since he was venerable and holy, and he brought me news from the royal court every other day along with some cooked potatoes, nuts, bananas, and cured fish. Even though I was not yet suspected of involvement in the kidnapping, the feeling in the royal circles was that things could get worse, the missing son was a portent, so nobody was making a move. The old man let me know he was trying to keep the king calm and assuring him of my best intentions. I shared with my dog the food I was brought, but he didn't seem hungry. He lay in the center of the hut with his muzzle pointed at the door and his eyes bright and deadly.

This hut I had been brought to that day was my living quarters, my hiding place, and the shrine of my ferret, not necessarily in that order. Once I had arrived at it, I had never ventured more than a couple hundred yards away. When the old man came, he took me out of my hut for short walks out of kindness, and because he was afraid to come in with the dog in there. The dog leapt and played behind us, in front of us, and all around us. Now and then it bared its teeth at villagers who passed too close. Everybody but me seemed afraid of it. When I was alone in the hut with my dog, even the old man was afraid to come in. That truly impressed me—I mean that there was something that impressed the old man. I loved my little dog.

It couldn't possibly have done the old man any good to be seen with me. People were sweeping the streets with the green branches of trees. It was a purification. The sweeping parties had begun their work at the very center of the village, at the king's compound, and were working outward hour by hour, day by day. They would sweep away any demons who were preventing the crime from being resolved and any devils who were preventing those who were responsible from being identified. Because there was a certainty that someone inside the village must have been

173

involved, since the king's son's whereabouts were always kept as a mystery from day to day, suspicion radiated outward and fell everywhere. When the sweepers passed us, they even swept the feet of the old man, but avoided mine. He grabbed a branch and swept my feet too and the ground around them. The sweepers paused to witness this noncommittally. The sweeping party stood back and exclaimed, "Ah!" as one man. Then they resumed their work, moving again and again from the center of the village outward, so sweeping all devils before them meticulously.

A band of youths waving machetes in the air ran up the lane toward us. Like everybody else they were hunting for the demons who had stolen the king's son. They seemed drunk. Their leader held a small flag of the country over his face as he ran. It had green stripes. It was so worn that it was nearly translucent and he was able to see through small rents in the fabric. He thrust his face covered by the flag toward mine. The flag seemed to give him daring. He peered at me through it. The old man shoved him on his way. There was practically a war fever in the village. The old man took me out for short walks only. He understood that if I stayed in hiding all the time, the people, some of whom had become used to seeing me about in the immediate vicinity, would wonder, but if we walked around a little from time to time with a normal unfrightened air, it would dispel suspicion somewhat. The goodness of the old man was an unending surprise to me. I was grateful to my friend the old man, for the atmosphere held extreme uncertainty. His interest in me seemed even more unaccountable than the kidnapping of the king's son, which had an air of fatality.

The moment I'd heard the bad news I'd had no doubt that the son had been kidnapped all right, and wasn't just out hunting or gone missing on some lark, which was what a lot of the villagers kept hoping at first. This was the first time I had even heard of such a son but as I learned more about him my feeling became confirmed. The king doted on him but in the view of the people the boy was spoiled and weak. The general opinion of the son was very poor, and he was much less popular than the king.

So nobody was concerned about it out of love for the boy but because it totally upset the apple cart around here politically or culturally. It inflamed and worried the king. That was the point of it everybody knew. Enemies inside or outside the village meant to weaken the king's hand. Even now the bands of youths were hunting for traces of him not out of concern for his well-being but out of fear of the old king, or what might happen next. My opinion became that maybe a faction in the village had done away with him. Spies and emissaries in outlying territories having brought back no news of him, the rumors now had it that he had been killed, and this immediately struck me as the truth, too. I feared the worst. My position was very doubtful and perplexing. The idea was to lie low, act normally, and hope things blew over.

I spent a lot of time wondering what niche I was really occupying politically in the primitive village without being able to understand it in the least. I trusted the old man implicitly, and my gratitude to him was total and humble. He had adopted me in a fateful way and such things counted. Since these were my true feelings, and they were good and proper ones, though I would no longer have made the mistake of trying to clumsily express them, they set everything in order between the two of us. This was ironic under the anxious circumstances. He could have washed his hands of me out of concern for his own safety. I felt so helpless that I never questioned him, never begged for news or anything else, never expressed my wish that he come back, each time he left. He seemed to like me, if for no other reason than that I had come here into his territory, the "other not-Benin," mysteriously. He believed that proved his responsibility the more mysterious it was. Along with such other talismans as the pony, the teapot, and my dog, the old man was a part of my story, but he didn't seem to know if it would have a happy ending.

I often thought about the fleshy netting that surrounded the square where festivities occurred and the dancers inside it. I wondered if the dancers were dancing. We were far enough away that it was hard to say for sure, but it seemed to me awfully quiet over that way.

I had the little dog to care for, who loved me, otherwise I would have had a lot of time to think. I had to meet the hunters to acquire some scraps for him at least every other day, for the old man did not always bring enough. The old man never fed the dog and did not concern himself with the dog, although I could tell he observed the care I gave the dog, and approved. After all he had been there too at his birth and somehow arranged for me to be the central witness at the creation. He wanted me to take care of my dog, and I did, of course. But he himself had no connection to it. He regarded it as significant to my fate, and also he must have felt some objective regard for the dog, as a sort of charm, but not affection like I did. We always took the dog with us on our short walks around the neighborhood, for that reinforced the impression of normalcy we intended to give out. The thing was that the villagers were leery of the dog, and in their eyes you could see they thought of the dog as a power that I had. This was a fact, the dog was a power that I had acquired, how I didn't know. So I was impressed by it too (but I wasn't impressed by myself). In fact, the obvious loyalty of the dog to me was quite as important to me as the old man. This made me all the more aware of how little I must deserve it.

Every day there was a dance of propitiation in the village and sometimes when we walked a few steps longer than usual I caught sight of the dancers behind their net, clinging blindly to the fleshly net or fence that enclosed and nourished them. My feeling was close to envy for their blessed state. The net seemed to protect them. In the frenzied atmosphere of danger that the kidnapping had brought on, the dancers laced their hands and feet about the net with extra energy. If I had had such a net to cling to, I wouldn't have faced the ambiguous situation I was now in, not knowing whether I should hide or flee, or how to go on hiding or how in the world to flee. My position was unsustainable and precarious. With an uneasy and horrified sympathy, I remembered the shipwrecked colonialist and the

176

spiffy safari guide that I had bumped into the day I arrived in the village. They had seemed pitiful and I had despised them. Was I like them already by now, misplaced and abandoned, having overstayed my welcome? I was stuck here with no way out. I was a complete anomaly in the village, surrounded by danger, and vulnerable.

One day we took a longer walk than usual and when we heard the monotonous otherworldly music that the dancers danced to, it made me wish to go farther and approach them, and against his better judgment the old man followed along. For once, he was following me. I could see the doubt in his eyes. They were the only ones who were not disturbed out of their routine by the disappearance, or at least they were still dancing, with greater abandon. Every day that the king's son was not returned to the village they seemed to cling to their net all the harder. People placed a lot of faith in them, brought them food, and considered their dancing sacred. I noticed that some of them were jumping onto the net much more frequently than I remembered. Some of them climbed right to the top of it. Once several climbed up together and seemed to want to touch or cling to the same strands of the net. Under their combined weight the net sagged dangerously, and I feared it was going to break. We went back once or twice to see them again.

The propitious sweeping with green branches went on tirelessly and rhythmically. It accelerated hour by hour and the chafing seemed to seek a climax and resolution, like the drums. I fed and walked my little ferret dog. As for taking my little dog to the North Pole, I forgot about that mission, or pushed it aside as far as possible from my mind. There was only so much guilt and foreboding I could bear. I could have never remotely imagined winding up in the situation I was in, confined to the kingdom with fear and tension mounting. It was easy to believe that I as an outsider had fallen under a cloud of suspicion, but thus far what with the old man and the dog every allowance was being made for me. This might not last. The old man and I didn't speak directly about these things, and any impulse I had once had to ask questions was long banished. I took each day as it came and the evil and boredom thereof. My old tendency to be light-hearted and jaunty had disappeared without a trace. I felt we were very vulnerable. Maybe not the dog, I didn't think he could be killed. But me. The old man had his position to save him, but the longer he hung around with me under his wing, the more he took his chances I thought. Sometimes I thought of the goddess and her teapot back in my friend's kitchen in Chicago. I conjured up that teapot as she had suggested that I do, and it made me feel better as pleasant memories will. But try as I would, it did not help me in my present circumstance, I wondered why. I hadn't learned the trick of it. I knew M and I should not have cut out of that apartment that night so fast. After all my travels and seeming progress, I was back in a tight spot far worse than the Clark Street night club. And M was long gone. How I missed her and wondered about her. I tried to enjoy the obscurity of the scene as once I had found solace in the anonymity of the poolroom, and stared into the dim pathways outside my hut on which no one walked.

On the twelfth day after the king's son's disappearance, the old man came brusquely into the doorway of my hut (or the ferret's shrine) at high noon, when the sun poured straight down through every chink in my thatched roof and dappled the earthen floor with white glints and raised the heat to broiling. Something was afoot and I must bestir myself. I was so used to sitting as still as a statue with the blues in my little hut hour after hour it was excruciating to force myself into action, but I was overjoyed at a diversion. The king and his retinue at that very moment were on their way to a sacred grove where I must meet them, that is, put in an appearance, the old man told me hurriedly, not wasting any words, and so we set off, the old man at a dignified pace ahead of me, my little dog trotting faithfully at my heels with his awesome firepower, product of a mysterious birth.

We arrived at the sacred center of the territory about an hour before the king and his retinue showed up, as was appropriate for a commoner and a foreigner like me. Even earlier would have been better it was whispered. Anyway I was doing as I was told. There was a state of emergency. We should have been waiting here our entire lives for events to unfold as everyone else had, or such was the baleful look the king cast on all when he had taken his chair and we finally approached. Some of the wretched commoners did look as though they had been broiling in the heat since the early morning. The king stared at me with particular apprehension. There was little doubt I was suspected of knowing something about the matter of the missing prince. This began to have me very worried. I was almost shaking, to tell the truth, by now, in the presence of the powerful and distraught king. In his eyes you could see he suspected everyone, and that included me. As soon as he glimpsed me, he stared at me a long time suspiciously. He must have heard about me, but it was something else seeing me. It stoked his fears. As business proceeded he cast his baneful eyes my way now and again. Had we met prior to the trouble he was in, he would have considered me a novelty, perhaps, but now anything novel might be a portent or a telltale sign. The bottom line was that to have his son vanish or be abducted raised a question of how well the king's juju was working. A powerful king should never experience any such distress. He was ready to latch onto any scapegoat.

In the meantime it was an hour well spent, for we ran into an old friend, you might say, who was ready to help, the sight of whom was like a ray of intoxicating sunshine on the beach, proving you never learn. The old man seeing my consternation, for I was practically sweating bullets by now, whispered to me that we would meet "a friend." There was someone he knew here who would help me. I got the sense that in the scheme of things I was "the honored guest" around here to some of these people, like the old man, and they thought my predicament was improper and even shameful. At some point the clutch of ministers and sycophants around the king broke up for refreshments under the date palms before the serious business began that would take all afternoon. In the mixup that ensued we edged through the crowd in her direction, and causing my heart to take off like a wild Arabian horse, she found a way to draw near us discreetly. The old man had spoken quickly to her under his breath as we arrived at her side, explaining my situation. Casting her eyes down, in a few simple words, she expressed sorrow that I was in a jam with the king, and promised she would help me. Her manner was modest and regal at once. She was connected, sincere, knew right from wrong. It might be I had been mistaken for someone vaguely of importance, or maybe CIA. Sensing my wonder, she whispered, "I was a slave in the time of King Solomon, no big deal," as if to put it in perspective, and give me the facts as well as hope.

She pulled out from beneath the diaphanous folds of her silken gown a carved icon and thrust it into my hand which she squeezed for a moment, whispering, "Give this to the king!"

"What—why?"

"You have to give the king something," she observed matter-of-factly, smiling indulgently at me.

"What is it?"

"It doesn't matter. Something for the tourist trade. The king likes any little thing. It's the gift that counts, believe it or not. They are not so avaricious. Well, they are, but I mean they want everything, so anything will do. He'll assume you don't know what is valuable around here. You're a fool, obviously, he already knows that, but well intentioned toward himself, he would like to believe. Better you are a fool, believe me. He'd be suspicious if you actually gave him something costly. They are trying to narrow down the suspects. He'll be assuaged and flattered for the moment, at least for long enough that we can do something about getting you out of here. Everybody likes to get a little gift, okay?"

There she was! In an unusual costume for sure, but we were far away from home. I was so happy to see her. Just in the nick of time. Yes, far from any beach, nightclub, or fancy restaurant, under a black veil, concubine of a visiting Moslem dignitary, but there was no mistaking her, and her usual semi-wry tone, and erotic shock waves pounded over me like a tsunami. I would have liked nothing more than to be sitting on the beach with her eating a ham sandwich or something, and certainly touching her face, and kissing it again and again, even though at this moment this would be impossible because of her veil. Or at least we might get something really good to eat. In the rush to be off to get to this audience with the king I had missed lunch. Life was worth living again, and my dire predicament was but a momentary impediment.

Instantly her appearance suggested that good fortune was at hand at last and an escape route did exist and would soon enough be shown to me. Love burst forth and bloomed like a flower in the desert after rains. Naturally she wasn't quite in her accustomed character, but I was well used to her predilection for playing some part or another. I had never been so glad to see her. I wasn't the only one who had done some roaming since we had parted in the hospital, not that that surprised me. I stared and stared at her under her veil. The mere strangeness of M's appearances no longer impressed me. A lot of water had flowed under the bridge since her days as a real estate broker. It was just the mystery at the core of things. There might even be a chance for love, no room for wondering about it in the melancholy vibrations that socked me, whose captive eyes glimmered like dead stars under that veil, who was so beautiful and a slave, notwithstanding that the last time I had seen her she had not even been human, but a lovely little pony named Smoky in the not-Mississippi. A pony was one thing but a concubine wearing slave anklets under her shimmering robe above her dusty bare feet was another. Even the pony had seemed to smile and dance compared to the tragic expression of a woman who had been bought and sold for centuries. My old girl friend who had escaped on that tour bus was nothing to this, and I wished she could see me now.

She was so grave, so calm and wan, as much as I could see of her face under the veil or hood. And she had black skin, soft and glistening. Her dark brown eyes were deep wells. They gleamed like precious stones hidden in a bed of velvet. She cast her eyes down before me, let alone the king. She had the dignity of the mysterious though enslaved female, maybe a captured queen. There was no fun left in her this time, she was all seriousness, and probably danger. She would stab you with her dagger in the blankets. Maybe she would stab the king and get me out of here. Things had been atrocious beyond knowing or mentioning for millennia. Her face behind the veil vaguely revealed itself only to waver and disappear for moments at a time sinking out of sight like a brown stone cast into the depths of a black pool or like the reflection of the moon in a flowing stream. She signaled me by not signaling. Promise, pleasure, and alarm glowed to me in electrical pulses from her face under her black headdress. I sincerely wished to caress that face, but at this moment her owner appeared, a fat man bearing a scimitar at his waist, with a retinue of thirty or forty bodyguards and henchmen. He was a close friend or accomplice of the king no doubt. This time she wasn't amusing any Moslem gentleman who owned her with any wild pranks, loud laughter, sly hoots at his pals, or walking out on any of his parties! She wasn't even being invited to any parties her abashed sad black eyes told me, not the kind she could take over with her antics anyway. When I whispered to her through the air words of astonishment, endearment, and commiseration, her whole being retreated under her black garments, under a burden of mystic woe. It would have meant

182

instant death for both of us, for sure. Above all I must hide any sign of recognition. I turned my gaze elsewhere and guarded my expression.

She wasn't having it for a second. (Maybe it wasn't M at all, I could be mistaken, and what a mistake that would be!) She knew her place, beyond imagining greeting me from a physical and social distance that spanned the Sahara desert and reached into the inner sanctums of the present-day Moslem feudal social structure, an angel more than two thousand years old and fresh as a dove. Those black veils are very sexy. My heart ached with forlorn hope as if I had carried a tomb like the pharaoh's full of bitter secrets in my breast and the acrid jealousy that coursed in my bloodstream was heavy, that she had suffered such depredations and been owned by so many males far more powerful than I, and that there was nothing to do about it, and no way she could escape her present fat owner with his scimitar and guards, for more than a precious moment. Her spirit embraced memories of an austere and tormented past yet remained mysterious and beautiful as a thousand years of black star-studded nights and crescent moonlight scented with Zanzibar clove. She possessed the secrets of the utterly enslaved and downtrodden but most enticing worshipped feminine of the imponderable ages past.

Sensing some of all this, she drifted close once more as some palaver and laughter among the retinue was taking place, and put her hand surreptitiously on mine, and whispered, "See ya later by the poolroom, guy, ha ha ha!" scaring me to death that her owner and bodyguards might hear this and think she meant like the pool in the oasis under the date palms or something. What would they know of poolrooms. But that would be okay because they would go to the wrong place, not familiar with Clark Street. She would help me escape, she as much as hinted, risking her life, and then we'd meet up again very soon. She winked at me as she slipped away, and not a moment too soon because a new psalm-singing crowd of servants, wives, officials, and bodyguards, with the king in the middle of it, had come back from the oasis, and everybody fell back, and M faded away to find herself where she belonged in a constellation of factotums and slaves belonging to her husband, who stood in front of the body of pilgrims, ambassadors, and foreign emissaries among whom were two white men in dark suits and white shirts with button-down collars and horn-rimmed glasses who I guessed at a glance were from the American embassy, probably CIA. I knew it from the surreptitious glances of disapproval and disgust they threw my way while trying to pretend I didn't exist and was beneath their notice. They were going to have to question me later to cover their asses, in case this turned into a diplomatic crisis. But my spirits were up and I was ready for anything.

"I would like to believe you," I insisted as she fled, feeling put out at a familiar note of condescension even if it was two thousand years old, as well as fleetingly remembering Mayor Daley's grandson that she had foisted on me, what that had led to. Unlike then I was so grateful she had appeared in my predicament. Actually I wanted to know anything I could about the icon she had laid on me, because I was afraid the king would think I was trying to pull something on him, get in his good graces, and deceive him with a trinket. He might ask me something about it.

"No, you wouldn't like to believe me at all, would you," she replied on an exasperated half lament that reminded me of when she had asked me to touch her face in the nightclub and cried out that I wouldn't. This time I couldn't have done so, even if she had asked me again, because her face was veiled and inaccessible. But now I wanted to so much.

She tightened her cloak around her with a flourish and following up with certain hand gestures patting herself here and there at the seams as if she were checking that she was all sealed up very properly, a customary feminine gesture I'd noticed in the local Mohammedan culture. She moved away from me in stages, inexorably, stopping several times to talk with head bowed to someone who spoke to her, the crowd around the dignitaries swallowing her up inch by inch. And at every inch of her progress away from me I felt a new pang of longing for her. She was a rather substantial woman around here apparently. As usual, no matter how much she irritated me I was sorry to see M go. I had been keeping up an unwarranted casualness and confidence to myself.

Not only was I in fact innocent but wouldn't have known how to carry out a kidnapping for the life of me. The little carving M had given me to give to the king was some kind of dark wood whittled into the shape of an open little boat, like a wide canoe. Inside it was a white pebble that was distinctly egg-shaped. Then when I took a closer look at it its resemblance to a boat diminished and it reminded me of the white bowl in which my dog had been born, this time in it a stone egg. I glanced down at my little dog, and was relieved to see him at my feet, panting lightly with the tip of his pink tongue hanging out between his sharp white fangs.

I felt better having such a curiosity to give the king, as she had promised, and clutched it for dear life. But then I took a yet closer look at it and I saw that it wasn't a stone at all, but it really was an egg. This was hardly a piece of tourist art I was sure, although not knowing the difference really. But it was most unusual and seemed to have a mysterious significance, and I was sure the king would quite like it. I would have liked to keep it myself as a memento, it was very cool and magical. I was certainly innocent of having anything to do with the prince's disappearance, that was a fact! Surely the king's wise men would figure that much out. When I spotted my guide the white-gowned old man a little ways away in the crush, he nodded to me solemnly and, I thought, reassuringly.

Then he had taken me by the arm and brought me into the king's circle, and the king's guards and servants had parted just enough to let us through, knowing the old man as a trustworthy vassal of the king. The guards instantly stepped back in place behind us, sealing the circle behind us as we approached the king. For a while we stood in the intimate circle about the king and remained silent as various business was being taken care of.

When at last the king seemed to take notice of us and turned to me and fixed me with his cold and woeful stare, I held out the boat or bowl with the egg or stone inside it and proffered it to the king straightaway, who definitely appeared delighted to receive it, and stared back and forth from me to it and cradled it in his lap, as a pleased smile just barely but unmistakably touched his lips. As usual M was quite right, as far as it went, or wherever that might take us. At once the egg cracked open, and a white dove emerged and gracefully flew about the king's head a couple of times before taking off into the wide blue sky. The king laughed with pleasure, and looked so pleased and relaxed. He took it as a good omen in general, and a sign regarding the fate of his son, I could tell, and I thought to myself how clever M was. Then I thought maybe she knew something about the kidnapping herself, but was smart enough to keep this hidden.

But the king's mood instantly shifted, as if hope in the circumstances was too much to bear. He suddenly let go with a torrent of words and then lamentable sobs and cries, rising to true biblical style lamentations, wild implorings of his gods, by whose force and apparent spontaneity it was my turn to be impressed, while tears of anger and grief shot straight out of his eyes.

"He's crying about Alomar, his son," the old man my guide whispered to me, in a flat voice, as if it were not obvious.

"I'm praying for his safe return!" I asserted loudly to the king, which was certainly true. The old man winced at this demonstration but otherwise did not move. I had been praying nonstop for the return of the king's son, not entirely selflessly. I was surprised by the intensity of my own response though. But it was just that I was moved by the king's great and genuine grief, which seemed to have been released by my gift, and the flight of the dove. I was sincerely sorry for him. The old man translated my outburst from not-English to not-Benin, after a discreet moment, since it was his unenviable duty to do so, and the king appeared to wait for it, and there was a dead silence, a queasy sort of calm. Why was it? Didn't they think an American, an

186

mzungu tourist, knew how to pray and would pray? I glimpsed one of the American embassy men squinting at me over the tops of the crowd's heads, a look of blasted annoyance or disbelief in his eyes that I found annoying. The CIA guys would disapprove of me on principle, just for being here and interfering with their jobs. They suspected I would give break their chops, and then turn to them for help.

Were the prayers of an mzungu interloper suspect or perhaps feared to mix up in the traditional imprecations in an unwholesome way? The king's consternation seemed to increase, or his inclination to give vent to it, and his royal visage disintegrated before our eyes in a spasm of sobs. By the desperate looks in the eyes of his advisers it was a critical moment. The old man though was cool beside me. He was keeping calm. In the end he muttered to me, "By God, Alomar was a nice boy, he really was. When he was a child I gave him his first little bow and arrow." The old man, himself overcome momentarily, put his hand to his eyes and wiped away a tear. The king calmed down eventually and regained his stoic dignity and the air of a man who had serious plans for discovery and revenge afoot. My guide shifted his feet carefully and folded his hands before him.

The helplessness of everyone in the face of the loss of a sweet and kind prince, who had fallen among evil influences at least, if not kidnappers, just got to me and I was moved to speak out again from the heart, "I'm sure God is watching out for him and will return him safely to you, dear king!" I wasn't even thinking of myself, and was just imagining the king's understandable agitation. The CIA guys cast me more looks of shocked disapproval bordering on official alarm.

Again there was silence as my remark, like an omen, was digested by the king and the crowd of sycophants waiting for his response. They watched him apprehensively. The king seemed to accept my input in the general melee. He moaned and cried some more softly. He seemed at his wits' end, reduced by exhaustion to trembling and panting. He clutched M's little boat in one hand

and fingered the fragments of eggshell (the dove having burst out of it) with the tip of a finger, while he tore at his face with the other hand, his hands expressing the two sides of his consternation, desperate faith and implacable fears. I was glad to have thrown a little weight toward the former. For the moment we seemed downright acceptable, or at least forgotten, and no one was studying us.

"Time to go," said the perceptive old man aside to me, bowing deeply to the king, and pushing me ahead of him out of the assemblage, bowing as I went too. Behind me I could hear one of the advisers begin a speech in a chanting sort of rhythm. My dog, which had been patient, calm and unobtrusive this whole time, emitted a low threatening growl as we passed through the outer parts of the crowd, some of whom looked surprised to see me. They pulled up their skirts and stepped back from the dog. Everybody took up a melancholy song of praise which trailed away behind us as the old man nudged me up the empty street back to my hut, my little dog bounding playfully and dangerously beside us. Mission accomplished. Making our appearance like that had been meant to assure everybody of my innocence and fortitude and it seemed to have worked. Anyway, I *was* innocent, wasn't I? All of a crazy sudden, I wasn't so sure.

"How do you think things stand?" I asked. "I fear the worst about Alomar. Did I do the right thing? The king seemed in a bad state. Do you know if they have any leads on the crime?"

"After the worst always follows something else, anyway."

"Something better?"

"Yes even death is sometimes better . . . when they find out about Alomar. I don't think things can remain like this much longer. Looks like the king will die of grief himself if there is no news soon. If something has happened to Alomar, he will die of heartbreak. But first he will kill everybody!"

The old man was talkative. That was more words than I had heard him string together at one time. He must have had a lot on his mind. As my guide, he must have a professional stake in my safety. He seemed to concern himself in how things would turn

out for me, it was a mystery to me why, but I certainly
appreciated it. He was clearly concerned for how things stood in
the kingdom as he had to live here and it was home. The welfare
of the state was at risk, and unknown enemies were at work. He
loved the king, and above all he loved the poor prince Alomar,
remembering his boyhood, whose fate was unknown. He didn't
care if Alomar was a playboy, as I had heard. He had known him
since he was a tiny boy. When we arrived at my hut, the old man
did not go away to tend to his other business as he always had
before, but slumped down on his stool as I did on mine. From
under his gown he pulled out a string of "worry beads" and
began to caress them and count them off between his fingertips,
worrying and praying.

"Alomar will return, if God wills it," he mumbled softly,
tendentiously I thought.

I understood that people like my guide thought like that. But
it exasperated me under the circumstances, since in this case
God's will would affect me so directly. I decided to question him
further and get beneath or inside that sentiment and see if it
contained anything, like a plan. I burst out, "So do you really
think there is a chance God will return Alomar to the king?
Otherwise what do you think I ought to do?"

The question took him aback but he knew I might well ask
such a question. But he just repeated, "Well I don't know. It's
God's will." We were at an impasse. In the Western culture from
which I came, it was also sometimes customary to make good-
hearted declarations about God's will based on total ignorance.
Fear and paranoia hung over the whole village like a fog, in
which to try to probe into the question of God's will was not
only hopeless but fraught with danger. Thus he sat still with his
beads. I was innocent (I hoped). There was every reason to throw
myself upon God's mercy, for I didn't have the least idea where
I was, why I was here, or anything else. It was not-Benin, even
not-not-Benin. I watched the old man depart finally with a pang.
My dog sat confidently in the doorway of the hut casting his eye
about viciously on passersby and reassuringly to me. He seemed

to be able to see through the mist deep as a fog that had descended over the village. There was not even a stir of breeze.

As always my little feral dog made me feel better, with his electric fur and bright eyes. Just a glance at him and I felt braver and happier than I ever had before I'd acquired him. Turning to him, I knew that things might not turn out for the best, but with him by my side I'd be more likely to get through whatever was cloaked in the old man's idea of God's will. There was bound to be trouble, otherwise why had God equipped my little dog with such a pointy nose for sniffing things out and such white fangs for slicing and biting, and given him to me? My dog was the efficacious spirit of this swarming earth, the dog-eat-dog earth. He was a cheerful, powerful little blue-eyed dog, the one that did the eating. Who knew what one was capable of until the time came? We would go down fighting, the dog and me. I occupied myself feeding him and petting him, and then just sat there listening to him pant in the heat while he kept his eyes on the doorway. The quick rhythm of his panting abolished time. Above all I was solaced by my pet feral dog. He would take a few serious bites out of somebody if it came to that. Bad as things were, I felt ready for whatever was to come.

The next morning the old man showed up looking much more cheerful. He looked like he had had a good night's sleep in spite of things, something I could not say for myself. As usual he had little to say beyond allusions to God's will but he seemed to discern a ray of hope. He sat in the doorway of the hut with the sunshine falling over him playing with my dog, who seemed to love the old man as much as it did me. The old man didn't usually play with the dog. The actual fog had lifted over the village although the miasma of confusion and consternation resulting from Alomar's abduction certainly had not. It was a nice day outside today though. The old man said, "Let's go to the market and get you something better to eat." I was for that. It was true I subsisted on a diet of gruel, or porridge, an occasional piece of fruit, and bits of indescribable dried meat brought to me at odd hours by one child or another.

190

The market was not its usual bustling self, but people did have to eat, so there were a few hundred people milling around, inspecting before buying, judging and weighing items, smelling things, palavering with each other in a circumspect way, since it was bad luck to talk openly about the one thing that was on everybody's mind—missing Alomar. The old man roamed down the aisles casting appraisals right and left. He seemed to have something in mind in the way of provisions and I followed along glad for the change of scene. We had left the little dog in the hut with the door closed and latched. He hadn't seemed to mind being left behind at all, not like your average dog, which would have been crying and whining about not being taken on a trip. No, my little dog seemed to understand a lot of things, and took its cue from something in the old man's bearing. He knew its presence in the market would not be called for. The little furry beast stood in the dead center of the hut facing us, watching us leave, its mouth slightly open, its white fangs glistening and its blue eyes throwing out electric sparks. An immense and immanent power radiated from it in all directions, more like a talisman than an animal. It was not your usual animal, as I already knew from having witnessed its magical birth.

An uncanny and somewhat troubling thought came to me that there was something about the dog that reminded me of that dwarf at the circus back in Chicago who had tried to kill me with a burning golf club. I say somewhat troubling, and not *very* troubling, because it was only its unfathomable blind power, its fangs and bold four-footed stance in the center of the hut that reminded me of the primordial energies of the dwarf. For the dog loved me. Mayor Daley's illegitimate grandson had always had a hard-on for me, as it were. I would have liked to see a fight between the dog and the dwarf. I had no doubt the dog would win. The dog's feeling for me was unalloyed.

The attitude of the little dog toward me, its "master" (if I could be called that, certainly in name only), was diametrically opposite of the dwarf's. It had the same incalculable power, but was on my side. The dog loved me and would do anything for

191

me. It didn't judge me. I thought of the dwarf if it had only been on my side. The comparison broke down because aside from its deadliness the dog had an unrivaled charm and grace. Even if the king's henchmen should suddenly come for me, the little dog would stand its ground and protect me. They'd have to kill him to get me. And I doubted the little dog could be killed. No, I don't think so. The little dog I was sure was an "eternal" dog, so I thought. I had seen him created. So any enemies would be in for it. He was perfect in being without limit in his protective and vicious dog nature. There was no way of knowing where anything connected to him would end, for he was unstoppable.

Having traipsed through most of the market and the sparse crowds, we came upon a fascinating woman seated before a table in the entrance of a stall. She arose on seeing us approach and I vaguely realized I must know her from somewhere. She placed the tips of her fingers to her broad forehead and then touched them together before her breast, and greeted my guide warmly, who bowed and made affectionate and respectful gestures with his hands coming out of his gown. She was not the usual black or mahogany non-Benin tribeswoman, but must be a Syrian or Indian trader, by her flowing black locks that hung down over her breast and her sand-colored complexion. How I knew her was a mystery, but she looked familiar. Her eyes were jet black contrasting her desert tinted skin and her expression very calm and knowing. A slightly ironic knowing twinkle in the corner of one eye that seemed to be looking away from you.

The woman was dressed entirely in white like the old man. Not only did they know each other but their flowing white gowns indicated some spiritual or tribal affinity. After greetings all around, I noticed her wares spread out on her table upon which her extended fingers rested. These fingers now reached out and proffered to me a kind of dumpling or round croissant, sugar coated, and bearing as an icing or decoration a beautiful crystalline shape that I recognized as nothing else than a snowflake. In the middle of the non-Benin desert! I took the snowflake encrusted pastry from her elegant hand and to my amazement it was quite cold as if it had come out of a refrigerator. That must be why the snowflake had not melted. But as I held it in my hand and the warmth of my hand flowed into it, the snowflake was completely unaffected. I examined the other pastries on the table, and it is true, as they assert, every snowflake is a different pattern, and so were these. They looked so delicious and I at once sank my teeth into my pastry and inside its delicately crusty skin was the most delicious warm honey. Slowly I ate up this tidbit and slurped down all the honey, and I was marvelously revived by it and energized.

"Imported from the North Pole," she remarked and beamed proudly.

Dusting off my hands of the crumbs from this treat with satisfaction, and smacking my lips, I turned and saw beyond the tradeswoman a piteous sight in the mouth of the stall. A beautiful white rabbit was bound in cords and tethered there. The white fur of the rabbit was even whiter than the gown of the woman, which was very white. The rabbit's fur gave off a radiance purer than snow, and it was a delightful and dear little rabbit. Seeing it bound in cords as it was, ready for the slaughter probably as the ingredient in some stew, made me very sad. I tried to tell myself this was nature's way, and everything in nature is constantly eating up everything else, and this was just the natural fate of the rabbit. But its twitching little nose and the whiteness of its fur stirred feelings of horror and despair out of all proportion in the middle of the teeming market scene, in which various small creatures were being sold in this manner. Suddenly I realized that the rabbit reminded me of myself, my own dangerous situation. I was like the rabbit waiting for my fate, which depended on whether they could find the king's son Alomar, and if they could not, then the whim of the king would fall on me, as on the rabbit. I was overcome with the most pitiful terror and sorrow watching the poor rabbit stir slightly in its bonds, awaiting its cruel fate. It could be me next. Why did nature bestow such a beautiful white coat on a poor creature meant for destruction? From somewhere in the stall, which seemed abandoned otherwise, some snakes and a horrible looking brown rodent crept forth and peered around craftily, before setting around the rabbit and beginning to devour it. I tore my gaze from the heart wrenching and terrible scene and found solace in my friends, who wore white just like the rabbit, but a different shade of white. They seemed beautiful and vulnerable like the rabbit at this moment. Nobody big enough to eat them was to be seen immediately about.

They came together to my hut about ten o'clock that night. I must have been waiting for something, without quite realizing it, as I was seated on a low stool in the entrance, the dog at my feet. M was veilless, as she had been in the market. I felt I had never met a woman so impressive as this, she seemed spectral. They were both bare-headed, something rather rare in people of any standing in this community, who always had something or other perched on their heads. The old man wore no hat or headdress, for a change. His white skullcap was missing—for the first time, revealing a silver-grey head. Seeing them together, I suddenly put two and two together and realized they were father and daughter. Her lustrous black hair hung loose about her head like a gypsy. It was only that I was not accustomed to seeing M with African hair braided and oiled, as her head at the market had been coiffed more in the local tradition, and her brown skin discreetly tattooed. Her hair tonight flowing to her shoulders made her look free, like a wild mare on the plains. The way they moved together, a gesture each made while staring at me cupping their respective chins in the hand, the soft comments they delivered to each other under their breaths, and finally the old man's look of resignation and sadness when it became apparent that the plan was for M and me to leave together this very night, all tipped me off at last what I might have guessed about their familial connection. He was about to say good-bye to his daughter! I was overwhelmed by emotion.

"If you were surprised to learn about my husband, think how surprised my husband was to discover I knew you," M laughed. "Being a Muslim he's not exactly understanding," she

194

added with an exaggerated foxy wink that was so much her
trademark I could have exclaimed with the joy flooding me at
the familiarity bursting through her exotic air of having seen two
or three thousand years of monstrous and magnificent history.
We could have been back in Chicago (but we weren't), except
she seemed to hover in the air like an apparition. I checked once
surreptitiously to see her feet on the ground. They were.

"He's going to stick me in a crate and ship me home."

What she meant by that I had no idea, not being acclimated
around here, unless she meant it literally. Her husband,
surrounded by bodyguards, was a guy, I was sure, to phrase it in
the vernacular of my homeland, who "did not play."

The old man made a sharp indecipherable movement in the
air with his hands before his face like warding something off and
sucked in his breath. His face went a little ashen and his eyes
glowed with knowledge and resolve. "In a crate. He wouldn't
leave here alive." He snatched the air a second time.

"Actually he intends to put me on his private jet and send
me to Paris where his government is posting him," explained M.
"I would go baggage class, ha ha."

"What!" I exclaimed.

"In cargo. This is done believe it."

"When you get back to the States, here is a list of things I
want," said my guide.

The old man tendered me a carefully handwritten list on a
ruled sheet torn out from a schoolchild's notebook, the first item
of which was "12 cases of Pepsicola." I didn't read further, but
folded the list carefully and put it away in my hip pocket, then
upon reflection transferred it to my shoe for safekeeping.

"Make sure Melusina has everything she needs as soon as
she gets there. Obviously she'll need some new clothes in the
latest American fashions."

"I'll do my best," I said with what I intended as a confident
tone. The idea of my being in charge of M, even in so small a
particular as a suit of clothes, made the prospect of our
successful escape seem that much more unlikely.

195

"It won't be a particular problem. It will be much easier for you than you imagine."

Really? I glanced at M for a clue of what he meant by that, but she had pulled back the sleeve of her white jellaba and was studying her wristwatch.

"What's the news on Alomar?" I suddenly thought to ask.

They both stared at me. After a second, the old man said, "Everybody knows he's dead, except the king . . . and you, I guess."

"That's too bad—"

"No it's not," M interrupted. As always the joke was on me. At least I felt myself getting back on recognizable ground.

"Even the king probably knows it but he doesn't want to face it," said the old man. "When he does, he's going to be struck again by the coincidence of your coming here just when his weak son is taken away and killed. Who can blame him? I'm struck by it too, aren't you yourself?"

"Alomar was a cheap playboy and an asshole. The kingdom is better off," said M, her voice trailing off, like it was no big deal anyway, one way or another.

"Not as far as the king is concerned." The old man glanced from her to me intently for a second and then rubbed his hands together like he was washing them of something while he stared at my little dog. Out of the folds of his gown he retrieved a small dead bird and laid it before the dog, who wolfed it down with most of its feathers.

"When you leave, his certainty will be complete. All the same for that very reason you two must now leave. And not in a crate."

M's light gown glowed in the darkness and her black hair shimmered in the starlight as if the oil of gladness had poured down on her head from the heavens. A silence ensued while I pondered their remarks and fondly watched my dog eat. Now that he mentioned it, I reflected once more that it was sort of a coincidence that the kidnapping had occurred just after I had showed up. I had wondered about it myself, and could easily see how a superstitious old king would draw certain conclusions. I followed everything the old man was saying, including how we must split, though I didn't want to leave my guide, especially now I realized he was M's father. Perhaps there was a secret connection in events I didn't understand in fact, I thought ominously. I suspected that there was. Answering the question that must have formed in my eyes, M said, "You were brave and ingenious to come to us in not-Benin at such a precarious moment."

I was? She seemed almost to imply I might be of help to her, and them, somehow, a mystery. I could no longer clearly remember how I had gotten here. It was an uncharacteristic remark from M, but I had to admit it had taken a little courage and effort on my part. As much as I hate to pack. I didn't say more as such a compliment from M was rare indeed. But any compliment from M would be followed by something else altogether. She loved to set you up. But then she unaccountably added, "I'm really glad to see you," very softly, and I got my first glimmer that things had really changed and M was now to be my guide and savior. At the same time deep down in my soul I wondered how anyone could be glad to see someone so shallow as me, especially M, it was a mystery.

"This is the moment the gods chose to strike Alomar," observed the old man, his eyes boring in on me. "Not you."

"I didn't do anything," I agreed, still worried, ambivalent about the road ahead.

"Exactly. Why you arrived at this time has always been dim to me. Alomar was something of a wastrel and given to Western indulgences. He has enemies and rivals plenty so there is not much mystery about that."

"I'll say!" She threw out the backs of her hands, brushing something unwanted away, a Mediterranean gesture. At this I suspected that she had had some involvement with Alomar, apparently not to her liking (or mine either), and maybe even in his disappearance for that matter (but I doubted that). I no longer felt a lot of sympathy for kidnapped Alomar, who must have

197

been a jerk and made some enemies in his short life to hear tell. What astonished me was the naturalness of the relationship between Alomar and me, and that something I had done (or not done) and the fate of a stranger could be associated so casually, and causally. I stared lovingly at M, so glad she had showed up again, who was going to help me escape, an ineffable creature, on the surface a wily Syrian tradeswoman, who probably knew the kidnappers, who knew how everything had gone down, and how we would escape tonight.

"This is not-Benin, and you are not-you," opined the old man tendentiously and cryptically on his accustomed note.

"Kings always try to get one-up on the gods," remarked M.

"So there is every chance you'll escape cleanly," said her father, as if that followed.

"They're always getting their people and everybody in trouble because of their royal ambition to be a god themselves, which fails generation after generation, and one king is deposed and the next one takes the throne, only to be deluded in his turn. They want to figure things out god-like, get revenge, have god-like powers and make the people miserable. The people always pay for it. Alomar was waiting his chance to be king, but they got him first."

"Now is the time," interjected the old man into her diatribe. "They'll look for you to try to leave just before daybreak, or even as early as three in the morning, but not at ten o'clock with everybody still walking around. Tomorrow I'll say the Americans came and got you."

That, with its possible implication of making the king mad at the Embassy, was an amusing notion. On the other hand, just the thought of U.S. officials struck me with fright and an unutterable boredom. The CIA guys would want to know "if I knew anything." What did I know? Anything to avoid such a fate as that in the old man's off-hand remark, even being captured by the king's men, would be better.

"You have to leave *right now,*" M's father insisted.

I was more than ready. I didn't have much to carry by now. My dog didn't brook being carried. The old man rose, embraced me, and hugged Melusina. Suddenly she solemnly bowed to me (which I took in the driest fashion and had to exert all my will power not to break out laughing, little did I realize how serious she was), and turned and kissed her father on both his cheeks. At the same time her appeal was overpowering and I loved her deeply, although my awareness of that fact came and went. She stared at me lovingly too. We were about to hit the trail.

Then her father embraced her and held on for a while. They parted with mutual assurances that they would meet again soon, which they clearly believed. That was reassuring. I could believe it too, the way M got around. M smiled at me intimately and sincerely. It was time to go. Her aspect had changed completely, for she no longer seemed an ambiguous creature to me, maybe because I must depend on her completely. Her gown billowed in a slight stir of breeze, and her face glowed confidently. I finally admitted to myself the wisdom she must possess which went past my understanding, but it was obvious at this moment.

"You have my list, right?" the old man mumbled to me anxiously. I assured him that I did, thinking how paltry any such favor I did for him would be compared to how kind he had been to me. As my eyes touched his for the last time, I became aware once more of the deep kindness in them. He had adopted me for no good reason as soon as I had stumbled into his village. I wondered with gratitude how it had come about, as there must have been a reason. Then, as we moved into the shadows with M in the lead, he called out again, "Never forget, you have to take your dog to the North Pole, that's where he likes to live—don't forget it if it takes a hundred years!" It reflected the change my relationship with M seemed to have undergone that I almost felt such a mission might be possible with her by my side. It was the last thing I heard as Melusina, my little dog, and I slipped into the night beyond the village.

Following along on the night trail behind M, who had surfaced after three thousand years in captivity, and obviously knew a thing or two, I admitted to myself there was no life without her. Now she'd come across the not–Sahara Desert, first a Nubian princess with a husband in the diplomatic corps of an ex-French colony, then in the garb of a devout but shrewd Syrian tradeswoman, just in time to save me. Her air was completely different and I realized I had never understood her. A dreamlike atmosphere prevailed more than ever.

Swinging her arms formidably, head thrust forward boldly and alertly, eyes spying right and left for any trouble, we walked and occasionally trotted down a footpath leading from the village deeper into the forest. At the farthest outskirts of the village we came again upon the ring of dancers, ever in motion, behind their living fleshy net, singing and chanting, round and round.

Ah-li-vet! . . . Ah-li-vet! . . .

All live it, I suddenly translated this to myself. Yes indeed, *all live it,* even us, even me. We were no longer looking over or through the fleshy net from the outside, but out from under it since we had stumbled into it blocking our escape and encircling us and were now in it on the inside of it, no longer visitors. *All live it!* Now that we wished to leave, we were caught in it. It clung to us unwittingly and tenaciously as a fishnet and held us in. As if the village trail had been a labyrinth that had swallowed us up and led us to this entanglement or living truth, we found ourselves one with the dancers in their trance. A tremendous nostalgia overtook me, a weariness, I wondered if I had always

200

been inside the net without knowing it. We could join the dance and lose ourselves in its overpowering rhythms and never leave. The king could not touch us if we danced in the circle. We didn't need to escape, we could just give in, and be lifted up by the net. It was an unexpected and terrific temptation, one hard to resist, for we were stuck in the net hand and foot and the question was how to get out, and even if we could. I felt myself being sucked in by the music, and the strands of the net coiled voluptuously around me. I doubt I could have broken free unaided.

It was up to her to get us out of this village and first of all out of the fleshy living net. We were entangled in the net now and could barely move. Even the little dog seemed helpless and panted listlessly, its head and one paw stuck fast in the pulsing web. To my surprise M just pulled on two strands and kept yanking and stretching them until she made a hole large enough for me to step through and she followed. The dog jumped through after us. I think I would have not wanted to touch that strange, protoplasmic flesh-trellis without M. Well, when you think of it, for a woman who would tell people in the row ahead of you in the movie theater to eat their damn popcorn more quietly, a fence on which dancers sprouted like cucumbers was not insuperable even if it kept the dancers rooted to it. She just grabbed it, and held it open for the rest of us. Nevertheless it was a feat of straightforward courage I would not have thought her capable of in the old days.

This all happened as in a dream for I did not have the volition to have broken free from the fleshly net. I think I would be one of the dancers to this day if not for M. I wondered again fleetingly if I had always been one of them without knowing it. Finally, we were leaving the endless village behind. We were free. Our escape was suddenly not only possible but real—real as the night into which we plunged was real. The sight of the magnificent forest before us was mysterious and beckoning. We entered into it with gratitude and abandon. The king would interpret my flight from the village in only one way. If there hadn't been a connection to me before, there would be now when we disappeared from the village before Alomar was found. He would know what to make of our running for it. This knowledge lent wings to our feet, as soon as with characteristic boldness and dexterity M had made an escape hole in the living fleshly net. Excitement and adrenaline pulsed through us as we broke free and strode ahead, bounding like the little dog.

We had a long way to journey to get not just past the border but beyond all influence of the king, as his spies were at work everywhere, and we would have to travel circumspectly, staying off the roads when we could and going where we would not be expected to go. We were headed out of the village in the opposite direction from that in which I had once entered it, so I had no idea what country was up ahead, as geography has never been my strong suit. The idea was that the king and his henchmen would suppose I would go back the way I had once come, not go deeper into his kingdom hoping to come out the other side. Eventually we must find our way to a city with an airport, I thought, otherwise how would I get the old man the Pepsicola and other things on his list? Where that would be I left to M without question. The little dog trotted by my side, blue fire in its eyes, its white fangs menacing. Then it would be off to the North Pole. Now and then it looked up at me with a powerful love and expectation.

Nothing made me so happy as my little dog, except for Melusina herself, who whispered encouragements to me over her shoulder, as we pushed through the stout undergrowth and occasionally took to the road only when it seemed safe. In the early morning hours we slipped between the first huts of a new strange village, staying off its main streets, sticking to the outskirts, our little dog scouting ahead of us, sniffing out dangers, sniffing for the forest again, which loomed black before us sooner than expected. We rushed toward it, the dog bounding happily. It had been only a minor village. A cock crowed behind us. No sooner had we gotten past without incident than suddenly emerging from the forest came a lone warrior with a long gun, coming back to the village from a hunting trip, and fierce and murderous as he looked, the second he caught sight of the little dog who bared its teeth at him, he fled off the path as fast as his feet would take him.

Occasionally M extended her delightful hand back to me, exquisitely soft and strange, in a new color every time, because of the starlight through the forest boughs, and her customary changeableness. We subtly changed direction, slipped off one unmarked path to another, took a fork in the trail. I gave up trying to keep track, and after an hour my dependence on her felt more absolute than ever. I had even flunked out of the boy scouts in my youth. The forest was primeval and the path winding. I was glued to her now, in the depths of the forest, my eyes ever fastened on the small of her lovely back (what little could be discerned or guessed of it through that Moslem gown).

We emerged on a clear path worn smooth and packed hard by countless feet. We were on the Trail of Respect, she strangely whispered to me, the Trail the warriors always took when they left the village to fight a war or to find game. Burial parties to inter the dead took this path too and anybody on any important mission who wished to shed all doubt and attain purity of purpose that would ensure success came on this way heading on their mission—anybody that is except women who were never allowed on the Trail and if they were even seen in the forest in the vicinity of the Trail of Respect could be killed. M, as usual, was the exception. The last place the king's soldiers would expect to track me down would be on such a sacred trail, I hoped. Foreigners above all were definitely never allowed to go here. So to attain purity but also to be where we would never be expected was why we were on the Trail. M explained all this to me over her shoulder in breathless fragments so as to reassure me and keep up my spirits.

When she reached back to take my hand in hers, delectable and made for pleasure and discreet as a sex slave's who had done no work for the past three thousand years except deliver expert caresses, I was hit by a jolt of desire for her under that white gown that almost knocked me off the Trail. I stumbled with longing for her, but this was not the place, and now was not the time, and she was all business, fortunately for us. Under the perfumed canopy of the forest, with an ordeal ahead of us, but well begun, I wanted just a moment of surcease in her arms. Life was at stake, both hers and mine, I fell against her, who stumbled, and pressed back to keep her balance, and the two of us tumbled off the Trail for what turned out to be the cushion of the forest floor—and crawling on it, she careening one way and I another, I lost touch with her and found myself tripping in a circle, stumbling over roots, fearfully alone, nothing between my outstretched arms, off the Trail, under masses of vegetation that dripped dew and hardly let in a breath of air.

M was gone, my dog was gone, I was in the midst of a pointless maze of flowering lushness. I'd been reckless and now look what had happened. Vines slashed at me and dribbled blooms the size of cauliflowers in black silhouette against the starry sky. Elbows of tree limbs smacked me down and roots reached up and made me trip. The silence was round as a ticking clock and every minute counted as the distance between me and my companions grew. The jungle night sang to me in suffocating soundless refrains that I had fallen off the Trail. I stumbled on in sheer unremitting horror at my mistake, waiting to be excused, exorcised, or executed, by the owner of this Trail, not understanding what a mistake it had been all right. I had not kept my spirit pure and my mind on business on the Trail of Respect and my punishment had been swift.

There was no sign of M and my dog had vanished. My heart was beating like an African drum and I seemed to lose and regain consciousness after having stuck my finger in the spiritual equivalent of an electric socket along the jungle wall of the Trail of Respect. I was lost completely in the forest and would have given all I had (which was nothing) to hear the dancers in their fleshy netting singing over and over *Ah-li-vet!*

Finally I heard a muffled bark way ahead. My little dog! They were so far away by now I only barely heard it. I pushed toward the sound as fast as I could pick my way through the vines and broad sharp leaves and tangled branches. I could not find the path again and just crashed through the resisting vegetation getting cut and badly bruised with every leap and step. It was as if the last spark of some forgotten instinct should have saved me, that he should bark, my little pet dog, loyally calling all my senses to attention.

When I caught up to them after an hour, the harsh exertion of the run had restored my lucidity. But as I fell to the ground beside them I didn't think I could go another step. "I'm sorry, I'm sorry!" I protested to M sincerely. The dog licked my hand, which was criss-crossed with bloody cuts. I was in a state of shock but at last I was serious. I realized some part of me had been having an adventure but now I saw life was on the line and terror had me in its grip. M in the meantime had retrieved a cloth from some pocket in her cloak and wound it around her head in a regal turban so she seemed to stand six and a half feet tall. She was patting it into place with satisfaction as I caught up. She smiled at me forgivingly, something beyond that, with hardly any reference to me personally much less my near disaster, as if she hadn't missed me, barely saw me, saw beyond me, saw something that gave her utter serenity, paid me no mind, and figured I would catch up. I could keep up or not. She was more concerned with her appearance and the state of her attire. Patting her turban in place, she turned and strode ahead. I wondered if she had even noticed I had gone missing! I gave it all I had thinking to myself how close I had come to losing contact and finding myself alone in a pathless wilderness. The dog gave my hand a playful bite as if it was glad to see me and bounded before us.

We walked on till nearly dawn, I in a trance brought on by exhaustion, when we reached the "Graves of the Warriors," so she said, and in these "graves," cracks or folds in the side of a steep rocky hill, we hid ourselves and slept. This was a sacred place, on a sacred path, and thus it doubly represented safety for us. People were in awe of it and afraid to come here, and nobody would ever look for us here. It was no longer where any dead were buried, but it had been a gravesite in ancient, heroic times, which for the local people might as well be very recently, impinging on their lives and thoughts via powerful myths and tribal memory, she said. There were bodies down in the cracks, but long turned to dust by now. It was strictly taboo territory nonetheless.

"We could make a mint by leading archaeologists here," M observed. "Think of the artifacts and treasures down there. We could get a grant from the government or the Art Institute."

"Probably the Field Museum."

Our bed was a sheer rockface maybe half a mile wide, with many strange fissures and louvers, some of which went deep into the rock. The bodies of the slain warriors had once been slipped into holes which dropped straight down, and so were buried in the heart of the rock, where no animals would eat them, spirits trouble them, or living people ever find them.

As the first blush of dawn appeared like a profound intimation of trouble in the east, M located for us a wide slit that went into the rock at more or less a flat angle, so we wouldn't accidentally slip in, roll down, and never be heard from again, and there we slept pleasantly all the day long out of sight, in the deep shade, in the cool rock, with the dead warriors all around us, although I awoke repeatedly with the fear of sliding all the way in.

Well folded into the protective rock, protected by the taboo of the place from meddlers or chance passersby, replenished in waves of stony serenity from the other world, snoring peacefully with the honored dead, M and I chaste in each other's arms, the fierce dog curled at the lip of the cave, we didn't stir till at dusk the rose-orange searchlight of the sinking sun came in and found our hiding place and illumined for a few seconds the walls of our narrow stone bedroom.

Our journey resumed in the twilight. The dog caught a large rodent and breakfasted on it. M picked some luscious red fruits in a grove we passed through and stuck a couple of them in my hands. We bit through their rough skins and ate them as we went, the juice spilling down our chests. As twilight deepened, the forest came alive with friendly chatter of birds and monkeys. We came to the edge of a cliff overlooking a deep pool edged all around and half-covered by a luxuriant green bramble in and out of which flew an abundance of colorful small birds and big butterflies and moths. So suddenly did we strike upon the cliff hidden by ferns and mossy rocks, I think I would have fallen over the edge into the water had M not been with me to halt progress with her outstretched arms. We remained motionless in awe a long minute. The world seemed bursting to life with the coming night.

In the pool, the water was wonderfully clear and what's more, in motion, fed by a powerful spring, which rushed through and over the brambles, and spilled out to the edge of a further cliff or descent, where it fell and swirled energetically down in a series of pristine waterfalls, disappearing at the base of nearby dark green hills out of sight. In the last light the moths were luminescent and had velvet wings. The hunting birds flitted fast over the water, streaks of color. Out of the pool leapt hundreds of golden minnows, in the air their luxuriant fins buoyed them up and they gently wafted around us and circled our heads as though they had wings not fins. I observed they were flying fish, flying minnows, only they didn't ever fall back into the water, but floated and zipped around our heads like dragonflies curious about the intruders. When one hovered near my ear overlong I noticed it seemed to be drying out, and I grabbed it and gathering up some wet moss from the pool's bank, wrapped the precious fish in it to revive it. But M objected to this, and laid her hand on my arm. She pulled the strands of moss apart and the fish flew out and rejoined its companions, some of which I noticed had human faces.

I couldn't take my eyes from the water where it seemed to almost boil near its source hidden by vines and bushes—clear and cold. I watched it bubble forth minute by minute. Never had I seen such an oracle of purity and wildness undefiled. It seemed the pure origin of life itself. To have been shown a glimpse of it!—all was well, I was at peace. Surrounded by danger, the very soul of all life rushed past us and pressed us onward and would carry us to our appointed destination. One of the fish darting back and forth past my ear wore a petulant expression very much like the dwarf in the poolroom, Mayor Daley's grandson. I couldn't help wondering what its problem was, but was distracted by M, who unraveled a long strong white thread from her cloak and attached a pin to it, casting it straight into the heart of the pool where the spring rushed the fastest, and soon caught us a fat golden and black fish, nearly round, like a flounder, which she cooked on a flat stone. All fear had vanished, at least for the moment, and so did hunger, when shortly we had dined on the clean firm flesh of M's fish. The dog got its share, of course.

It didn't surprise me that we were wonderfully energized by the meal of such a fish from such a pool. The meal set us free to ramble on again confidently, now the sun was well set. The night was pleasantly cool and the stars came out to light us. Before we left the pool I noticed something hard to explain, for I hadn't seen M catch anything else, but three monstrous tiger-striped fish lay on the bank tied together nose to nose in a circle, open-mouthed, with tendrils like catfish and vicious teeth like sharks. They lay there working their gills forlornly, sadly expiring. Though I was overcome with sorrow for them, it seemed it was meant to be that they should die.

We eventually came upon a new road straight as a highway, and we progressed rapidly toward the not-Benin border now. That was my impression or hope, though M didn't say so, keeping her guard up. After the second night of traveling we might be beyond the influence of the king and out of danger of M's husband as well. No sooner did I have these thoughts, when the little dog ahead of us suddenly stopped, its long, pointed nose in the air, growling on a very low, violent note just audible to M and me. It hadn't barked, and deeply respecting its intelligence as I did, I knew that it smelled threatening humans and didn't want to give our presence away but just let me and M know. Its barely heard *grrrrrrrr* was heartening and reassuring. The fur on its back stood straight up over its muscles rippling down its back. It licked its chops and bared its teeth and took a few steps down the path pointing with its nose the direction from which the trouble would come, which was directly in front of us. I thought my little dog resembled a wolverine which I had seen once in a photo fighting a snake (a bad snake, a large one).

As quickly and quietly as possible we retreated back up the road a quarter of a mile and slipped into the forest behind some fallen trees that made a brushy little cave where we could wait, still close enough to the road that we'd be able to discern anyone passing on it. The dog stayed quiet now, alert, before us. About a half an hour passed, and a small band of men passed silently, not from the direction the dog had pointed, however, but out of the territory we'd left, from our rear if we had still been on the road. M raised her head to take a good look at their backs and concluded, "Men from my husband's country. I'm more of a danger to you than you are to me. There's more than one group of them, too."

The dog had not been wrong though. Another larger group approached the other way. Warriors were moving up and down the road in all directions searching. We stayed in our hiding place among the fallen logs for an hour until the warriors had finished reconnoitering and dispersed. As the dog gave no further warning, we set off again, walking a little faster, keeping a sharp eye out. The dog ran now ahead of us, now dropping behind, understanding perfectly that the danger might come from any direction.

"They are going back and forth between here and the border. They know we want to cross the border. They are circling around and there's going to be a crowd of them on every path. We need weapons."

"How far are we from the border?"

"Very near. But we can't go farther without weapons. Do you understand how serious this is?"

Certainly I did. It had been my mission for some time to reach the Far Country, where something waited for me that would round out things. The country began to descend. We crossed several streams and got our feet soaked. At each stream a guard was posted, and I was badly frightened by the first one, as the dog had not barked or even growled, and I didn't see him until he and M were deep in conversation. I tried to calm down. My dog had not so much as whimpered so I knew all was as it was supposed to be.

It was not a language I had heard before in Africa and it took a while before I suspected it was Hebrew. When they had finished speaking, and we passed on, as I had to go by the guard, I could not help noticing the scowl on his face as if he found it very disagreeable that I should move freely beyond his station in spite of all the persuasions and mollifications of M. He stiffened as I went by and gave me a piercing look but let me go on. After that the confrontations with the guards were not so alarming as M seemed to know them and have some means of identifying herself to them. Some of them were good natured and seemed to regard me in a friendly or at least tolerable way.

At the last crossing the routine was similar, except that the Israeli guard was more indifferent to me than hostile or friendly. I didn't count, or was just M's entourage. He was younger and obviously in awe of M, who did all the talking. In the streambed I saw the rusting hulk of some kind of military rifle. It gleamed an ominous pale yellow under a few inches of water, and as I leaned closer I saw it was bones, the skeleton of a gun, as if the gun had been alive, and this was its remains, in the shape of a slender bird—its delicate bony frame. Yes, the gun appeared to have been some kind of bird, for it reached out with impotent claws toward me as if wishing I would pull it out of the water and bring it to life again. In other words this was an old gun that had once been a flying creature. I regarded it for a long time.

M warned me that she would be away for a few minutes and walked away into the forest alone. The guard became friendly, offered me a cigarette, and spoke English to me with a strong accent. He remarked with a grin that it was good that we had come into "his" territory before I had gotten an "Arab knife in my ribs," as he put it. He asked me what I was doing in not-Benin, and as usual I had great difficulty explaining myself since I had no idea. I wanted to ask him the same thing. His smile had faded by the time I was finished mystifying the situation by whatever it was I mumbled. I didn't ask him anything.

He looked at me like I must be lying. But really I didn't know what to say even in the way of a good lie. However, he had no ill will and had just been asking, since M had explained everything to him. He yawned and I could tell he was just killing time. He glanced in the direction she had gone and relaxed. The silence between us finally became so oppressive that, since he had been so open in asking his question, I did ask him exactly what he, an Israeli soldier, was doing in not-Africa, and by now whatever superficial good will had existed between us was dissipated by unknowns beyond my imagining. Or it was just because no soldier of whatever nationality likes to be questioned about his mission, since privates in any army have no idea what strategy they are enforcing and don't like to be reminded of it. He didn't reply.

When M finally came back and interrupted our desultory nonconversation, she had abandoned her robe and turban and had donned a khaki army uniform and a purple beret. We pushed on, the young guard giving her a firm salute in farewell. The path descended ever more steeply to another stream and as we headed down into the small valley, she explained to me the obvious that her bedouin outfit had been a disguise, she was actually an Israeli army captain. That is, she was some sort of Israeli irregular officer operating behind the lines. Her husband also was a double agent, and in greater danger than we were, for if we were caught we stood a chance of being exchanged for Arab prisoners, but it would be the end for him, beheading would be his fate. That fat guy with the scimitar and bodyguards! I was sorry I had thought ill of him, because he had occupied the king with some business while M and I had made our escape. She had doubly good reasons for her caution in never telling me any of this until now but it had never been because he was after us. I was very sorry for all the ill will I had been bearing him. You never know.

"What are the Israelis doing around here?"

"This ground is full of diamonds, gold, oil, uranium, lithium, all kinds of 'ums' you name it. Wealth, dollars, shekels, and crazy minerals they're going to make intelligent rockets out of in the future and new telephones that provide you such great answers you don't even have to ask questions. The Americans are here behind the scenes of course. Like you, for instance."

That was the least of my concerns and I let it go. Now we passed more and more soldiers in uniform on the paths and each time M exchanged salutes with them, they stiffly and very respectfully saluted her back because of seeing some emblems on her cap and blouse. Once, when we were briefly alone, between soldiers, I remembered something, "Melusina, while you had that veil on, I couldn't, but now I'm going to," and reached out to caress her face, but she turned my hand away.

"Now you do it? We have business to take care of! We're here!"

My hand, in falling, awkwardly brushed her breast, which was soft underneath that army uniform. The tension set up by the stiff khaki cloth and her yielding breast created the more desire. I struggled to regain my seriousness. It seemed I could not understand this was life or death, or didn't care. We came to a small clearing amongst the trees. A squat cinderblock warehouse with a corrugated steel roof stood out incongruously in the green forest. Lying all over the ground outside the building were gun skeletons like the one I had seen in the streambed.

"Melusina, these guns look like birds," I said.

"Yes, they have hearts, lungs, bones, and wings, and they die, as they once lived, those guns. They have a life of their own and that is why they are extra valuable. Like I told you we need some guns if we're going to try to cross the border. But that's not the model we're after. We want the *other* model."

We entered the armory. Inside, we watched the women armorers at their work. The basic material from which the guns were made—the *other* model that M wanted—was meat. I mean raw red meat. Loin sections, whatever, were being sliced off bones and laid in silver trays for chemical treatment. After the chemical process, the meat was aged. By this means it was calcified, hardened, and turned green, the proper color as well as consistency for guns I surmised. At the other side of the room we saw examples of the finished material, dark green, grainy, hard and lustrous as jade or some kind of tough plastic. Now the stocks of the guns were stamped out and fitted with tiny wings which began to flutter. Their inner parts were machined and polished, and put together, greased, and oiled, and on a firing range a woman in a labcoat wearing ear protectors was testing them one by one as they came off the assembly line. It was a very good thing I had taken that target practice at the family reunion, I reflected, if I was going to have to handle a gun now. I was impressed how the woman personally ascertained each and every gun was in prime firing condition.

While I was absorbed in watching the different phases of the gun-making process, M had disappeared again and when she came out of a restroom in the corner, she was wearing a white robe and a white turban once more. So we were headed back into the bush again and she had donned her appropriate disguise. None of the Israeli armorers batted an eyelash at this. She was a known secret agent around here and could change at will. We had just stopped here to pick up some weaponry. She took a green gun for me, two for herself, and outside we found the dog standing guard for us, its eyes ablaze, its fur standing on end, and its teeth sharp as razors. It was all alone in the open. None of the guards were anywhere near it. You wouldn't pet such a dog. It had the air about it of belonging in the military as much as a colonel.

We left immediately down a path into the forest. After a few minutes, M stopped and confronted me with an honesty that told me we were soon to cross the border. She opened her robe, showed me a gold crucifix, and said, "As you can see, I really am a Christian. And these guns are made from—"

"The meat that perisheth not," I finished her thought for her.

"Exactly. They shoot straight and kill you dead, believe me, if you are not one of the faith. After which, you and me, we will live again to see another day. We are not far from the border now!"

Our little dog bounded ahead with something trailing out of its jaws. He had stolen a bone from one of the temporarily dead guns lying around on the ground awaiting resurrection. Suddenly he stopped short, sniffing the air, and dropped the bone. At the same time M's gun, which she had pointed before her as she ran, began to act like a diviner's rod and wouldn't point up the road any more, but insisted on swinging to the left and pointing into the forest pulling her along behind it. She took off in that direction, or was practically jerked through the air by it, leaving the road, and almost her feet, and the dog and I followed. Moments later came the pounding feet of a squad of bedouin soldiers as they raced up the path toward the base camp and armory. As much as I didn't care for that young guard who had waylaid me I wished I could warn him. I figured the Israelis could take care of themselves. M didn't hear a thing as all her attention was on keeping up with her gun, which she had gripped for dear life in her two hands outstretched before her. Full speed it pulled her on, now right, now left, the dog and I leaping bushes and fallen limbs and barely staying up with her. Whether it had life eternal, that gun had a life of its own, and she grasped it with all her might to keep it from flying away from her. The gun led us on and on. Abruptly the forest came to an end and silver mists floated before us over a wide expanse of river. She lowered her gun at last. That is, the diviner's rod had found its target and pointed at the ground. Dawn was breaking. This must be the border ahead. The green gun had shown us the place we should cross, as well as where to camp today.

We sat down and rested in some high grass only a few feet from the river while we waited for some transportation across the water to the other side and freedom. M full of confidence it seemed now so close to freedom pulled off her headdress and shook out her hair, which had turned back to that delightful strawberry blonde I remembered and loved. She laughed in her old way like we were on the beach of Lake Michigan. From her knapsack which I had not noticed till this moment she pulled out a picnic lunch—ham sandwiches! Whether a Coptic Christian or not, if she was an Israeli agent she was not kosher. Handing me mine her eyes were shining with fun, as we both must have remembered the morning we had first met. It might have been these sandwiches were made from that very ham she had insisted I enjoy that morning, I imagined. I very nearly relaxed since with our escape all but accomplished, she was her old self again and ready to have some fun. In fact, she had turned into her strawberry blonde, sexy, and slovenly self again, looking at me like I badly needed help.

Meanwhile my little dog had not relaxed his vigilance and he suddenly began to give out his low growl. He sat on his haunches and stared back up the trail into the forest, his eyes fixed and glittering. M and I leapt to attention just as a new band of the king's warriors burst into view and shouted with triumph when they saw they had found us. They were exultant to have found us at the last moment as we were just about to cross the river. They rushed straight at us but they had not reckoned on the dog who bolted forward and ripped huge mouthfuls of red flesh from their knees and haunches right and left. His speed and efficiency were absolutely amazing. Several of them lay on the ground screaming in agony losing blood rapidly. The others realizing they could not get by the dog reached for their bows strapped over their shoulders and pulled arrows from their quivers. They let loose a volley just as a small dhow powered only by a sail arrived at the shore and we dashed through the water up to our thighs and leapt aboard, a rain of arrows falling around us.

Until that moment the dhow had been of that strange but familiar two-dimensional variety of watercraft but as we jumped in, it acquired depth sufficient to gather us in and for that matter, the dimension of time, or timing, had been perfect. The Arab running the boat let loose a cord and the sail flapped sideways and caught the breeze and we were soon out of range of the arrows. My dog jumped in the water after us once we were out of danger, and he was a powerful swimmer, quickly reaching our side. M grabbed his belly and I caught his forelegs and we hoisted him into the boat. Shortly we were in the middle of the river as the breeze was fair. By some miracle we still had our ham sandwiches and finished them off with a great appetite relishing the open air after the closeness of the forest. We stared at the gleaming expanse of water before us feeling victorious.

But right in the middle of the river, no sooner had we finished our repast, and the dog licking some tasty warriors' blood from his chops, as we anticipated the farther shore, which had begun to approach, than an icy blast of wind caught the sail and ripped it clean from the mast. The temperature dropped dramatically below freezing and a fine hail blew violently from the sky.

The dhow was equipped with a small outboard which our driver fired up, but as we neared land we could see the docking was entirely icebound and we couldn't get near. Up the river we roared faster and faster in hopes of making some landing before everything froze over. For such a small motor we achieved terrific speed, and once nearly ran over some swimmers who were performing a feat of endurance in the cold waters. Each time we saw a small beach in the jungle our hopes shot up, but everything was getting coated with rime and the hail and snow were building up. Blocks of ice protruded far into the river from the shore and I wondered how we would ever get to land again. The only explanation for this I could come up with was that if we couldn't get the little dog to the North Pole, he had brought a bit of the Arctic down to us, and so it seemed. He stood on his hind legs in the prow and sniffed the frigid air with delight, panting wildly, his tongue hanging out.

216

In our light clothes we were about freezing to death and I wondered if our strange trials would ever cease. Again and again we passed frozen clearings, which our guide slowed to inspect, only to veer out into the open river again, when suddenly he cut the motor, and made a wide loop back towards the last landing we had passed, and slowly we approached a gray-white beachfront looking no more hospitable than the others, except that a band of native people were warming themselves on shore by a fire, whom he seemed to know. They had kept a narrow path into the river clear of ice and now they waded out to pull us in.

I'd wondered if we were ever going to make it before freezing to death but at the last moment we did. They had a big fire going on the shore. But we didn't need it, for as soon as we hopped out of the dhow and stood on the ground, everything melted, the sun came out, the temperature shot up, and we were in the fiery tropics once more. A lot of wild friendly talk ensued as everyone welcomed the change, except the dog, who had been in his element.

Although we had made it across the river, and the border, and found ourselves on the other shore, maybe in the Far Country by now, I hoped, it was still necessary to conceal ourselves, as there were spies everywhere. We were quite exposed here and M did not like the idea of pushing ahead thoughtlessly. Her idea was we must still travel only by night even if we had made it safely across. It was just when you had met with success that you must remain doubly cautious. Now that we had made it out of not-Benin never had M seemed so wise and sure-handed to me, so I was ready to be patient. It had grown very hot again once we were off the exposed river. I was just as glad M wanted us to hide and rest, for it would have been hard walking in the extreme heat. The river had returned to its torrid self, and it must have been just a passing snowstorm. The green life along the bank was thick and torpid. The rest of this day we spent under water—or at least up to our necks in it. The river dropped off sharply from steep banks. The water was about eighty degrees. Through a green slip in the thick bushes and vines, we climbed down into the golden black water neck deep only a few feet from shore. M paddled around and cut some hollow reeds for breathing tubes, if we needed them. We hid ourselves in a pocket nearly sealed off by stands of blue reeds and rafts of purple water lilies.

The little dog rooted himself into a shady spot close by. No one would ever spot him and if they did, they'd think he was a wild animal and soon find out too.

In the end we took turns sleeping with our heads resting on the bank, while the other kept watch. We heard hunters only once all afternoon, if that's who they were. M suspected everyone, every sound almost. Two long canoes full of gowned men cruised by the opposite of the barges on the Missouri River I had seen that day at my family reunion, bursting into our vision through the reeds with their vivid roundness and fullness ready to roll over everyting. M had selected a good pocket in the lush vegetation with an angle of visibility onto the main current such that the canoes were visible to us, and we potentially to them, for only two or three minutes. But they never looked around. They seemed so close we could have reached out and touched them. The canoes were so full of tribesmen they seemed about to burst at their seams and elbow each other off into the river, and their prows thrust up out of the water at every stroke by the full crews. The animation of the crews and the coursing long boats was extraordinary. It seemed to me the excitement had to do with the missing Prince Alomar, even on this side of the river. They were still looking around for him I guessed.

We ducked under water and breathed through the reeds till they'd passed. This required keeping a firm grip on one's tendency to panic because the air came through the tube only a very little at a time in a thin stream that required not only patience but imagination to assure oneself that it kept coming. Dozing off was an unpleasant experience for one was woken by one's mouth and nose filling with water.

Right by my head was a beautiful purple flower, the largest among dozens produced by a water plant with silver leaves. Under water I opened my eyes, and in the surprisingly clear water I could see all about me the delicate stalks of the plants rising from the bottom.

When the canoes had passed, it was my turn to rest my head on the bank and sleep. Children's voices woke me from a confused slumber. M touched me to whisper the danger was somewhat downriver, if it was danger, for it just seemed to be children playing loudly. Perhaps they might give us away. After a while, when it was clear from their shouts that the kids were entirely preoccupied with each other, I swam out a few yards— just for something to break the day's tedium, and M didn't seem to mind. Treading deep water against a slight current, I was able to see down the shore far enough to spot a commotion in the bushes just as one child, perhaps the smallest, received a shove that sent him splashing into the river, who managed with an agile move to catch another by the ankle, tenaciously holding on to pull him in too, and the two tumbled and thrashed, whooping. The sense of peace and innocence of children's games weighed on me with delicious nostalgia. To have been a kid again like these on the riverbank and not a hunted man! To have been able to splash about and enjoy this water and not have to cower uncomfortably in a nightmarish sleepy haze in it. I wondered vaguely if by crossing the river border we had finally arrived in that "Far Country" by now in spite of our caution. I supposed I would find out.

The pack of boys played a game amazing to watch. One of them had a large tortoise, which he raised against his chest by the edges of its shell so that the animal's scaled belly was exposed and for a moment I thought the child was wearing a yellow breastplate. He took one step into the river, lowered the tortoise into the shallow water, and let it go, and the boys at once stopped their fighting to swim after it. Soon one of them stumbled up onto the bank clutching the big tortoise to his own chest, and now released the reptile again, and this was repeated again and again, a dozen dives and retrievals, until at last the tortoise managed to escape or they just let it go. The tumult died down. I thought it wise at this moment to drift noiselessly back into hiding. But they were leaving the water. Their laughter and chatter trailed away, and the kids must have disappeared back into the forest or home to their village.

The purple blooms glowed and bobbed about my head till I felt my retinas burned by their hot color. I was mesmerized by their harmonious undulations in the feeble current. They no longer seemed individual flowers but an upsurge of living spirit, a dancing swath of purple life dividing the water and the sky. Time hung so heavy, and each waking into the needling sunshine was so painful that the blossoms which had been a grace took on the quality of a giant purple wound festering at the edge of the river whose waters were poisonous.

A voice boomed over the river, "THE FLOWER ARRANGEMENT IS CORRUPT BECAUSE DONATIONS ARE GIVEN TO IT!" I about jumped out of my skin and my head came upright out of the water and I glanced around, but not even a chorus of hunters could have produced that voice. M to my amazement said, "Yes, I heard it. I guess you want me to tell you what it means." As I was doubly speechless to hear that, and weary enough not to take umbrage at her characteristic tone but just stared blankly and pitifully at her, she softened. "We're not far from a sacred place. You may hear a thing or two now, as well as see something all right."

Silence deepened as day departed and evening came. All life had headed home to the cookfires. A few minutes later, she pointed over my shoulder and said, "Have you seen that?" In the air one of the blooms seemed to be floating, as if it had come dislodged and just risen straight up in the air like a balloon whose string had been cut, or like Smoky, I thought with a pang. But on closer appraisal I could see it was a perfect sphere, lustrous as a ruby. I thought it must be just one of the purple spots before my eyes caused by staring at the flowers overmuch, but M said, "You ought to polish that."

I reached out and managed to touch it. But the touch of my finger sent it away in the air. It rose to a height and slowly faded from sight. I stared after it for a long time but it did not come back. "Too bad," she said, "but you'll get another chance, you always do." When I looked down again I saw something hideous on the shore I had not seen before, a pair of gigantic vertebrae with clumps of decaying gray meat still attached. M said it was a kind of huge reptile that lived in the river that was hunted for its nourishing flesh. Those sections must have been too heavy for the hunters to carry away. They had taken most of it. The hunting must be good around here and the meat plenty. Even as I looked at it, one of the vertebrae came loose from the bank and fell into the water with a resounding plop and slowly sailed off in the current ponderously as a tree stump. I tried to imagine a lizard or something large enough to contain under its skin such bones. My own bones felt vulnerable under the water. Perhaps there were piranhas in these waters. I wished the night would come and we could pick up our journey, giant snakes or no giant snakes, and get on with it. It was human snakes M was concerned about, she said, because near the border were spies and foreign agents aplenty.

M must have read my impatient thoughts and she told me we would leave the protective river soon and the first thing we would do when we left the border behind tonight would be to visit the sacred temple in the "city" and make our offerings for our safe journey and our crossing out of not-Benin into not-not-

221

Benin. Like her father she spoke of everything in double and triple negatives whereas I aspired to a simple positive, a unitary Far Country, which I hoped to reach at last. She knew that though. It was just her way of keeping me honest, and serious. You didn't just slip into the far Country by happenstance but achieved first a new way of thinking. The way she alluded to a city while we were yet in the depths of the wilderness made me realize it wouldn't the usual sort of city. I pictured it as a far ranging fabulous jewel of a city with four sides like a "diamond" but ruby in color shimmering through green forest boughs from a long distance yet, as we approached. I began to be certain we must on the outskirts of the Far Country and perhaps it and the city were the same thing. As she was describing our sacred itinerary to me, my eyes rose and I saw in the bushes over her head two green-and-yellow parrots with their orange beaks crossed against each other like lovebirds, and took this as a good omen. They seemed to be kissing and caressingly pecking each other in purest love and homage to God, bringing the tips of their beaks together and then crossing them and rubbing them along their sides. Their beaks made the sign of the cross and I began to be hopeful.

In the blazing late afternoon, about five o'clock, M and I held each other gently under water. This happened so innocently and thoughtlessly, without a word from either of us, seemingly even without our intent, with so little transition from sleep and dreams, it seemed but a dream too. We hardly sent out a ripple over the surface of the water, and if we made any sounds they were indistinguishable from the natural sounds of the forest and its birds and insects. And yes, under water, intertwining among the slender silver stems of the water plants, holding our breaths as we plunged down, with our feet rooted in the mud, I touched her face fleetingly, and it glistened strangely. All in all it had been a restful interlude, even under water. In spite of some disturbing sights and the feeling of being still on the margins, things were peaceful. Everything had changed.

Afterward, I was not actually certain I had touched her face, however, it may have been I only brushed her ear. Things were confused as it was the sort of lovemaking you don't do but just happens to you. Now we would enter the Far Country, I felt certain, although M didn't call it that. When the little dog appeared above us on the bank, sitting on its haunches, yawning, and grooming itself, we knew it was time to go. Dusk had not yet quite fallen, but in the forest it was shadowy, and after the dazzling water all afternoon the path before us at first seemed impenetrable and dim. The dog took a little swim before we left the river. He shook himself brightly and dried off, but we could not shake ourselves and M and I dripped water down the trail the first few steps, particularly M with her long white gown, which stuck to the curves of her body. Her skin had grown a dark olive shade again and her hair returned to bluish black which she wound tight under her turban with a flourish.

Soldiers could be heard approaching us in a quick step march heading back toward the river, though we couldn't see them. It happened so fast we had no chance to hide ourselves before they came around a bend and were upon us. In spite of a moment of panic, it didn't matter because we were safely across the border and for all I knew in the Far Country. Anyway they couldn't touch us here apparently, for neither the dog nor M seemed worried. We just stood in the open road as they flew past and around us. They couldn't do anything to harm us and didn't seem to remark us. Even the little dog seemed surprised and didn't even bark. We held onto our imperishable green guns and maybe that seemed to ward them off. Some of them veered into the verges of the undergrowth going around us. In their midst appeared a shining chariot just big enough to hold one passenger pulled by two of the soldiers.

The golden cart nearly ran us over before we jumped out of its way. The passenger seeing M craned his neck and half stood causing the rickshaw to careen momentarily on one wheel. "Hey baby!" he called to M and grinned and waved at her. He seemed to be drunk and wild in contrast to the warriors who were pulling him who did not look our way but dug in and gained speed at once dead serious. He was staring back trying to get her attention.

"Hey yourself!" she called back scornfully, lowering her eyes and her gun.

As quick as that they had disappeared up the trail the way we had just come, back toward the river.

"That was Prince Alomar, in case you didn't know," she said to me.

"You're kidding!"

"No I'm not. Such a fool. But it's not him, it's the idea of him that the people depend on. They won't be worrying about us anymore now. We're free."

"He seemed to recognize you," I remarked drily, but she did not reply.

With our green guns in our hands we followed a path along the river for a number of miles until long after midnight. At one point M vanished and it was just me and the dog bounding beside me but I didn't worry. Far ahead I glimpsed a tawny lean lioness out hunting, her head low and her stealthy movements following the contours of the forest floor. Her footfalls on her big sure pads were deadly and powerful. The lioness seemed to be leading us or rushing before us to scout out trouble.

The forest began to thin out and we found ourselves on a hilly plain under the starry sky. Black horses appeared out of the mists and thundered gracefully beside us, kicking up their heels, snorting, their manes streaking like flags. One nipped at the gun in my hands and took a big bite out of it, flung its head to rip out the meat. With that it raced off with its friends, clods of earth flying, starlight gleaming from the horses' black coats rippling over their flanks. My green gun grew itself back into a fully loaded and functioning lethal weapon in less than a second. One horse had stopped, however. It was a mare and it must have a colt for its nipples were full. But it wasn't a colt but a little golden headed child running by its side. Finally the child ceased its play and turned to suck from the mare. I paused to watch this spectacle, as there was everything of strange tenderness and goodness in it, as astonishing as it was. There was something disturbingly familiar about this child though, and after a moment I thought it must be the dwarf, because of the way it had mounted on top of the horse and was swinging its legs as if it were the little master of all it could see. At this, I hurried on to catch up with M and my dog, who had burst far ahead of me. I ran a while and soon enough caught up with them. When I glanced back over my shoulder I could see the tiny child playing in a patch of wildflowers, innocent and wild. I was relieved to see it wasn't the dwarf after all, apparently, but I wasn't sure.

A soft gleam on the skyline and a faint throbbing in the distance suggested human habitation and activity far ahead. These slowly became unmistakable, and M's step brightened and quickened the more, as we headed right into the thick of it, not going to shy away from people any more, for this must be the temple and sacred grove in the "city" she had mentioned at the border, where all visitors were pilgrims, no one could rightfully touch us, and perhaps the taboo was strong enough that they wouldn't.

As we headed ever deeper into the Far Country, I felt more at peace than I had in a long, long time. Even though this country was new to me, I felt a strong attraction to it. This had everything to do with M's familiarity and even expertise regarding the culture around here. I was happy to be in her capable hands. We were passing through exquisitely cultivated tracts of farmland. Unexpectedly the smell of water filled the air. The river which must have curved around became a solemn, ponderous presence again beside us. It was like coming upon a trusty old friend, for it was the river that had separated us from the hostile warriors. On a rise in the land we caught a first glimpse of a vast lake or even the sea. The river rolled forward eagerly to meet it. The city must be a port, with the fertile land at its back. M gazed on it with equanimity and expectation.

Dawn was not far off when we reached the sacred city's busy outskirts. We were part of an early crowd, as people emerged from sidepaths, on their way to market with baskets of produce and loaves of bread and platters of fish balanced on their heads. Or maybe these were sacrifices. We joined the people who trudged beside us without notice. M stepped off the path and led us through a slip in a grove of trees into a pleasantly laid out park. The dog stood guard as she stripped off her white turban and gown. Underneath she was wearing the simple garb of a peasant woman, a flowered cloth wound about her and knotted above her breasts. We found the path again as it entered the city and moved along as one with the boisterous throng. A bright thread of silver in the east suggested morning as we broke onto a vast marketplace, still dark and half-deserted, illumined in splotches of bonfires, flames in braziers, and dancing torches. Vendors were just setting up, and we dodged goat carts, wheelbarrows, baskets shouldered on swinging poles, baskets on uplifted women's foreheads piled with fruits and fresh breads in mounds eight feet in diameter and five feet high—baskets the size of delivery trucks balanced on the women's foreheads. Down one aisle after another we made our way through the labyrinth of the marketplace which was getting more active by the minute as we passed through it.

The ghostly mists of dawn rose up and parted revealing a tumult of business being established for the day until there were no more empty rows for us to dart down and we struggled ahead through the thick market day crowd. As I distinctly saw M palm a piece of fruit from one stall, I grew bold as we passed an unattended stand and grabbed something for myself, a small round red fruit like a plum, but with lots of little seeds instead of one large one. As I bit into its supersweet delicious flesh, the sun came over the treetops and flooded the market with full delightful daylight. Like colorful beads on a thousand necklaces, glistening red, purple, and yellow fruits hung in intricate displays revealing at once the generosity of nature and the care of man, and woman, for most of the market stalls were manned by women, and that sensation of giddy gratitude I had been experiencing periodically all morning welled up inside me as I chewed the tiny sweet seeds and swallowed the nectar.

"THE DAY WILL COME WHEN YOU WON'T NEED THESE ANY MORE," boomed that voice again, taking me back from my pleasure. The fruits? How could you not need delicious fruits like these? Nearly tripping on the hem of my robe (I had acquired a robe somehow), I looked around uneasily not wanting to be the source of a disturbance, but nobody seemed to have heard the voice except for me, and M of course. I looked into my hand in which lay a round, desiccated black apple. Then in a rush of inexplicable horror I dropped the withered, coal-black apple and holding the skirts of my robe raced to catch up with M who was moving ahead, lively and determined. I had fallen so far behind I would never have seen her if I hadn't recognized that daub of seablue, seagreen glimmering gauze no bigger than a seabird way ahead in the sullen, earthen colors of the workday throng. She had changed costume once again, this time to that watery sheath she had worn that time she had laughed sadly at me from the top of a tall building in America before she had dashed herself to pieces in the street. The memory overcame me. She wasn't going to pull a stunt like that again? I couldn't afford to lose her now. Maybe she was just having one of her jokes. Holding her azure veil over her mouth over which she stared at me with some irritation, she scolded, "You'll make us late." For what? I wondered.

This was a great river town, the outer suburbs ran along the river for miles, and the river was wide, flowing toward the sea. It was a seaport too, with miles of beaches crammed with fishing canoes, and wharves that supplied the market. The market stalls were full of fresh and salt water creatures for sale, both great and small, fish swimming in buckets, and laid out dried and salted, tigerstriped, speckled, pink, green, and brown, fish round as vases, stingrays like kites, barbelled fish, and clean-shaven, giant eels, starfish, and pails overflowing with wriggly eels, white and black crabs, blue crayfish, water snakes, baby crocodiles, fish roe, fish heads, shellfish, snails the size of loaves, frogs, turtles, sea urchins, and animals I'd never seen before, from both the sea and the river. Hidden in the scaly, finny, slimy, slithering, beshelled profusion until at the last moment I nearly ran into him surfacing from the waves, rolling before my eyes like a giant terrapin or hermit crab, then disappearing again so perfect was his adaptation and disguise, a coat encasing him head to toe and a headdress too made entirely from clacking shells, hundreds of colored shells like fat beads or countless facets of crab-chain mail protecting this old wizard, nothing but gnarled fingers and wizened face showing as if floating independently of the rest of him which seemed to belong more to the stalls and pails of snails and lobsters he sniffed at, than to himself in his long robe of horn creaking and cracking, he fingered sea slugs, inspected shell-less blobs with naked antennae, as if he might offer them a home in his cloak, until what magic, what potion, or tasty soup on this old fellow's fire would they grace?

Water rushing away from the river in a canal for irrigation, or hygiene, or perhaps it were some sacral purpose, bisected the market and blocked our path and we had to follow along it. Fires lit this channel every fifty feet or so and into the fires attendants with baskets hanging from their shoulders threw handfuls of a powdery matter that made the flames leap up pinkly, giving the water an intermittent rose glow sweet as syrup. Swimming in the roiling, oily, flame-lit waters, some gliding by fast, others fighting the current and even moving upstream against it, giant snakes poked their goggle eyes the size of baseballs into the air to stare at the people like watchdogs guarding the trough. You wouldn't want to fall in. I couldn't be sure where the market ended and the temple began—they seemed to blend into each other somehow—but perhaps the snakes in the trough made the demarcating line. On the other side of the rushing canal Melusina in her blue-green sari stood waiting for me, I wasn't sure how she had gotten over there. I walked on a ways until I crossed on a narrow bridge to reach her. At this moment, as I thought to look back for him, I realized the dog was no longer with me. For a moment I worried about him, but a glance at the crowded stalls of the market suggested endless stray, slimy treats for a little dog, sloshing over the sides of buckets and things, reassured me. No wonder he was tarrying someplace, nibbling at starfish and sea urchins, and anyway he'd be well fed. I didn't doubt he'd catch up with us later. No one would be able to steal that wily and vicious creature. He must be having a feast of marine life. He'd find us when he was ready, but I felt uneasy without the dog.

A black monkey, almost dead or moribund, keeling over at a forty-five degree angle, tied to a stake on top of a table, stared at me with hollow eyes. To the top of its head someone had affixed a silver disc like a crown, which gave the final touch of the horrifying and macabre. When I looked more closely and I saw the creature was black because it had been roasted and burned in a fire, and its skin was charred and cracked, the cooked flesh showing pinkly where the skin had flaked off, it seemed to be not a monkey at all, but a cooked child, stuck on a pole, wearing a silver crown.

"Why . . . can it be . . . a child?" I whispered.

I clutched M's arm for support as I nearly lost my balance and fell against the table.

"It's the child," she said matter of factly.

At its feet was a bowl into which people had flung copper coins, and M threw a few pennies into it. I breathed a sigh. That made sense of it. It was some sort of pagan religious effigy. I had read about such things in anthropology class in my one year at college, the stuff of scary tales and science fiction, too. "Oh, I see, it's a fertility symbol," I mumbled. M lost her temper. "Will you have to understand everything? Either things should be positively thrilling, but mainly there to make you feel good, or else they go in a glass box, further proof that the world is as boring and convenient as possible!" That seemed very unfair and I was on the verge of losing my cool when all I wanted was to keep from losing my mind. I suspected we were not yet that far into the Far Country after all. Some bad old vibes had crept into our exchange that reminded me of times when we had not been on the same wavelength at all, me and M.

"Come on, this is not the northshore of Chicago," drawled M in a familiar tone, pulling me on. I knew what it wasn't, but wondered what it was. We passed great piles of dried dead animals on pallets, the way hides are stacked one on another. But these were the whole animals dried and stretched out in mounds fifteen feet high, various in color. I stared at them, but kept my mouth shut as we passed by. I didn't need any more of M's observations for the moment. I wondered at the meaning of it if there was one. We were no longer in the market but on the edges of the temple grounds.

In a square in what may have been the center of the town thousands of years ago stood the ruins of a temple, no more left to it than a stone staircase, a half dozen marble pillars, and a few piles of chalky rocks where walls had once risen to a roof now open to flocks of birds and the elements that were steadily wearing it down. Surely this was of some archaeological interest I was about to tell M, remembering how she had wished to bring tourists to the Graves of the Warriors where we had slept. I was about to laugh and give it to her when I noticed three fascinating symbols carved in the top step of the temple, on the left the moon, on the right the sun, in the middle something I couldn't make out, something enigmatic that moved me deeply but obscurely, part shelled creature, an insect, riding sheaves of corn, and partly a man in a cowl with his arm holding his cape across the lower part of his face while he peered out at me with penetrating living eyes. I was compelled to walk toward this carved symbol, which shifted as I moved. The man ran away, but in a snail shell, in sheaves of grass, something graceful and flowing touched my imagination, promising to put to flight the whole accustomed order of things.

"Come on," said M. "We're late."

Late for what I wondered, as if in such antiquity one could possibly be late or early for anything. Still, I harkened to her for I expected something up ahead in the way of a fruitful sacrifice. I turned and over my shoulder stared blindly back on the trials and tribulations of countless ages, expired under the gaze of the strange symbols, which seemed yet to live dimly on, far off in time or the universe somewhere, their last traces in the stone washing away inexorably, hinting at eternity.

We ascended the steps, how I wasn't sure, even as I stared back at them. On the floor of the temple was a lamb with no head. I'm not sure why I hadn't seen it at once except that it was so bright around here. The poor lamb was no longer bleating; all was silence. The slaughter had just taken place, still fresh. But no priest or executioner around. No blood either, everything neat and clean and done up right. The headless lamb stood quite alone in the temple. It had been skinned too, but again so freshly that the lamb still stood on its own legs, though just now it was beginning to slump, to fall to its knees. It nodded its headless neck to me in the most pathetic gesture that would have been gruesome if it hadn't been so terribly, terribly sad. The stump of neck was an abyss of pathos as if somehow it still possessed the power of sight and appealed to me. The stunned tears stood out in my eyes at the sight of the slaughtered lamb. I felt the meek and strange power of everything in the temple.

"You can only make out the pity and horror in such a thing," said M, dragging me on, "not the deeper truth."

Just then men approached with plates and knives. They were going to butcher the lamb for a feast. I wondered how I was going to deal with such things if they kept on coming at me at this rate around here in the temple. I hesitated, thinking vaguely that I should take some meat, or that there was someone I ought to take some meat to, but M was insistent that we keep going, which was fine by me as I had no appetite.

I had the queer apprehension that Melusina was right and that my reactions to everything were inappropriate and false. This thought cheered me up, because I was not so different from anybody else, and in that case not only I but everybody is wrong, not a new idea of mine but one that didn't usually cheer me up so. I insisted on it to M that it was not only I who was wrong.

"Oh my God, they must all be right! Come around here with me!" We were heading up a rocky path at the side of the temple. On the other side of the temple was a very different sort of a church building, a homey, familiar little redbrick structure that could be nothing else but a small hometown Baptist or Methodist mission. I had seen plenty of them in not-Africa already without really seeing them. They so reminded me of home, as mzungus bring their own boring architecture with them tirelessly, and had so depressed me with the thought that Americans or Englishmen were over here telling people what to do and believe in, that I shunned them, refused to even see them. But this one was very strange juxtaposed on the ancient temple. To see such a little homey shrine was comfortable and welcome as a slice of apple pie just at this disturbing moment. We climbed down the side of the temple cliff to approach the brick church. The service was breaking up and people in their best Sunday clothes were coming out the doorway, so M had been quite right in fearing we'd be late. She now seemed to relax as if we'd made it in time after all, although I couldn't see why, since the church was letting out. The crowd surging out soon engulfed us, and this seemed to be to M's liking who indicated to me we should just follow along with them. An usher was aggressively passing the alms bucket, as if they hadn't collected enough inside. He thrust it against my chest. But I hadn't even been in church and this was just what I disliked about churches, their materialistic and greedy side! What did I care if they wanted to build an addition—or send another missionary to not-Africa? We were in not-Africa, maybe they wanted to send a missionary to the not-States. Well, I supposed I could contribute to that. I pulled out all of my remaining not-Benin notes (because I had hidden a few in my shoe) and thrust them in the pot. I recalled the story in the New Testament of the widow's two mites. It struck me I had given my all quite effortlessly and I felt pleased. Then I remembered the voice we had heard boom over the river which had said something about the flowers being corrupt because you gave a donation to them, and I questioned M about this anxiously.

"Well, you always make a distinction, don't you?" she replied, her voice rising. "With you being on the right side of things!"

I really didn't get what she meant by that and the petulance in her voice was all too familiar. For a moment I panicked and believed she might turn on her heel and disappear, or just float away into the sky, or break into a hundred pieces. Someone in the crowd remarked loudly enough to be heard above the hubbub, "The goddess must return to the watery realm." I wondered what was meant by that and found it alarming. But I recalled the goddess with her teapot from the northside of Chicago and the recollection was very pleasant. M gave a good-natured sigh and squeezed my hand.

At least it was a familiar Christian scene, even if it wasn't maybe the Far Country yet after all. I walked with M and the African crowd in their Sunday best, following a path that led to the left from the church, down behind it, down a slope, in a downward spiral quite sharply, so that the church was no longer visible any more above the heads of the crowd behind us when I turned to look. The noon sunshine was now blinding in any case and it was not possible to see beyond the throng in any direction, and we had descended into a pit. The grass was very bright green on either side of the path, and then a hill stood up ahead of us abruptly with the black mouth of a cave yawning near the top of it. I was only barely conscious of any of this because I felt very real and not a tourist and ready to see things as they really are in all their sacredness or whatever.

Among the African parishioners in their threadbare but starched and ferociously clean dark suits and bleached white shirts and brightly colored dresses I was astonished to realize the guy in front of me was a white guy. He looked like a real down-home country Baptist all right, with suspenders and a bald head and patches of sweat under his shirtsleeves. Once when he turned his head I recognized him and tried to remember from where. It was one of those things. He was an ardent believer, mumbling a prayer out loud to himself, and punctuating it with fervent Amens and Thank the Lords, all delivered solo. He hummed a hymn to himself, inserting a few holy roller phrases, a regular one-man choir. Really, the zealot was extremely funky in his stained white shirt giving off an odor. Next to the left suspender was a round black spot so intensely filthy black I was unable to tear my eyes from it, spot yawning black as the mouth of the cave above our heads from which now issued a loud moan. Where was he coming from and what vision had he mislaid? The impression he gave was of no longer caring, sure God was on his side in a self-righteous and even belligerent sort of way. He stretched his arms up toward the cave and gave out with a hallelujah the next time a loud moan rained down on us. He was bending his torso forward rhythmically in time to the hymn he was singing to himself. This ardent and funky believer began to sharply depress me. I became uncomfortably aware that hideous groans and moans were issuing from the ugly black cave over our heads. I looked to M to see if we could move to another spot in the crowd that had by now stopped right below the cave, or better yet get out of here, but M just patted my arm. I felt a sharp erotic pang for her out of place in the sacred setting.

A real scream came out of the cave directly above us making my hair stand on end. Somebody was being seriously tortured. I turned around and asked a young African man wearing a midnight blue suit, immaculate white shirt, and wide tie from circa 1940 that misguided missionaries must have provided him what was going on in the cave, and he replied, "The saint is being martyred." The screams of torment became louder and no longer stopped, or stopped just long enough for the saint to get his breath and start again. It was a sobbing inhuman howl from devilish tortures beyond imagining. The sustained, awesome shrieks were certainly most terrifying. When believers of the Church speak of the old martyrs, they never conceive of anything like that noise. A woman now stepped out of the cave and slowly made her way down the hill to the crowd. Her hair was full of light and she wore a long white smock like an acolyte's. She held a little book before her that seemed to guide her footsteps. The African behind me whispered into my ear, "The disciple, the priestess." Gently the people at the front of the crowd pushed a dark man forward toward her out of their midst, a handsome young man whose chest was bare and whose hands were bound behind him, with a glowing and transfixed expression on his face worn with such conviction it almost obliterated his features in an insane look of rapture (so it seemed to me). "Alomar! Alomar!" cried the watchers as one. It was the King's son! But it couldn't be. The disciple took his bound arm and led him up the hill and into the cave. The last thing I saw of them was the beatific smiles on both their faces. Soon a second voice joined the first and there were two martyrs being made. It was a duet of raving howls. No wonder the king had been worried. I wanted to protest to M that she had said the band of warriors heading back to the village were escorting Alomar in their midst in that chariot, but M took my arm and held it so firmly that the words stopped in my throat. My beloved little dog had disappeared someplace, I remembered, with a sickening, dropping sensation.

So this was where the king's son had been taken all along. The priestess came out of the cave once more and started down to us. This time she had put away the book and was carrying a torch, its flame barely discernible in the bright sunlight. When she had come down from the hill the crowd parted for her and she started through it. As I watched her approach me, I enjoyed some exquisite feelings I can tell you. By now the noise from the cave was a steady roar, like a subway train at rush hour. The priestess calmly picked her way, sometimes hesitating as the people pressed back from her. Patiently she let them make way for her, which they did with alacrity. If she was playing "tag," they didn't want to be "it." Her smile tranquilized everybody especially after she had passed them by, while the mighty roars of Alomar and the other saint seemed to paralyze some, to give others the shakes and cause their eyes to roll up, and to open the throats of many in hosannas and song. The crowd was babbling in tongues. An unknown but certain eternity presented itself to one's capacity to hope beyond the screams of enormous pain. The woman kept getting closer and closer. No one in the crowd bobbed his or her head more devotedly, sang his songs more religiously and hopefully than the white guy in the suspenders in front of me. I couldn't take my eyes from the crude black spot next to the left suspender, which suddenly leapt a foot in the air as the priestess shoved her torch under his nose and touched him, surprising him and indicating that he was next, who now backed away in fear and doubt holding his hands high in supplication. He almost stepped on my foot. I was glad she was after him and not me, I can tell you. But M was calmly squeezing my hand. I had a look at his face in profile as he turned aside to her, a study in being profoundly and impossibly caught out. His head seemed to want to keep bobbing and even to move forward toward the woman, but his feet kept shuffling backward. His body was going two directions, the top toward her fatal embrace and the bottom in reverse out of town. He was nodding harder and harder in panic and he let out a yowl of awesome apostasy, under the priestess's fingertip, that torch breathing sulfur under his nose and singeing his stubble. Then they reached for him. Hands of the crowd reached out for him from every direction, helping him forward as if kindly. Everybody seemed glad he had won the prize and not them and they meant to give him their support. To his credit, he regained some control though he didn't stop groaning in fear. He allowed himself to be propelled forward by the crowd and by the acolyte, who suddenly turned around and gave me a beautiful, beatific smile, the smile of a Mary or a Beatrice I might say, hopeful of peace and promising wisdom. I was not entirely reassured.

As she went back up the hill leading him by the hand, her hair lifted with the light as in a breeze and even his bald dome diffidently shone. She and her torch had transfixed the new victim, who stumbled after her, still singing to himself. I caught hold with my eyes of that black spot on the guy's shirt by his left suspender and followed it all the way up the hill until it was swallowed by the total blackness of the cave. The black spot and the entrance to the cave blended into one blazing abyss. Soon it was a threesome of roars and howls, a regular barbershop quartet minus the one cast to the lions, was my involuntary defensive black humor, as I had no real defense any longer, smirking to myself in a silly way, sweating in the heat with the moans from the hill threatening me with madness, had it not been for M's presence on my arm.

Gravediggers got to work on a plot of land to one side of the hill. Now and then we could hear their spadework, and see shovelfuls of dirt fly through the air. An African priest in a white smock like the acolyte's marched to the side of the graves and sprinkled seed into each of them. At once flocks of sparrows swooped down and pecked at the seed. One of the sparrows flew over to me and perched on my hand. I stared over at the freshly opened graves. There were four of them. The priest finished planting and scattering the seed and walked back up the hill and along with others helped bring down the first body, and then next came Alomar's, and then the old boy with his suspenders. While this was happening there was a commotion behind me, and I and the rest of the crowd were pushed aside by a procession bearing the burned body of the child, who was to be buried next to Alomar and the others, so someone explained to me. Reeling, I had room in my religious feelings of awe to be relieved of an overpowering curiosity as to who all was to be buried, since that made four. But then somebody said, no, the child would not be buried.

For the moment the leaders of the procession made some fuss and set the child down under a great tree, with its back against the tree, which I would have said looked strangely like a fir or pine tree had this not been an equatorial country. I was moved to take a closer look at it and the resemblance increased because the people had tied little cakes and balls of popped corn to its branches so that the child was sitting under the tree like one big overdone, well-cooked Christmas present. Around the tree the sparrows were swooping as they were over the open graves full of seed and I was touched that the people had put out the

237

popped corn on the tree limbs out of some obscure symbolism and now the birds were flocking to it and being nourished by it also. I wanted to have a look at this charming sight and I walked up close to the tree only to find something more grisly, but perfectly normal, I supposed, going on. This huge tree was very old and had lots of dead limbs and dead portions of trunk also, for the birds were flitting past the cornballs entirely and clutching the bark of the tree to peck at it and root out from it little slimy white grubs. No doubt this was completely normal and natural and struck me as slightly repulsive only because I had been expecting some sentimental Christmas card scene of the sparrows pecking the Christmas balls, while instead they of course preferred succulent pale larvae for which the old tree was one huge nest. Reality as always provided a symbolism of another order if only one could ascend to a position from which to actually understand it.

With a pang I realized once more that my little dog had disappeared, when we entered the temple grounds, and I no longer had my little loyal, vicious ferret pet. It made me feel naked and vulnerable. I wished for my little dog with all my heart and missed him terribly. I wondered poignantly if I would ever take him to the North Pole, and feared not.

The screams from the cave having ceased, the Christian psalm singing of the parishioners had come to an end, too, replaced by a purely African chanting backed up by drums hidden somewhere in the throng. It was the rhythmic atonal chorus of the dancers back in the village square hugging what imprisoned them, their fleshly, pink, protoplasmic net, and crying, "Ah-liv-et! All live it!" This music cried out first and foremost that it would never end. It had only been hidden by the hymns. It had no beginning, middle, and final refrain like ordinary songs or the Christian hymns, but went on and on forever as long as it amused the chanters to keep going, till they fell down asleep, and maybe replacements would keep going then. It was hypnotic, heart-breaking, eerily beautiful as it always had been. Now and then the psalm and hymn singers would grow enthusiastic and take it up again and their gospels and good news would drown it out for a time.

All the bodies at last brought down from the cave and placed next to the graves, there were just three, not counting the cooked child. But someone had said the child would not be buried after all. Although the people surged forward, I found I had no desire to see things up close, to see the bodies, to witness the burial details. Moreover I had to take a leak, and I drifted away toward the very back of the crowd, as it pressed past me. M watched me leave with her mother's smile saying she'd be keeping an eye on me nonetheless. She let me drift off confidently, I felt. A terrific tension was building, either in the crowd, or just in me. Also, I wondered who the fourth grave was for, if not the child. An overwhelming need to relieve myself reminded me that I had seen a latrine building behind the church, and in spite of a spasm of disgust I entered its low door and stood over a long tin trough with several other men. A wave of loathing of self and everything struck me to think I needed to do this at the moment the bodies were going into the ground with proper ceremony and flourish. The men on either side of me were drunks, bums, hangers-on, who were probably here just because beer was being passed around by now and they were pissing it out. It seemed to me I was one of them, pitiful and seedy. Nevertheless we were all children of God. The drumming and chanting grew louder. I could use a beer. It struck me I had made no progress at all, and was just as much at odds with myself and everything as I had been in my poolroom days on Clark Street, before M had returned.

Our piss in yellow streams arced down to the galvanized tin trough and splashed and flowed. Once in midstream I glanced down and was amazed to see a tiny firefly-like creature hovering under the rim of the trough as if caught in a storm. As I gazed at it, I saw it was the dwarf. In horror I jumped aside protecting myself in case any spears or missiles might come flying at me from the dwarf in my vulnerable posture. Considering his new tiny size, they would be small enough but might hurt just the

239

same depending where they landed. Spattering the floor and readjusting my flow downstream of the creature, who gazed up at me with imploring eyes, I finished up as fast as I could, undone by the ludicrousness of the vision as well as by a certain shimmering fearsome beauty in it, guarding certain tender parts in case he threw a bolt of lightning. I fell to my knees and reached toward the child to take it out, who, small as it was, grew even smaller. The child had golden hair and a cherub's face like the one who had been sucking from the mare in the field of wildflowers, only it had shrunk to the point of disappearing. That is, a minute ago, it had been about the size of a very small sparrow and now you could have brought it out of the pit with a teaspoon. Its eyes were as black and limpid as its hair was golden and curly. I begged it to come out, to follow me. It was just floating under the lip of the tin trough like a bumblebee or firefly, buzzing and dying in there, though I thought it could have flown out or flown anywhere, but it meant to stay just where it was. My only hope was to coax it forth, but when this didn't work, I tried child psychology, and announced I was leaving and it could come with me if it wished to, but if not, I would leave it behind now, it was entirely its own decision, and I left. This was just the same sort of calculating behavior I had utilized on M's child during the church carnival to get him to cooperate, which hadn't worked.

In the open air, I had the feeling he was following, but at a discreet distance, shy as a deer, keeping a distance so as to "keep watch over me," said a voice in my ear. I felt humbled and abashed. It wasn't trying to kill me anymore, but like an angel was looking out for me, even in the damn latrine. He had sought me out at the lowest point of my existence. I had the idea that after all my travels I was back where I had started and had made no progress. The tiny droning animal hovering over me seemed to do a preternatural surveillance as if I counted to somebody. I couldn't help thinking to myself that an answer might be forthcoming. The familiar idea that I had to do something, execute a mysterious task, carry out an errand for somebody, or surmount some challenge departed a little from me, happily, although not entirely. Over the burial crowd a small silver sphere was floating, translucent as a bubble of mist or foam, except one sensed it was impregnable and not fragile, hard as the disc of the daylight moon, although it was not like the daytime moon but something uncanny. I found a slightly elevated position at the foot of the hill from which to watch the burial proceedings. The silver disc grew larger and larger and as it grew, it sank toward the earth, where it finally came to rest, and disgorged a personage. I could only partly see it for the sphere was half-hidden from me by the crowd, and I could not see who had climbed out of it, someone important, no doubt. Or it could be the dwarf once more himself. But the child flew off to greet this personage, buzzed past my head, off and away. A feeling of suspense rose in me, or somewhere, as if something was coming to completion.

As much as I wished to see who the mysterious fourth grave belonged to, an overpowering force made me hang back. I both wished and didn't wish to know. This caused the suspense to intensify to the point of being painful and demanding resolution. I have always felt there was a question to be answered, as long as I can remember. I don't know about you, but I've always sensed there was something missing, something I didn't understand. I've always known something needed to be put right. But it's a fearful thing and you shrink at the prospect.

As soon as the bodies were buried, the sky grew black, and a breeze came up, thunderheads shot up high in the sky and raced toward us threatening a drenching downpour, but it wasn't to be an ordinary rain. All the people gasped, gazed upward, clutched each other, but didn't run away for cover. They held out their hands expectantly palms upward, wanting very much the refreshment that was coming. The air moved violently and seemed to open up everywhere at once. The turbulence grew stronger and stronger, and the wind steadily increased and began to whistle, and suddenly on this wind was borne a rain of golden winged seed which poured down and pelted us all, and the people stretched up their hands to it and stuffed their pockets with it, and our hair and mouths were filled with it, and it planted itself everywhere in the ground. Holding up her hand to shield her face from the pelting golden seed that fluttered down so thickly it reduced visibility to near zero, M had found me and stood close to me peering at me. I believed she wished me well and surely might even love me in her way.

"This is a fertile place. All our needs will be met here, and we're going to live here for a while," she said. "It's going to be nice."

"It's all hard to believe," I replied in a daze.

"Fortunately for you, it doesn't matter what you believe, since it's happening to you."

I wished to ask her who the one who had stepped out of the silver disc was, and also who the fourth grave was for, as I had a feeling she would know everything, but I had lost my voice. The winged seed kept flying through the air torrentially and covered the ground with bushels of gold. The lushness, bottomless fertility, and grace filled me with the stark wonder. "All is well," I heard someone say behind me, and thought it might have been the personage who had stepped out of the silver disc. I was glad to hear it!

"Listen, my parents used to have a business in this area— they were in the hotel business. Their old inn is still here and it's abandoned. We can buy it for a song and fix it up and that's where we'll live, in the holiest region of the world."

"Wait a second, we left your father in the village."

"Don't you want to accept this blessing and enjoy it?" Ironically this was substantially the same thing she had said to me about that ham, I recalled, and in the same objectionable tone. She seemed so appealing and innocent again.

"How will we get him that list of stuff?"

"Do you suppose my father needs a case of Pepsicola?"

"Well . . . that's what he said . . ."

"Do you suppose that old man is my father?"

"What?"

"God is my father."

"Well, sure, we are all children of God."

"God is also my mother."

"Okay . . ."

"Old Buwelo is not my father. He is a fine person, and he took good care of you. I love him. He's my friend. My father is not from this world."

My thoughts plodded along behind. I supposed wherever Melusina wanted to be with me would be home for me from now on. I knew she had entered upon a successful career in real estate and had every reason to believe she knew the ropes when it came to properties. A guy passing me by at this instant slightly grazed M but bumped me with his elbow hard, and turned to apologize. "Stranger, you are the guest of God!" he said heartily. At this, I gave up thinking. I loved M with all my heart. It was a new deal. I didn't have to think anymore but let her do the thinking.

She was wearing her old tight blue jeans over her sexy legs like she used to and her hair was strawberry blonde. Her sunburned face with wrinkles around her eyes suggested her old abandoned attitude toward life, but now also a commitment that didn't brook half measure. Where once M had been languid, opinionated, and crude, she had grown attentive, insightful, and wise. She was the guide on a guided tour and the only guide in sight. She knew all the secret listings of the sacred property around here, some of it valuable beyond any price. Everything I could see and sense stood out so sharply and discretely, every winged seed, every person in the crowd, every blade of grass on the hill, each thing or being no matter how insignificant with its own fate to live out, a strange fate, crying for an answer, seeking "home." The wings of the seeds were sharp and dry as they still occasionally flew against my cheeks and struck the backs of my hands. Every tiny and large thing loomed up at me with its undeniable claim and it was too much to bear the sad multitude. The fearful suspense that had been raised concerning certain identities of burial victims and visitors from space, the unaccountable mounting tension in the air that had culminated in the storm of grain, and her really incredible real estate proposition merged into M suggesting peace and harmony in the village but at the same time I felt my feet losing the ground.

She was the woman I'd known but no longer so obstreperous! I clasped her fondly in my arms, so soft, pliant, and full of good will, I felt. Reassured, I indulged my desire to kiss her and squeeze her and she responded and grew warm in my embrace and in turn squeezed back and caressed me so enticingly. For a moment ours was the pinnacle of bliss. M was the beautiful stuff of dreams, her scent an ambrosia of the gods, her flesh the food of mortal desire. A large black and gold snake crept across the grass and twined up Melusina's leg and stared at me with sad, and sleepy eyes. Out of its mouth appeared a golden-headed hatchet. "Bury the hatchet!" I thought, and realized it was time to make up with M for good and accept my need for her without qualification, that what she had to say to me was beyond true, it was necessary for my salvation, and I would do anything she said. This was the climax to every adventure we had had together and everything that had happened between us since the morning we had met at the boarding house. So I would live with her here at the inn she had described as she wanted me to. I desired it too very much, and I could hardly escape the awareness that I was meant to dismember the snake with the golden hatchet.

When I looked at her again she had acquired that foxfur jacket of hers with the red silk lining that flashed over skintight blue jeans. That gave me a shiver. It was almost night. Fireflies were out. One of them hummed through the air and sat on her shoulder. That was such a charming and unheard-of thing for a firefly to do that I knew she was charmed and the moment fateful. I looked a little more closely at the firefly, which was not blinking but glowing steadily, and saw that it was not a firefly at all but that tiny child again, aka the dwarf. It was sitting on her shoulder swinging its legs just like Mayor Daley's grandson had in the poolroom, but not so menacingly this time, rather contentedly like a little kid in a swing, on M's shoulder. Then it began to grow into a more normal sized infant, which M cradled in her arm and petted so happily.

"You don't think I know something about real estate?" M asked me laying it on. "*Pah!* I know a good thing when I see it!" I didn't doubt it. She turned her attention to the child and cooed at it contentedly. She knew she had won again and why not since she was true. She smiled openly up at me. I hadn't a doubt in my mind that all was well with M and me by now, though I didn't understand my good fortune.

The last drops of the rain of golden grain had finally stopped and over the heads of the crowd I could see the four burial mounds, now filled in. This conclusive reality arrested me with a dropping feeling, as I still didn't know who was in the fourth of the graves. But it was somebody. The way they were laid out in a circle with their ends or feet pointed inward reminded me of the circle of "wings" or banners on the church grounds when M's kid had thrown his deadly silver club at me while watching the carnival. The graves began to revolve in the sunwheel and I gazed about with trepidation. Every appearance I had ever seen her take unfolded in procession, every garment which had adorned her from her jeans to her black veil, all peeled away until she stood before me in a simple brown cloak, almond-eyed, olive-skinned, unornamented, a simple Semitic woman vintage about two or three thousand years ago. I was attracted to her as much as ever but in a new exciting way. We belonged to each other and she seemed to be waiting for a signal from me. (It could be we would have to sign each other, for she might not speak English.) The irony was I didn't have the slightest idea what to say to her now, while she came from a culture where the woman never spoke first. M had never been like this, genuinely waiting for me to take the lead, rather than pretending I was about to, and it was enjoyable, even though I didn't know what to say or do. I had the impression that she would stand here submissively all night waiting for me to say yes as if I were her client in a holy land real estate deal. "So, your father used to run an inn around here," was all I could finally say, my voice cracking at first, unable to help smiling that M meant me to swallow this fantasy.

"Yes, he did," she said quickly in a small serious voice, immediately covering her mouth with her hand in a gesture almost of apology for having spoken, a very middle eastern gesture suggesting modesty and seriousness. Her voice was sweet and the modesty sent a chill through me. Women in this culture could say yes or no although that was about it, in public. There was a whole crowd around us regarding the graves with awe. M had at last persuaded me she held a secret superior to anything I would ever learn on my own. She had done this all at once by the mere tone of her voice. But I couldn't quite bring myself to say yes to her, since in the end I was just who I was too. Not that it mattered what I said.

The concept of "the truth" was one I had always paid lip service to while my college education had rendered me incapable of ever entertaining such a thing. But Melusina and what she had for me were true in a way I couldn't deny. Standing next to the ancient and ever youthful Semitic woman I became aware I was alive. Whoever she was, she'd always had that effect on me, and she'd always be with me, giving me a hard time, sending me on treasure hunts where there really was a treasure. Whoever Melusina was, she was connected to everything real, and since she loved me, so was I. Here was my treasure. She didn't look at me directly, that being the middle eastern culture around here. She was the mystery that was about to begin. Apparently, the dwarf was an innocent babe now with no dwarflike qualities about him left at all. She turned her attention to the infant child as she had been doing for the past half hour.

At her feet lay the golden hatchet, next to it the coiled snake. I wondered what would happen when I chopped its head off. Slowly, almost as if it were asking me to do it, it stretched forth its neck and looked up at me with its beseeching, sad, and sleepy eyes. What happened was that M had stepped back in alarm, the lopped-off head of the snake oddly pointing right at me, accusingly, still staring at me, now in a mocking manner.

Far from ingratiating myself with the gods, I was overcome with sorrow, as it had been a very fetching and pitiful snake. M began to lead me somewhere. M and everyone else around here could even murder people, sacrifice them, while the sky opened up and rained golden seed, and if I wanted to join in and do my part, I put the wrong foot forward. I decided it was time to stop trying. On the other hand, there was no question but I'd had to kill the snake. I had done so, even if it wasn't quite the thing. Following M, hand in hand, I became grindingly aware once more I no longer had my little ferret dog and I couldn't believe he would wander off and leave me alone. No, I had been there at his birth in the pedestal. He had always been mine. I remembered how he had chewed up the warriors by the river who had nearly caught us, maiming several of them, and knew nobody could steal or hurt such a dog. Finally, I thought that he must have decided it was time for his trip to the North Pole. It was instinct. He had taken off. He hadn't meant to leave me but it was just what had to be. The likelihood of this brought me some peace in the matter momentarily. But I had not taken him to the North Pole as instructed. The strange mix of feelings I had was that in spite of my best intentions, and a few good omens, things were getting out of control, everything was coming to a head, and my little dog couldn't help me anymore. Then it struck me my little dog had been a dream. For all his viciousness and blue eyes, I had just dreamed him up. Could that be, with those warriors he had chewed up? The likelihood of this overcame me, but what followed then was, what hadn't I dreamed up?

M made a sign at me and smiled so pleasantly. She made a certain welcoming motion with her hand that indicated we would take a little walk. She handed off the infant to a tribeswoman who had been watching us and drew off her veil and let it fall about her supple shoulders. Her high cheekbones were revealed and long straight black hair. Her skin grew a little darker or perhaps we were leaving the lights of the temple. I knew she wouldn't disappear anymore and was able to accept this and relax. So, we would live here together in these Mediterranean parts. I guessed she was going to show me around. Maybe I'd get used to it and gain some understanding. We went for a walk now along the shore of the great lake or sea into which the wide river, maybe it was the Jordan, drained. I was given to understand this was the Dead Sea, while something hinted to me it might be Lake Michigan. I supposed it was neither, but someplace new.

There was only a sliver of a moon, and it was very dark along the shore, and the black waters made their presence felt by their whispering silence. I was full of passion, not only for her, but for the life I hadn't known existed until stirred to life again by her, still new and beyond my grasp. The night was full of dark shapes of the new life. We didn't need to talk, we seemed to have survived something, or arrived somewhere, and there was everything understood between us as we approached through thick mists, at a distance along the shore, looming spectral white buildings, their tops lost in the dim clouds. I wondered if it was that inn she was so keen on, or another of her properties, somewhat too opulent and out of place on this desolate body of water, but they had a welcoming and protective air, old castles or mansions in the ether. The impressive sight didn't surprise me, nothing would anymore. It was unneeded proof she'd made good in her career. As we walked slowly and calmly along the barren shore of the lake or sea, M reached out and embraced me. She kissed me like she meant it and her almond eyes gazed up into mine achingly and searchingly, but finally peacefully. The black water was a shimmering expanse at the corner of my eye under the moonlight. On a passing breeze the distant drumming and the play of flutes flared up and momentarily dissolved into eternal silence. It seemed the moment to ask her, and so I did.

"Melusina, who are you, really?"

Instead of an answer, or as if this was her answer, she took my hand in hers and brought it to her lips, then her cheek. "I thought you'd never ask," she said. But at this I burst into flames. Beginning someplace at my breast, perhaps where I kept my cigarettes and lighter, although I didn't smoke much anymore, the flames engulfed me. Apparently I had gotten lighter fluid soaked into my shirt. I didn't think it could be explained like that but I resolved to really quit smoking this time as I ran for the gentle waves. Burning over half my body I ran like crazy and leapt into the black water. I struck out for the deeps and dove repeatedly. But when I came up for air, the flames still had not all gone out, and showed an alarming persistence. The water nearby me as well seemed to be burning as if not only had it not put out the flames but had itself caught fire.

A crowd had gathered, drawn by the strange occurrence and the bright flames. At this point the woman ran to my rescue, and leaning down over me from a pier to which I clung, splashed water over me repeatedly. But as the flames kept raging, she pressed me under water gently and held me there, and at last the fire began slowly to go out, although by now I was badly burned over half my body and almost unconscious.

She held me under the soothing waters, my face and breast a charred mass of flesh. She meant to extinguish all the fire to the point it would not flare up again. But she wouldn't let me up for air! She held me under lovingly, tenderly, but firmly, pushed me down and down, keeping me under till I gulped black water, and drowned. She smiled at me peacefully as if this were my only hope now or she was content to relieve me of my obvious suffering, which she had done. I was briefly aware of her kindness and wisdom.

Then terror and disbelief came over me as it became apparent that she had decided to take the opportunity of the accident of the fire to murder me. There was a look in her eyes that I did not understand, yet it held understanding and love. As I sank helplessly beneath the surface, through the ripples I saw her stand up, still smiling, and glance around as though to see who might have seen her push me under. She was detached, and serene, like somebody who had accomplished her mission, as she drifted away. She walked away on the shore through the crowd without haste, stopping to peer back at me once. I stared after her with desperation, but with resignation, under the circumstances, since she didn't look like she was going to return, and I had drowned. I thought I could part with my eyes better than I could part with M and refused to believe I might not see her again. She was no longer my touchstone with the unknown, however, for I myself had become the unknown.

By now I was sinking to the bottom of the comforting and cool waters. As I floated like a dead cinder in the embrace of the slight current at the bottom of the sea, I saw a man with a perfectly round face come toward me. He must have emerged from a cave far away in the sea floor. He was coming from a great distance and was but a flickering image of a fine fellow at first, tiny and insubstantial. But he radiated everything that is acceptable, and his approach was sure. Oddly he was carrying a silver teapot in his hand. Moment by moment he grew, till I thought his gait and shape looked familiar. He had sun feathers in his hair, but his face was blacker than the night, blacker than the waters themselves, blacker than my charred flesh. His face was round as the globe surrounded top and bottom and all sides by cheery frizzles like one of those old medieval prints of Father Sun with sunrays shooting forth, or the compass with the Winds puffing from his cheeks on an old mariner's map. It was the roundness that encompasses all there is. An inexplicable peace came over me. Suddenly I remembered him and realized I knew him slightly. I thought happily that I might get to know him better this time. I forgot everything, and all pain faded away. Black Sun Man sauntered through the waters toward me without intention and in no hurry. Sun and shade dappled the deep, and the fresh breeze of springtime stirred beneath the waves.

"Where you been hiding?" he drawled pleasantly, as he came near.

There was no way I could answer that, as I was very tired. But it was not a question that required a response. It was merely a friendly salutation. His voice had the reassuring lilt of the islands, from which, as I recalled, he had recently returned.

www.ingramcontent.com/pod-product-compliance
Lightning Source LLC
Chambersburg PA
CBHW020727210626
46807CB00016B/405